ORIGIN: UNKNOWN

ORIGIN: UNKNOWN

Edward A. Holsclaw II

Wendy M. Easton

AVENTINE PRESS / SAN DIEGO

ORIGIN: UNKNOWN

PUBLISHED BY AVENTINE PRESS
1023 4th AVENUE, #204
SAN DIEGO, CALIFORNIA 92101

EDWARD A. HOLSCLAW, II
OFFICIAL WEBSITE:
http://www.Fearmaker.com

ISBN: 1-59330-259-2

Printed in the United States of America

ACKNOWLEDGEMENTS

My heartfelt thanks to those individuals who supported and assisted me - my wife, Mylene, Mom, Dad, my brother, Shane Holsclaw, my sister, Tina Hunter, Michael & Lori Cutlip, Jeffrey Estep, Susan Ware, Marshall Nelson, Wayne Conley, Jamie Summers and Jason "Roadblock" Robinson.

- Edward

I would like to thank the following individuals for their support and assistance – My husband, Paul, Mom, Dad, Christy Craig Wilt, Patty Kelley and Ronette Willis.

- Wendy

For

our families

1

"Cheryl, I need some slack," Brian yelled.

Cheryl was standing on the edge of an abyss lowering her husband into a hole with a large nylon rope. Duncan's Pit was a dangerous cave on the outskirts of a small town in Indiana that was fit for only the most experienced spelunkers.

Cheryl met Brian during a caving expedition more than eleven years earlier and they had been inseparable since. They shared a passion for exploring the most remote and treacherous caves and Duncan's Pit fit the bill. For her, spending time in a cave with Brian was next to heaven. Her love for searching the vast depths of the underworld in the caves of North America was second only to her powerful affection for the man at the end of the rope. Cheryl took a long, deep breath and smiled to herself. For her, standing forty feet under the surface of the planet, was her summit.

She got down on her knees and looked into the void that her husband had descended into moments earlier. The beam from her helmet light was smothered by the extreme darkness and she couldn't see any light at all, although she believed that he was no more than thirty feet from her. "Hey, what's up?" she yelled.

"Nothing. Just taking in everything that I can. It's awesome down here. Give me a minute. I'll come up and let you come down."

It took Cheryl a minute to interpret what Brian had said through the echoes. "Okay."

She sat back away from the edge and waited for her lover to ascend from the depths. She turned off her helmet lamp and closed her eyes. She loved the dark. She found it quiet and peaceful.

"Hey, Cheryl?" Brian questioned from below.

"Yeah, babe."

"You hear that?"

"Hear what?"

"Listen."

Cheryl turned her light back on, raised her chin, and listened to the cave. "I don't hear anything."

"Give it a second. I think it's getting louder."

Cheryl cocked her head to the right. She raised her eyebrows when the sound hit her ears. It was a slight hum, completely out of place in a remote cave like this. "What is that? Is someone running power equipment in here?"

"I don't think so," Brian answered. "It doesn't sound mechanical or electrical. It sounds...like bees."

Cheryl let out a short laugh. "It ain't bees, sweetie."

"I know it's not bees," Brian growled.

Cheryl furled her brow. Brian was upset and it sounded like he was coming back up.

"You on your way up?"

"Yeah. Whatever it is, it's making me uncomfortable. I think it's heading this way."

Cheryl felt a cold chill run up her spine. For the first time in her life, she was anxious to leave a cave. "Well, hurry and get up here. I wanna get out of here."

"I'm doing the best I can."

Cheryl went back over to the edge to help her husband with his ascent. When she looked over the side, the volume of the buzzing took her breath away. Now she was really scared. She called out to her husband, but Brian couldn't hear her over the deafening roar. As he approached the top edge, Cheryl's helmet light illuminated his face and she could see his fear. She frantically began pulling on the rope, trying to help him complete his climb.

Cheryl thought she heard a yell from Brian before the cavern was suddenly whipped into a terrifying frenzy. She couldn't make sense of what was happening. The raucous noise left her disoriented and the picture formed by the beam of her helmet light was making her dizzy. Within the darkness, she could feel biting or stinging all over her body. She started flailing wildly at her attackers, even though she was in agony. But there were hundreds, or maybe thousands of the creatures assaulting her. They had found their way into her mouth, in her ears and even under her clothing. No part of her body was protected from the insects. She stumbled forward, lost her footing, and plummeted down the same shaft that her husband had been enjoying just a few minutes earlier. She landed on the base of the burrow with a blow that broke her neck ending her torment.

The creatures rushed from the chambers of the cavern - a violent powerful force that seemed to hover for a moment to take in the glory of the murders they had committed – then exploded into the early evening sky, covering the orange-blue dusk with an evil and vengeful shadow.

2

She knew the van couldn't keep up this pace much longer. *Please, just a little further,* she thought as she pushed her foot harder on the accelerator, willing the old van to move up the endless winding mountain road. *Why is this happening?* Again, her eyes flashed up to the rear view mirror and saw her sons' wide-eyed and frightened faces staring back at her. *Oh Lord, please just let me get them to safety.*

Della was startled by the crack of the radio. It had been maybe fifty miles since they had heard anything and now something was trying to break through the silence. The odd crackling gave her a flicker of hope. *Maybe we've traveled far enough. Maybe we're safe.* Della grabbed the radio knob and began scanning the dial, hoping beyond hope that it would pick up someone's voice.

"...the far northwest corner of the county is..."

When Della found the station it caused her and her boys to jump. Partly because in Della's earlier search for a station she had left the volume up, but mostly because the invasion of an actual voice in the van was initially unnerving. She realized that they had been traveling for hours now without having spoken. Della worried about how this ordeal subdued her normally vivacious children.

"Once again, if you are traveling to Mount Hope from the north or to Pesculla County, please turn around. The road leading to the summit is closed. There are several multi-car accidents and many abandoned vehicles. One of these accidents has damaged the bridge at the base of the mountain," the voice from the radio announced.

Della pulled to the shoulder and stopped the struggling van. Mount Hope was their destination. Their last hope. She closed her eyes, and covered her face. *Thank God they had made it across in time.*

Della almost gave into her desire to sob hysterically. But stopped when she again glanced in to her rear view mirror and saw her frightened boys. *No. I have to maintain control for their sake.* She sure missed Ash. He was her rock. He would know what to do. He always knew what to do. For fifteen years, Della relied on his steady presence in her life. She always felt that she and the boys were anchored to a rock that was unalterable. Now the link to that anchor had been severed. For the first time, she and the kids were on their own, lost in the middle of a storm.

Della took a deep breath and pulled the van back onto the road. A deep and painful sadness consumed her. *Is Ash still alive? Will I ever know?* Her tears started flowing again, but she was determined to maintain control, not letting her sons see how terrified she really was. She punched hard on the accelerator causing the van to lurch forward and spit pebbles in its wake. Mount Hope was where she was heading and she was going to get there. She was determined that her kids survive and that determination gave her a new strength. There was no turning back now.

Mount Hope was a small, mostly abandoned vacation town at the top of a mountain slope that was fairly level for about three square miles. It was located in the mountainous Rockhills Canyon of New Mexico. A Navaho tribe discovered it while looking for a deified site for their religious ceremonies. The hills and valleys are resplendent with hidden trails, passages, and caves. Mount Hope was rediscovered in the 1920's by a group of adventurous college kids, but it remained relatively untouched until the early 1980's when a group of yuppies decided it was an ideal vacation spot and set out to develop it into another Lake Tahoe. However, after the initial burst of energy and funding, the group's savings and credit ran dry and they were unable to find any venture capitalists willing to take on this venture. After ten years of blood, sweat, and tears, the group gave up and left the crest to be reclaimed by nature.

Ash had heard about the abandoned place from a colleague. He brought Della there on their first anniversary and they both fell in love with the it. Except for the monstrous, boarded-up resort by the lake, the area was mostly untouched. Scattered throughout the mountain's apex were modest fishing and camping cabins that were still rented out, especially in the summer months when the mountaintop was 10 to 15 degrees cooler than the valley. Ash and Della had chosen to build a vacation home that bordered a small lake and sat in the shadow of two sloping hills that appeared rust-brown because of fallen pine needles. In the evenings, when you looked to the west and the cabin was encased in the shadow from the hillside, the cottage almost disappeared from view. Because of this his camouflaged affect, the couple named the cabin their 'hidden villa'.

Running through the northern contours of New Mexico, Snakebite River is completely uncrossable except by bridge. The river winds through the hills of Rockhills Canyon and into the low valleys of River View. Mount Hope, by some geographical anomaly, is almost surrounded by the river. A small strip of land enabling access to Mount Hope from the valley is, however, almost impassable by foot.

Louie Bishop's small voice broke Della's thoughts. "Mommy, I'm hungry."

Before Della could respond, Louies' older brother, Ricky, spoke up, "Be quiet, Louie, Mom's gotta worry about driving right now. We'll eat when we can."

Looking back into her boys' needful eyes and certain that no one was following them, Della looked for a place to pull over. Ahead to the right was a boarded-up gas station. She parked next to the garage and got out of the van to try the doors. There were two short two-by-fours screwed to the wooden roll-up garage doors and into the wall on either side of the door. Della went back into the van and grabbed the small toolbox that Ash insisted she carry.

She located a small crowbar, walked back to the garage, and slid the lip of the crowbar under the two-by-four on the right side. She gave it a hard yank and the weathered wood crumbled and splintered under the force. She went to the other side and easily removed the two-by-four. She quietly prayed that the door was not locked on the inside and gave it a hard tug. It opened about a foot and a half and stopped. She couldn't budge it.

Exasperated, she went back to the van, to get the boys to help her with the garage door. She told them both to pull up on the door as hard as they could while she laid on the ground and bench pressed the door. On her mark, all three tugged and pushed on the stubborn door until it slowly began to give. At once, it sprang on its track to the ceiling, and started coming back down. Della held the door up and told Ricky to find something in the garage that might help hold the door up. Ricky found a long board and pried it into the track. Della lowered the door to rest on the board.

"Good job, Ricky," she told her son. "Let's get that van in here and get some rest."

She started to pull the van into the garage, but thought better of it. She stopped, pulled out, turned the van around to face the road, and backed into the old gas station. She cautiously got out of the van, careful to avoid anything that might be lurking in the shadows. Della looked down the road to make sure nothing had followed them, pulled the board out of the track and let the door fall shut. Then she took a broom handle and wedged it into the track above the door to prevent anyone from opening it. She returned to the van and turned on the battery-powered camping lantern that Ash also insisted they carry in the van. *Thank you, Ash,* she thought.

Della looked at her boys and was suddenly very worried about Louie, her little cricket. He was barely five years old and smaller than most four-year-olds. Because he had always been so small, she babied him, which Ash had warned her would quell his independence. Now, she desperately needed that independence. Ricky, on the other hand, was her little man. He was twelve years old and independent to a fault. Now that Ash was not with them, Della knew that Ricky would be her strength. They both resembled her - blond, fair skinned, and most of all, strong-willed. She hoped that indomitable spirit of theirs would now be an asset.

"Are we there, Mommy?" Louie whispered.

"Not yet, honey," Della replied as she climbed between them. "Not yet."

She crawled to the backseat and unfolded it into a bed. She pulled two pillows and a blanket out from under the seat and made a makeshift bed. Then she retrieved a can of Pringles and a box of strawberry Pop-Tarts from under the middle-row captain's chairs. Della also grabbed a six-pack of bottled water. "This will have to do until we get to the cabin," Della said.

Louie's hungry, Della thought. *That's good. The knot of fear in his belly must be loosening.*

Della and the boys ate quietly, reflecting on the last several days. All of the questions the boys had bombarded her with in the last several days were now moot. After a few minutes, Louie fell asleep with a Pringle chip in his mouth. Della grinned at him and asked herself how many times had that happened before. Ricky let out a big yawn. Della covered them both with the blanket and kissed them on the forehead. Taking the lantern, she turned and slouched down in the captain's chair.

As she had so often in the past few years, Della found herself in a state of wonder over the way her life had turned out. Before this craziness, she would have easily said it was perfect. At least, as far as she was concerned, it was as perfect as she dreamed her life might be as a young girl. As a child, she would lay in bed night after night dreaming of what a normal family would be like, hearing her parents engage in their nightly battle in the front rooms of the house. As she grew, her dreams became refined and simple: a man who loved her and the well-adjusted children she hoped to have someday.

Her parents' fights had always been the talk of the neighborhood, but even then, no one was prepared for how it would end. One day, after a particularly severe quarrel, Della's mother arrived at her school with her attorney and announced that Della was going away with her. Della's father apparently caught wind of this and brought his own attorney to make a counter claim. The argument that ensued was renowned and didn't end until Della's mother lay dead on the elementary school grounds from two gunshot wounds. Her attorney was also shot, but he survived. Her father waited for police to arrive and allowed himself to be arrested without incident. Della didn't say a word. She just turned around and walked back into the school through the gauntlet of shocked and crying classmates. Two hours later, she was sitting in the Child Welfare Office as strangers discussed her future.

Now, looking at her sons, Della silently swore to do everything possible to keep them safe and make sure they always had their mother. Della pushed down on the lever on the side seat and allowed it to fully recline. She was reaching for a blanket on the floor, but fell asleep before she seized it.

3

Ash Bishop was awakened by an alarm and muffled sirens that crammed into the small, dark Chicago hotel room in which he slept. He reached over and turned the switch for the lamp repeatedly with no luck, while his arm brushed a glass of water to the floor. His tired senses came to life.

What's going on? he thought. He jerked the covers off his bare body and quickly, but cautiously made his way to the window. He peered below from his ninth story room and could see the flashing lights of police and emergency vehicles.

Fire! His mind screamed. That must be the fire alarm. He impatiently felt his way around the dark room and quickly dressed himself. He could now hear the bustling of people in the halls outside his room. Grabbing his wallet, cell phone and other things that he carried in his pockets, he took a quick look out the peephole. All he could see were blurry movements. He forcefully pulled open the door and looked back and forth through the hotel emergency lights.

Ash stopped a lady in a white robe. "Do you know what's going on?"

"I think it's a fire!" she trembled as she brushed by him.

Okay, he thought. He knew the exercise. He was the Emergency Training Coordinator for the Colorado State Police and Emergency Training Academy. One thing he knew was to stay calm and keep focused during an event of this kind.

He moved carefully down the stairwell of the Chicago Wellington Hotel, the site of his weeklong enhanced homeland security training. He was only three days into the training.

Maybe it is only a false alarm, he prayed. He tried calming the people as he headed down the stairwell and helped out where he could. He came upon a mother with two small children who were having a hard time making it.

"Ma'am, can I help?" Ash looked into her tearful eyes.

"Yes, please." She barely got the words out.

"What's your name?" he asked the little boy.

"Brent," he whispered.

"Everything will be alright. We'll be outside soon." He bent over and picked up the toddler. He thought about his own family.

I'm glad they're not with me in this predicament, he thought.

As he took the last flight of stairs, he could feel the group relax and gave a sigh of relief. Ash reassured Brent and his family that everything would be fine. But when Ash opened the stairway door to usher the people outside he was shocked by what he saw. They had gone from the confusion and alarms within the hotel to even more chaos outside. Sirens from all directions pierced the night with their ear splitting wails. Ash had to cover his eyes from the blinding lights of the emergency vehicles.

Ash placed Brent beside his mother.

"Everything will be alright. Just go over and stand next to the others across the street," Ash winked at the children.

They nodded their heads and did as they were told. Ash on the other hand wanted some answers. He walked to the police cruiser nearest to him. He pulled his wallet out to show his badge to the police officer.

"Hi, I'm Ash Bishop of the Colorado State Police." Ash managed a smile.

The officer nodded and sighed. *This emergency had to happen at this hotel,* he thought. He had been swarmed with homeland security personnel since he arrived. All wanting to help, all wanting to share their advice. *I don't need this,* he thought, but as a professional he knew he could not just blow them off. So he took a deep breath and said, "Mr. Bishop. I'm Patrolman LeSalle of the Chicago Police Department. What can I do for you?

"Just curious, what's the situation here?" Ash asked.

"A fire alarm must have been tripped on the main floor. Not to mention we are getting multiple power outages throughout the city," Officer LeSalle paused and looked away momentarily. "And get this, the radios are lit up with disturbances of assault and battery, murders, breaking and entering. I don't know what to think of it all."

"Damn, I guess whenever there's a blackout some people can go a little nuts," Ash offered an answer.

"I wish I knew," the officer continued, "the fire department is about to call this a false alarm and then I'll be off to fight this freakin' crime spree. It almost reminds me of the Rodney King riots of Los Angeles."

"Well, thanks for the info and take care," Ash said.

"You too," Patrolman LeSalle answered.

Ash walked over to join the mass of people from the hotel. He stood speechless pondering how safe it really was to be on the street during all this mayhem.

Suddenly from the far side of the hotel, a couple of shots rang out. The crowd, from which Ash stood, crouched down and looked in the direction of the fired shots. Then the few rounds turned to an all out war zone. The group screamed and ran for the hotel. Ash's training told him to assist his fellow officers. He ran through the throngs of people and vehicles and into battle. Grabbing his side, he reached instinctively for his Glock, and then remembered that he didn't bring it. After all, why would he need it for this training? He didn't like taking it with him on the plane. It wasn't worth the hassle.

Up ahead, he could see the police officers running around the far side of the hotel and he followed them. *What good am I without a firearm?* he thought. Ash didn't care. He would manage.

As Ash rounded the corner of the hotel he was stopped in his tracks. There were hundreds of people charging the police. It was hard to see what exactly was going on in the light gray haze of morning. But he knew one thing, and that was something was very wrong here.

Ash observed the officers in the front being attacked and overcome by hordes of people.

"Fall back, fall back!" the voice of a police officer screamed over the commotion.

Ash noticed that he was one of the few still left to fight off the irate mob. He turned and made a mad dash for the hotel, but as he drew close enough to see, the hotel was also under assault. Noticing that he no longer heard gunfire, Ash turned and looked over his shoulder.

Damn! What the hell is going on? he thought.

The hordes of crazed people were close enough that he could smell the pungent smell of body odor and urine. Ash eyed an opened door on a police cruiser and dashed for it. He clumsily entered the cruiser and locked the doors in the nick of time before the vehicle was besieged by the multitude of angry people.

"Thank God," Ash said as he could see that the cruiser was still running. The car started rocking back and forth while being pummeled by the crowds' fists, feet and even a head, which cracked the back windshield. He realized the mob was silent except for the inhuman growls and shrieks. *What's wrong with these people?* he thought.

"Damn you!" Ash shouted and shifted into reverse. The attackers one by one flew from the car. He slammed on the brakes and all that remained was a teenage boy that hung onto the hood staring coldly into Ash's eyes.

This is crazy! Ash thought, as he stared in shock at the angry boy before him.

Ash shifted the car into drive and punched the gas pedal. He headed for an opening stretch of road. The boy rolled to the left, lost his grip, and rolled over and away from the moving vehicle. He gazed in his rear view mirror and noticed that the attackers had not given up the chase, but he lost sight of them as he rounded the corner.

4

Della awoke startled. Surveying her surroundings, her anxiety abated. Her sons were asleep, the garage was quiet and the sun was beginning to make its way through the dusty aging wallboards. *Well, we made it through the night,* she thought. What lie beyond the walls of their temporary shelter was unknown and as much as she would have liked to stay, hidden inside the garage until Ash found them, she knew her best option was to keep moving. Mount Hope was close and if everything went smoothly, they would make it there before sunset.

Easing her way out of the van, Della quietly made her way to the garage door. Leaning with her ear against the soiled plank, she listened. Hearing nothing but the soft New Mexico wind blowing steadily by her, she turned and peered through the crack looking for movement. Nothing. *Good,* she thought, *better get moving.*

The old garage door moaned and complained loudly as it slowly rose, succumbing to Della's steady pressure. The welcoming sun shone through the van's windows, bathing Della in its warmth. Although the early June sun had broken free of the horizon an hour earlier, it was already heating up. Inside the van was even warmer. Still Della shivered, trying not to think of what lay ahead for her family, she concentrated instead on the peaceful, warm day outside her windshield. She wondered if she would ever be able to forget the horrors of the past two days.

* * *

The Twin Pines Valley Shopping Center had been packed that day. It took Della almost two hours longer than normal to finish her 'to do' list. Both she and Ash had, for one reason or another, been putting off buying the boys new tennis shoes for weeks now. Today she had been determined to cross that task off her list. Unfortunately, the annual sidewalk sale had started that morning. After hours of maneuvering through a maze of seasoned shoppers, a quick trip through the supermarket, and a stop by the local dry cleaners, Della and her two weary sons finally walked through their home's front door.

The boys, who had a few minutes earlier complained of sore feet, dry mouths and aching legs, jumped immediately from the van and ran full speed to their favorite activity, the back yard play set. Della was left again to carry the groceries alone. She thought about calling the kids back to help, but thought better of it. They had been good at the mall, only asking to visit the toy store six or seven times instead of their normal dozen or so. They deserved a little kid time.

Dropping the grocery bags onto the kitchen floor, she punched the "on" button to the kitchen radio, preparing for some alone time while she made dinner.

"...if you've just tuned in, this is not a hoax. The President has issued a state of emergency in 27 states and has ordered all citizens not to leave their homes..."

What? she thought. *Did she hear that right?* She put the eggs she had in her hand down on the kitchen counter, walked over to the radio and increased the volume. Static. She tried tuning in another station. Static again. *What's going on?*

Della walked into the living room, picked up the remote and sat on the edge of the sofa. The television flickered snow and then a picture. A pretty blond CNN correspondent was reporting from Chicago.

"As you can see behind me, Stan, things here have gone from bad to worse." The camera panned to show a downtown Chicago street; the shop windows were broken out, glass and trash littered the street. Cars were on fire and overturned and screams could be heard in the distance. The camera zoomed in to show a lady's clothing shop whose front window had been smashed and clothing ripped and thrown across the street. Della thought she saw a mannequin without its arm lying halfway out of the store's entrance.

Gasping loudly, she realized when the camera panned in closer that there was blood covering the mannequin and that the mannequin was actually a person. Jumping to her feet, she dropped the remote control, trying to quickly change the channel to find out what was actually going on. FOX News was just switching to a press conference from the White House. The President was speaking.

"Without a doubt, make no mistake that your government will get to the bottom of this virus. We have some of the world's best doctors working on a cure at this very moment. We will find a cure." His usually clean-shaven and professional look was replaced with unkempt hair, day-old stubble and weary eyes. He was worried; Della could hear that in his voice.

Virus? What did that mean? And what's happening to Chicago?

The President continued. "Outbreaks have been occurring throughout the world and we are urging all citizens to protect themselves and their loved ones by staying indoors and locking your doors."

Della switched the channel again and this time the camera was actually showing a mob of what looked to be angry people chasing a half dozen screaming people down a street. The cameraman was safely located on a rooftop and Della could hear him unabashedly crying as he filmed the mob overtaking the terrified people. She changed the station again and saw yet another cameraman filming a mob smashing windows and breaking down doors of the shops on a different street.

Suddenly, it hit her. *Chicago! Ash!* Grabbing at the phone and dropping the receiver twice, she finally managed to punch in Ash's cell phone exchange. It was ringing. Good.

"Please answer, please answer," she chanted quietly as it rang.

"Hi, this is Ash, I'm not available to take your call right now, please leave me a message and I'll get back with you as soon as possible." Ash's recorded voice resonated through the phone line.

"Ash, I just saw the news. It showed Chicago, and I can't believe what I'm seeing. Are you all right? They said to stay inside. Nothing like that has happened here yet, but I don't want to be here without you if it does. We're too close to too many people. I'm not sure what I should do. God, I wish you were here. I'm going to take the boys to the cabin. If you get this, try to make it to the cabin. I hope you're all right. Please, please try and call me and let me know you're safe. I love you, Ash. Please be careful. I'll take care of the boys. I'll take..."

The line went dead and Della stood staring disbelievingly at the phone. Had she really heard what she thought she had heard? Seconds went by, as Della stood in the quiet living room, suddenly aware of the stillness in her home. The rhythmical ticking of the grandfather clock echoed throughout the room. Frozen, Della's eyes darted around. It had always been her favorite room of the house. A room where the four of them had sat and played, watched movies, and mostly just spent time together as a family. She had chosen a light cheery color scheme, light green walls, to complement the tan carpet. Ash had insisted on oversized furniture and the boys loved curling up in the overstuffed blue and green chairs with their pillows and favorite blankets.

The boys were playing in the back yard. Their uncomplicated laughter made its way through the closed windows and doors, surrounding her, allowing her consciousness to grasp the circumstance and the gravity of the situation.

Oh my god, the boys! she thought, snapping herself out of her stupor.

Running for the back door she screamed for the boys, "Hurry, get inside quick, quick, quick!"

"What Mom?" Ricky asked, upset that his game of tag had been cut short. His short hair was plastered to his head with sweat, his puffy cheeks red from the physical exertion.

"Something's happened and we've got to get to the cabin quick," she hurriedly told her oldest son. Instinctively, she pulled both of them closer to her.

"Can you go downstairs and start bringing up everything Dad has in his emergency room?" Della asked, her wide-eyed son.

* * *

"Louie, you can help Mommy carry them to the van," Della told her youngest son.

That day seemed like a distant memory now, as if it had occurred not just a few days ago, but in another life. Trying to keep her mind on anything other than their current situation, Della began to make a mental inventory of the items she had hastily packed in the van that day. Did she remember everything? It had taken a little over an hour to empty Ash's emergency supply room downstairs. Most of the boxes and bags were sealed and Della was unsure of their contents. She had allowed the boys only minutes to fill a bag of things from their room as she quickly emptied their pantry of canned food into plastic bags.

Once the van was mostly packed, Della ran back into the house quickly surveying it for anything else she might need. Her eyes lingered on the photos sitting on the mantle of the boys in different stages of their lives. Her heart ached because she had to leave those cherished memories behind. Quickly, she ran to the desk, jerking open the bottom drawer; she emptied the drawer of CD's. Grateful that Ash had insisted on copying their photo collection onto disks last summer.

Now as she navigated the van towards the final stretch of their journey, she questioned if they would ever be able to return. The familiar warm sensation of tears pooling in her weakened eyes threatened to spill over as she thought of her beautiful home now so far away. Memories began rushing through her mind once again as if she had unlocked a vault within herself.

* * *

Ash's hands were covering her eyes.

"Surprise!" he yelled, as he removed his hands to reveal his surprise: A two story colonial with white siding and red brick accents sat in front of her with a SOLD sign in the perfectly manicured front lawn. Della had opened the white picket fence and stared at her husband's boyish grin and the picturesque house that stood behind him.

"Ash, are you sure we can afford this?" she had asked when her voice returned.

"Sure, things will just have to be a little tight until my promotion pay kicks in but..."

"Your what?" Della asked the still grinning Ash.

"Oh, did I forget to mention, I got promoted?"

"Oh Ash!" she squealed, as she leaped into his arms, kissing him hastily across his face. "Why didn't you tell me? That's wonderful!"

"From now on baby," Ash said, sliding his arms around Della's waist and pulling her closer, "wonderful is going to be our status quo."

And he had been right. Life with Ash was a dream. They had settled into their home and soon welcomed two beautiful sons into their world of love. Life had been everything she had hoped.

Until now.

5

Ash peered over the ledge of the four-story parking garage. The city was shell-shocked, like a scene from a war movie. Cars, trash and dead people littered the roads and sidewalks. He checked his watch and found it was only 1:15 p.m. It had been the longest morning of his life. As soon as he left the hotel in the cruiser, he had to immediately stop because wrecked cars blocked the road.

I didn't even have enough time to radio someone from the cruiser, he thought. *The bastards were almost on me before I found that abandoned taxi. Thank God, it still had the keys in it.*

Ash took out his phone and tried again to contact his wife, Della. It was useless. The phone still showed no service and soon his cell phone battery would be dead as well. He missed Della and their sons. He just wanted to let them know he was alright. By now, he thought, the circus that he had seen in Chicago was all over the news.

He followed the signs to I-55 South towards St. Louis to get out of the chaos of Chicago. As he was nearing the interstate he had to stop. The daylight was even more dangerous than the night. The freaks, which Ash had coined the rage-induced crazy people, were killing anything in their path including one another. Moreover, they didn't show prejudice to any age, human or animal. He had attempted on several occasions to help others, but he always fell short because of the mob's sheer numbers.

"Leave me alone!" shouted a young boy.

Ash hastily moved closer to the ledge, but saw nothing.

"Stop it, leave me alone!" he screamed even louder. "Help! Somebody please help me!"

In the split-second after Ash saw the young boy, Ash opened his mouth to yell, but stopped short. It wouldn't have mattered. The boy was attacked by the three men, who brutally beat him to death and then ran off seeking more victims. One turned and looked up in Ash's direction, but Ash jerked himself back out of view. After a couple of minutes of standing quietly, he observed the three men running down the block.

"Damn!" he whispered as he released the tension of air he held fully in his lungs. He could see the boy's body convulse and jerk madly about as the blood around his head gushed out onto the hot sidewalk like molten lava. Then he stopped moving. It was over.

Ash bit hard into his hand and screamed silently in disgust. He knew there was no way he could have saved the boy. He wanted to do more than run a few of them over. He felt helpless. There were just too many of them.

Ash could hear the blind screams coming from all over the city, but it wasn't what he heard that concerned him, it was the absence of certain sounds that worried him. The sirens from emergency vehicles had stopped. *Did that mean they had given up and gotten the hell out of Dodge or did that mean something worse?* he wondered.

He had managed to snag a few bags of Fritos and a couple of Coke 2-liters from a looted store, and his stomach was reminding him that he was becoming hungry again. The radios from the different cars he had taken up to now offered nothing but static.

This is too much, he thought, while he covered his face with his hands and muffled a yawn. He needed to sleep. He got back into his car and laid his sweat-drenched body down on the gray cloth back seat of his borrowed dirty blue Chevy Impala, and hoped sleep would overtake him.

He thought again of his wife and boys. He wanted so much to see them again. Closing his eyes, Ash could see Della's image before him. Instinctively, he raised his hand toward her. He knew the image was not real, but enjoyed the memory his mind was replaying for him anyway. In their fifteen years of marriage, her looks had changed little. To him she still looked as fresh and young as she had that day so many years ago when he had caught her smiling at him across the crowded campus coffee house. Della complained often about the small lines materializing on her face and the pull of gravity in other areas, but Ash thought she was imagining things. The aging effects had, in his mind at least, left her untouched.

Ash smiled as he pulled a familiar memory into view. It was of Della outside in their backyard a few short weeks ago. She stood beside a laundry basket, hanging their clothes on the clothesline, while watching the boys play nearby. Her long hair pulled back hurriedly into her usual ponytail. Blond strands refused to cooperate and fell stubbornly around her ears and across her forehead. She was wearing one of his old dress shirts and had it tied at the waist and her dangerously short cut-off blue jean shorts that Ash refused to allow her to wear in public. He had seen his neighbor's glances and how their conversations with her lingered longer than they should have when she ventured outside in those shorts.

Ash could see her, pausing between articles of clothing to stretch, pushing the unaccommodating strands of hair out of her eyes with the back of her hand, letting a wooden clothes pin dangle between her full pouty lips. He remembered how the mid–day sun bathed her in its golden rays, leaving her long slender limbs tanned and sexy. Ash remembered wishing for ten minutes of privacy while he watched her bend repeatedly, retrieving clothing from the basket. *There was never enough time for the two of them,* he had thought. Never enough time to show what was in his heart.

In college, they had spent their days naked, wrapped in blankets in her apartment bedroom. Coming up for air only to call for take-out or to take their lovemaking to her shower. He could remember how much he loved her then and amazingly how much it had grown when other marriages seemed to crumble. His chest hurt. He tried to draw into his memories. To lose himself in her face. Her light blue eyes, the way the freckles danced across the bridge of her nose and spilled onto her cheeks, the deep intoxicating sound of her laughter, her beautiful smile. Breathing deeply he tried to recall the tantalizing smell of her neck. A unique blend of Obsession cologne , baby powder and raspberry shower gel. He loved her scent, the way she tasted as he licked and kissed her beneath her chin. The way she quivered when he let his teeth playfully nip at her skin. *God, how I love her. How I miss her.*

The sound of the stairwell door opening within the parking garage emanated throughout. Ash shot up to eye level with the window and repeatedly searched the area. His heart raced. Sweat ran steadily down his spine as he slid from the backseat of the opened car door to the floor of the garage. Stopping momentarily to listen, he heard footsteps and it was from more that one person. Ash hunched, grabbed his tire iron from the front seat and quickly ran toward the footsteps. Weaving in and out of parked cars, he drew closer to the strangers. He bent down on all fours beside a mini-van and saw two sets of legs. He warily moved around the back of the mini-van with the tire iron ready for action. His breathing picked up again at the fear of having to face those inhuman freaks again. Ash jumped out from behind the van and met his aggressors, who were facing the other way. Sensing someone was behind them, the two quickly jerked around and screamed.

"Please don't hurt us," the woman pleaded as the little girl grabbed her leg.

Realizing the two were not crazed like infected people, he said, "You two are normal...aren't you?"

"Yes we are," she swallowed hard. "Are you?"

"Yes, thank God! Finally, I have someone to talk to." He smiled at the two of them.

The woman smiled weakly back at him, but Ash could tell she was in pain. The little girl seemed to be in shock and who could blame her after what they had probably gone through.

"Are you hungry?" Ash asked.

"Yes," the woman answered weakly.

"I have some chips and pop over in the car and you're welcome to it."

"By the way, I'm Ash," he said, extending his hand.

"Ash, I'm Barbara and this is my daughter, Emily, and we would love something to eat and drink," she said as she reached out to shake his hand.

"Come on, follow me," Ash said.

* * *

As they consumed their not-so-nutritious lunch, Ash told of his perilous journey of how he got to where he was now. He also told them of his job and family life. Hoping to ease their mind and bring some normalcy to their situation, Ash asked Barbara their story.

"There's not so much to tell. Emily and I have been on our own now for more than five years after my ex left me. He barely has any time for Emily. Probably because he moved to San Diego, but that should be no excuse not to call her on occasion, especially on her birthday. I work for Simon and Hoekstra, here in Chicago, as a financial officer. We have made ourselves a good life. Emily is ten years old, but I swear she acts like an adult sometimes. Now... she's too scared to say a word. Who could blame her? We were very lucky to escape our apartment after it was attacked by those...people. We've been on the run since and hiding for most of the time. Do you know what's going on?" Her distressed eyes permeated Ash's heart.

"I'm not sure. I have had no contact with the outside world. My phone has no service, all the radios I've tried have no reception and you guys are the first normal people I've seen in hours."

"Well, do I have a shocker for you." Barbara looked intently at Ash.

Do I really want to hear this? he thought to himself.

"Ash, while the sirens were blasting all through the city and then throughout the gunfire, we sat in our apartment, switching from news channel to news channel. What they were saying was that this is happening all over the world. It's just not here in Chicago, it's everywhere." Barbara barely blinked as she continued her story.

Ash listened intently.

"And no one knows how it started, but people and animals alike are becoming rabid by what they think could be a major virus. No one seemed to know, but people appeared to be losing their minds and just start killing one another for no reason at all. They ran footage that was absolutely horrendous. On one station showed a group of infected people tracking down a man and his baby as they mutilated them right in the middle of the streets of New York. No one is immune from this virus, including the police."

"What else?" Ash asked apprehensively.

"The cable went out several times before they told us that the Center for Disease Control was working diligently to find out what we're dealing with. The only thing that they asked us to do was to stay indoors until they knew more." Barbara paused to think. "One more thing. The people that were infected were dying about twenty-four to forty-eight hours after being infected."

There was a short-lived moment of silence, while Ash took it all in.

"This can't be happening." He stood up and guardedly glanced over the ledge. Again, he viewed a few people running up the street, but could see by their swagger that they were the so-called "infected ones."

His thoughts turned to his family. He was pissed that he couldn't be there for them, but he knew what he needed to do. It was all planned out. Ever since 9/11, his family had worked out a plan to deal with a national, or in this case, worldwide disaster. Mt. Hope, their refuge and safety net, was their answer. Their own secluded mountain home away from all that was bad in the world. It was stockpiled with enough food, water and firepower to maintain them for years to come. In Ash's line of work, he was prepared for this. He hoped anyway.

He had to get to New Mexico, and with the state of things, it might take him awhile to get there. His chest tightened as he again thought of Della and the kids. Then he remembered how strong-willed his Della was and he prayed she would be there waiting for him.

He looked down to see Emily fast asleep next to her mother. Her now frizzy long hair and ragged pajamas showed the tough morning she had experienced. *She was a pretty little girl,* he thought. Barbara, on the other hand, looked unhealthy. Dark circles outlined her squinty eyes; her parched blue lips and pale skin told him that she was definitely sick.

"Barbara, are you okay?" Ash asked concerned.

"I think so. I must have over-exerted myself," she answered him, but sounded hesitant.

"Did any of the infected come into contact with you?" he asked.

"No, not even close. The only thing that..." she paused.

"What?" Ash asked impatiently.

"Well, I was bitten by a horsefly or some insect a couple of hours before we found you, but it's nothing."

Something told Ash to ask, "Where did you get bit?"

"Well," she paused, as if she where hiding something from him.

"You need to show me. Maybe it's nothing or maybe it could mean life or death for all of us, even your daughter." Ash didn't want to scare her, but he meant what he said and she could see it in his rigid face.

"Okay, it's right here."

She lifted her nightgown up slightly to reveal a reddish blue sore of some type that was raised an inch above the skin. Creamy puss ran from the wound as the arteries became visible and spider-webbed around the bite.

Holy shit! Ash was speechless.

6

"Mommy, are we there yet?" The innocent familiarity of Louie's question made Della smile. How long had it been since she had smiled?

"We're almost there, Louie, can you grab something out of that bag and hang on a few more minutes?" she asked. She was answered by incoherent mumbling and the rustling of a paper bag.

They had driven almost three days straight, and were now rewarded by familiar sights. Approaching the final stretch and about to enter the town, Della suddenly hit her brakes, causing the van to swerve dangerously across the road. Surprised yelps erupted from the back of her van.

"Mom!" Ricky screamed, as they rounded the last curve before entering the small mountain town.

What looked to Della to be a small man-made mountain of trees, broken boards and other large pieces of household furniture sat in the middle of the road, making it impassable.

"What the...?"

"Mommy," Louie said, obviously upset, "you made me drop my poptart."

"You guys stay put, I'll go see what's going on," she said, trying to control her panic.

They had been through so much; to be so close...this can't be happening! she thought fighting back her anger at the situation.

"But Mom, I want to go with you," Ricky protested.

"No, you stay here and watch your brother," she said, walking away. Then having second thoughts, she returned to the van.

"Ricky, keep the doors locked, and come up here in the driver's seat so you can see what's happening."

The van had stopped only a few feet away from a steep ditch. Anger again washed over her. What would have happened if she had not been able to stop?

"Hold it right there!" A male voice boomed from on top of the makeshift mountain. Della looked up to find a young man probably in his early twenties with a shotgun pointed at her.

"Mom!" Ricky had seen the man with the gun and had jumped from the van, yelling as he ran towards her.

"Ricky, get back in the car!" she yelled to no avail.

Ricky quickly jumped in front of his mom placing his 12-year-old body between her and the shooter, wrapping his arms tightly around her waist. Della untangled his arms from her and firmly placed him behind her, looking over her shoulder to make sure her youngest did not follow big brother's suit.

"Put away that gun!" she said, her anger now in full control. "What's the matter with you?" She pushed Ricky to the side and made her way towards the road block. "Can't you see I have children with me? You could have killed one of them. Or me! Then what would they do without a mother! What the hell's going on? I leave home to get away from crazy people and come here, to someplace where I think my kids will be safe and you put up this...this...mountain that almost causes me to wreck my van. We've driven for three days. I can't reach my husband. We were almost attacked twice on the way. I don't know what to do and now you...and this gun...almost shot me!"

Although she knew she was rambling and probably didn't make sense, she couldn't stop herself. By the time Della had reached the top of the pile where the young man stood, she was crying, frantically, wiping tears away as quickly as they fell, stumbling over tree limbs and angry enough to have taken the man's gun and shot him with it.

"Take it easy, lady," the young man said, putting his hands up in a defensive manner.

"I didn't mean nothin'," he said. "It's just my job."

"Your job is to scare the daylights out of little boys and cause car wrecks?" she asked, still angry.

She knew she should let up on the guy, but three days of worry and no news from her husband had taken its toll. Tears continued to stream from her eyes. She turned to see Ricky standing in front of the van holding Louie's hand, quietly watching their mother's tirade. Trying to calm herself, she bent over and put her hands on her knees and it seemed to be working until the guard spoke again.

"I'm afraid I'm going to have to ask you to turn your van around and leave the mountain, Ma'am."

"What?" Della asked incredulously. "You're going to ask me to do what?"

"I'm sorry, but we're not letting anyone in who doesn't already live here."

"What are you talking about? It's a mountain, you can't decide who comes or goes, it doesn't belong to anyone."

"That's my orders," he said. Looking over her shoulder at the two children, he continued, "But, I guess since you've come so far, maybe you can talk to Brady," he relented.

"Yeah, maybe that's a good idea. Take me to Brady."

The young guard slung his rifle over his shoulder and helped Della back down the way she came. Amazed at how treacherous the footing was, she supposed her anger helped her on the way up. Calming slightly, Della watched as the young man bent down to speak with her sons.

"My name is Billy," he said, extending his hand to Ricky. Ricky placed a protective arm around Louie and glared at Billy.

"Hey, I'm sorry about scaring you and your mom. It was really brave of you to jump in front of her though."

Ricky loosened his grip on Louie and looked skeptically at his mom for direction.

"It's okay, Ricky," Della said, and locked the van.

"Let's go see this Brady person before it gets any later," said Della, glancing towards the skyline.

Billy bent down, scooped up Louie in his arms before anyone could object, and started back over the roadblock. Della could see, now after her swollen eyes had cleared of tears and the anger had drained away, Billy's sweet lopsided grin and boyish mannerism. His short brown hair cut above his ears and well above his collar reminded Della of the kid down the block who played football for the high school and who in the summers mowed their lawn. Billy's long tall stride made maneuvering over the logs and branches much easier than for Della or Ricky. Standing at the top of the pile, Billy played and joked with Louie while waiting patiently for the others.

Once everyone was at the top, Billy said, "I can't go with you. I have to keep my post, but I'll radio and have someone come get you and take you to Brady."

Della was about to ask who this Brady person was, but Billy had already pulled his pocket radio out and had it to his mouth.

A few minutes later she watched as a white Ford Taurus made its way from the town down the road to the roadblock.

* * *

The man that drove the white car did not seem pleased to be playing taxi driver to a woman and two little kids. They rode in silence through the town. Della noticed that there were indeed people in Mount Hope. She noticed three men standing outside of the old lodge and more men standing by a fishing shack. She didn't see any women or children, but assumed that they must be around because she had seen toys and bicycles near where the men were standing at the lodge. Della also noticed that each man had looked displeasingly at them as the car passed. That, along with the fact that they each had firearms over their shoulders, made Della increasingly uneasy.

The car stopped in the driveway of one of the town's larger fishing cabins. Two armed men sat on the porch, both with unwelcoming expressions on their face.

"Who the hell is that?" the man on the left asked the driver.

"Oh, Billy went and let these three through." The driver growled and Della almost expected him to bark as he looked at her. "Brady's in there." He jerked his thumb at the cabin's door, turned on his heal, and quickly walked across the street to the old lodge.

Della could feel her sons pressing closer to each side of her as they passed between the unsmiling armed men on the porch to reach the door. She pushed open the door and saw the back of a tall tanned man. He was standing looking out the side cabin window with binoculars. Dressed in blue jeans and a tight slightly stained white t-shirt, she could tell he worked outdoors before all this had happened. His arms and back were sculpted by what probably was years of hard labor. He already possessed the dark rich tan that, at this time of year, was found only on teenagers who spent most of the Spring lying in tanning beds getting ready for swimsuit weather, or in this case on someone who spends his days outdoors.

When he heard the door close behind him, he lowered the binoculars and turned to face them. Della noticed he wore the same unfriendly expression. Looking down at the boys, Della watched a transformation quickly occur on his face. He smiled and walked closer to them. Bending down a few feet away, careful not to invade their personal space, he grinned at Ricky and held out his hand.

"I hear we got ourselves quite a little hero in the making here," he said, as Ricky tentatively shook his hand.

Grinning, he rubbed his rugged tanned hand over Louie's head and stood up. "Do you boys like ice cream?" he asked.

Both boys looked up eagerly seeking Della's permission to accept. She nodded.

"Yes, sir," Ricky answered politely.

"Well great. If I'm not mistaken, Missy is over at the lodge with the other kids dishing it out right now." Brady looked up at Della and said, "I can have Jake, my man outside, walk them across the street, if it's alright with you."

Della was torn. She hadn't let her sons out of her sight since this whole mess began. But she wasn't prepared for Ricky to hear what Brady might tell her. She didn't want him to worry any more than he already did.

"It's okay. Jake's a good man. He has three kids of his own over there."

Della nodded and Ricky took Louie's hand and walked outside with Brady. She could hear him telling Jake not to let them out of his sight. She was not sure if he was worried for the children's sake or about them.

Once back inside, Brady turned and motioned to a wooden chair on the opposite side of a cluttered desk.

"I know that Billy said you weren't letting anyone up here, but we do own a cabin here," Della began.

Brady's eyes narrowed a bit and said, "Ma'am..."

"Please call me Della," she interrupted.

"Okay, Della." He started again, "I'm sure you're scared. You're alone with two little ones, but I also know you don't own a cabin up here. I have a listing of all the sites right here and they are almost all spoken for, so unless your husband is here waiting for you, I'm sorry." Brady had unrolled a large yellowing map with the cabins marked off by red circles.

"I'm not real good with maps, Mr...?" She looked at him, questioning.

"Brady."

"Oh, right. I'm not real good with maps, Brady. But I do know where my cabin is. My husband and I designed and built it from scratch over eight years ago. I'll take you to it. It's just over this ridge. It sets between two little slopes and it's right up from the lake. At sunset it's almost invisible." The desperation was creeping its way back into her voice again. She felt drained from her earlier explosion at Billy.

"Della, are you talking about this cabin right here?" He pointed to a red circle on the map.

Getting up, she walked around the desk and studied the map. On it, she could see the lake and several little cabins, as well as the lodge. Searching for familiar landmarks, she took a deep breath of relief and said yes, that was her cabin.

"Do you have any proof that's your cabin?" he asked, still skeptical.

"Proof?" Why do I need proof that that cabin is mine?" She could feel her temper flaring once again.

"Well, there's already a couple who moved in there yesterday. They say it's their cabin," he said, standing up from the desk.

"What? Did anyone think to ask them for proof?" she said irritably.

"No, but...," Brady started to explain.

"You don't ask them for proof, but you demand it from me?" She stood up and started to walk out the door.

"Where are you going?" Brady asked, walking out after her.

Della turned around in the driveway, gravel crunching under her feet and looked up at him. His tall frame towering over her, he grabbed her elbow as she turned back around and started to head for the lodge.

"Let go of me, before I get really mad," she said through clenched teeth.

"Just wait a sec, will you," he said quickly, releasing her arm. "Tell me where you're going?"

"Why, what difference does it make to you?" She looked around the town. "I understand that they've made you king, but I'm not one of your loyal subjects." She glared at him and continued, "I am taking my children to *my* cabin and Lord help whoever is staying there. Now either get out of my way or come with me, it doesn't make any difference to me."

"Della," he began, "you just can't waltz up there and confront these people. Times are different now."

"Tell me about it," she said, looking around him to see Frick and Frack on the porch with their hands on their weapons, waiting to see what she was going to do.

"At least let me go with you." Attempting to smile, he added, "Please?"

Reluctantly, she relented and Brady followed her as she continued across the street to the lodge.

7

Ash wiped the sweat from his brow with his t-shirt and then looked at Barbara sleeping in the passenger seat and then back to Emily, who was asleep in the back seat. Both of them looked as if they didn't have a care in the world. He thought of what their life may have been like before. His thoughts were promptly erased as thoughts of his own family flooded his mind. He was worried and longed to be with them again.

I wish I could get some sleep, he thought. But his fears were keeping him from a much desired rest. He had some suspicion that whatever bit Barbara may cause her to turn mad. Ash contemplated what to do in case she did. Damn, her daughter would be there to see it all play out. He deliberated his alternatives while sitting in the driver's seat. He leaned back on the headrest and shut his fatigued eyes. Just for a couple of seconds, he reminded himself repeatedly.

* * *

Ash was jolted awake by an indistinguishable shrill screaming resonating throughout the garage. *What the Hell?* he thought. His wits hadn't quite kicked in, but he recognized where he was and what could be occurring at this actual moment. He hurriedly rose from the vehicle, rubbing his tired eyes and looking intently at the girl sleeping in the back seat of the Impala.

Then the piercing noise that echoed throughout the garage was there once more. It was Barbara violently vomiting and moaning. This moan was no moan of pain, but of gratification. Ash had to think fast. He quickly cracked open both windows and slowly closed the car door.

Ash had to check on Barbara, but was apprehensive at the thought that he might have to kill what she had become. He detested picking up the tire iron, but he had no other choice. Ash followed the foul stench and the bloody mucus on the cement floor. The vomiting and moaning had abruptly ceased. The intense throbbing in Ash's temples and heart seemed to be in a race to a finish line that wasn't there. He held his weapon ready while holding in his own vomit. He gagged at Barbara's atrocious odor.

"Barbara, where are you?" Ash called out. "I'm coming to get you Barbara."

Nothing.

"Come on Barbara. I only want to help. Your daughter needs you," he pleaded. Maybe she had passed out and was going to turn. Ash prayed that was the case. He looked back at the Impala to see that everything was still the same.

I've got to do something. He trembled slightly, but drew strength from his fear and sprinted as he followed her bodily fluids. He zigzagged around the parked cars to where finally the putrid fluid ended.

Where in the Hell is she? His mind roared. Ash bent down on all fours, making sure to stay clear of the toxic fluid and looked under the cars on either side for as far as he could see. Nothing was there. Chills overcame his body as the top of his head tingled with anticipation.

An inhuman screech rang out overhead. Ash looked up as Barbara landed squarely on his back. The impact caused him to lose his breath, but Ash still managed to roll out from under her. She had pounced on him like a predator. He started to stand up and was tackled full force and knocked back five feet again to the hard floor. He winced in pain, grabbed his back, and watched as Barbara growled and snickered at him. She was salivating to the point that white trails of saliva dripped to the floor. Through her matted frizzy hair her eyes stared emotionless and dilated. Her smell was atrocious as the stench of human waste and vomit blanketed the air.

He slowly stood up, never taking his eyes off Barbara. Ash noticed that his tire iron was nowhere in sight.

Damn, he thought, *what do I do*? He had no time to think as she shrieked and dashed at him. Ash didn't know what to do, but he did know that he needed to keep well away from her bite and her bodily fluids for fear he might get infected. So he ran. She was quickly on his heels; he had to think fast. He ran hard to the side of the garage, glanced back at Barbara's position, and planned out his next move. Ash sped up and swiftly twisted, putting the garage railing at his back. He challenged Barbara to come at him by standing in the open and shouting obscenities at her.

"Come on bitch!" He waved his hands to get her attention. "Come on!" he yelled at the top of his lungs.

Barbara screamed as she leaped in the air at Ash.

Ash wasn't sure how it was going to work, but he had few other choices. As she left the ground, Ash grabbed hold of her waist and turned slightly, hoisting her up into the air and over the ledge. He quickly let go and she plummeted four stories to the concrete below. Ash heard nothing as she hit, just an abrupt end to her screaming. Ash watched her twisted lifeless body and waited to make sure she was dead.

To his right, on the ground, Ash saw six infected people look up to him simultaneously and run in the direction of the parking garage as they disappeared from sight. "Oh shit," Ash gulped.

I wanted to wait until night, but now I have no freakin' choice, he thought as he ran for the Impala. Ash dreaded telling Emily about her mother. He quickly grasped the handle and opened the Impala's door.

"Where's my Mommy?" Emily demanded, as she attempted to make meaning of what was happening.

Ash turned the key that was already in the ignition and fired up the engine. He gunned the motor by accident and shoved the gear shift to drive, chirping the tires.

"Where's my Mommy?"

Ash could feel her eyes on him as he maneuvered around parked cars on his way down to the exit.

"Emily", he said pausing "your Mommy was taken away by one of the crazy people."

"No!" she cried. "You're lying."

"I wish I was honey. I tried to help her, but it was too late," he replied.

"I don't want to leave my Mommy!" she cried hysterically. "I want my Mommy!"

"Honey, she told me to get you out of here. She wants me to watch over you," Ash said, trying to comfort her.

"No!" she cried frantically.

Their conversation was put on hold as the mob rushed their car.

Damn, we almost made it out.

"What floor are we on?" Emily asked.

"The second," Ash replied.

Ash sped up. He knew the only way he was going to get out of the garage was by running over them. It was cruel, but he had no other alternative.

"Buckle up and hang on Emily." Ash glanced over to her to see if she did as she was asked. Ash buckled up, as well.

Ash could hear their furious shrieks, as one after another was thrown from the Impala. Several hung on while Ash swerved back and forth hitting other parked cars to knock them off. The crunch of bones became a numbing experience for Ash.

Finally, he pulled the Impala up to where the exit bar once stood, but now laid on the ground after another vehicle in all probability hit it in an attempt to escape the garage.

As Ash tried to depart the garage, an infected person slammed his head through Emily's window. Shattered glass exploded throughout the car, covering Ash and Emily with small shards. Emily squealed in terror.

"Turn away!" Ash hollered over Emily's cries and the man's shrieks of fury. The infected man was middle-aged and balding. His dull lifeless eyes and his pale, bleeding face protruded through the window. The diseased blood dripping from broken teeth seemed to seek vengeance.

Ash placed the car in park and turned sideways, pulling Emily out of the way. He kicked with both feet repeatedly at the man's head. The beating to the man's face only enraged him more. He somehow managed to thrash his fist hard enough around the broken window that he reached in and grabbed Emily's hair and yanked at her.

"Auuggh, he's got me!" Emily wailed.

"Just a second!" Ash said, as he kept lashing out at the man while unbuckling Emily. "Get to the back!"

"I can't. He won't let go," she cried.

Ash grabbed the man's wrist with his hand and twisted hard, which loosened the man's grip, at the same time kicking him hard in the face.

"Oh!" Emily cried as she pulled free, then immediately jumped in the back seat.

The madman still held small straggling strands of her hair.

At that time, the whole car was suddenly bombarded by a horde of the infected.

"Damn it!" Ash shouted in anger. "Screw this!" Ash swiveled around, shifting into drive as he punched the gas. The Impala jolted forward as Ash peeked around to see who hung onto the windshield. The mob pounded and screamed to get in, but Ash was more worried about wrecking. One by one they fell from the car. But the man in the side window never stopped his relentless attack. The crunch of the dead bodies that scattered the streets sickened him. But he had to survive and he had to keep this young girl safe. The foul smell of death was all around.

After the last of the monsters fell from his hood, Ash turned his full attention to the one hanging out of the passenger window. "Alright, your turn dickhead!" Ash said to the man in the passenger side window. He aimed the car so he would just barely brush an upcoming lamppost. Ash gunned it and told Emily to buckle up, again. The Impala got up to 50 miles an hour before they scraped along the lamppost. Sparks flew and a deafening screeching sound ended the man's time on Earth. The man was gone, but his head bounced on the seat and down to the floor where it rolled around several times before it rested under the front seat.

Ash slowed the car down to a coasting speed. He looked out his rear view mirror and all around the car. He was speechless at the sight of the thousands of dead people, pets, and birds scattered all about the city. He looked back to Emily.

"I know everything is scary right now. But I promise I'll take care of you and everything will be alright," Ash told the frightened girl. Although, he didn't know if he would be able to keep his promise.

8

Brady reached the lodge before Della and stepped in front of her, blocking the doorway.

"Before you get mad at me again, let me say something," he said, trying to impede another unpleasant situation.

"Go on," Della said, as she looked over his shoulder through the glass window, scanning the small group of children for her own.

"If what you're saying is true," he began, and seeing her face, hurriedly added, "And I'm not saying, it ain't, but if what you're saying is true, do you really want to go confront these people with your kids in tow?"

Della studied his face. A few minutes before this man had wanted her removed from the mountain, kids or no kids, now he was giving her parenting advice.

"No offense, Brady, but you're a complete stranger to me." She turned in a slow circle, spreading her arms and gesturing at her surroundings, "Everyone here is a complete stranger to me. With everything that's been going on, I don't think it would be in the boys' best interest for me to go off and leave them with complete strangers."

"Look, I know you're scared and angry," Brady began. He placed both hands on her shoulders, turning her to face him directly. "Hell, we're all scared and angry. We don't know what in the world is going on. The rules have all changed. But Della, look at them." He placed his arm around her shoulders and guided her towards the window of the lodge.

"The boys are safe now. There are armed guards all around this lodge; no one will be able to get to them." He turned her towards him again and held her gaze a few moments longer. "I promise."

Della stood for a moment and watched her sons. Inside the lodge sat a dozen or so children. If she had not been aware of the chaos in the world, she wouldn't have known anything was wrong from looking at the scene inside the lodge. The children were scattered throughout the large room. A few were gathered around a board game while others were lying on the floor watching a battery operated TV-DVD player.

Della noticed Ricky seated on an old orange and blue-checkered chair in between both groups watching the other children. Louie, however, had evidently become friends with a red-haired boy who looked to Della to be around the same age. The two were seated near the TV with a deck of cards. Louie was laughing and talking as if it were perfectly normal for the boys to be playing cards while a lethal virus attacked the world.

Knowing Brady was right, Della caught Ricky's attention and motioned for him through the window to come outside. Once outside, Ricky looked apprehensively first at Brady and then to Della.

"I'm going to go check out the cabin first, would you care to stay here and watch Louie for me?" she asked, carefully omitting the other less than positive details.

"But I should go with you Mom." Ricky looked at Brady suspiciously, "What if you run into another one of his goons?"

"Brady's going to go with me, just in case," she added reassuringly. "I need you to take care of Louie. Can you do that for me sweetie?"

"I guess," Ricky said, with his head drooping. "Just hurry back, will ya?"

Della gratefully scooped him up into a tight hug and kissed him quick on his reddening cheeks. Ricky had tried unsuccessfully to explain to his mother that he was too old for such public displays.

"Now, make sure you keep an eye on Louie. There's a water bottle and a pop in Louie's backpack if you get thirsty," she told him, as he was already making his way towards the lodge door. "And don't let him go outside. Do you hear me Ricky?" She was talking to the back of his head as he nodded and waved her goodbye. As usual, Ricky believed his mother was the queen of overkill.

Della followed Brady back across the road to where his Jeep was parked. "You said the boys were safe here, but you don't know if you're going to allow us to stay here, yet."

Brady looked into Della's eyes, "I gotta feelin' that you're telling the truth. I trust my instincts."

She smiled when he stopped to open her door for her and waited until she was settled before closing it behind her. Putting the keys in the ignition, Brady glanced over to find Della grinning.

"Something funny?" Brady asked.

"I'm sure it's just the situation, but it seemed funny that you would wait to help me with the door," Della said.

"Why?" he said seriously, "You think someone like me can't be chivalrous?"

"That's not what I meant," Della said, suddenly wishing she had kept her mouth shut. "I was talking about the state of the world right now and someone taking the time to hold open a door for a lady is..." She could not think of the right word. Miserably, she sank back into the seat. She hadn't meant to insult him, she didn't even know him.

"That's called gallows humor." The seriousness was gone from his face. "Finding something funny under a stressful situation that you typically wouldn't find funny," he continued. "I'm sorry, I shouldn't have overreacted. Residue from a former life, I suppose."

Della looked out the window at the passing hillsides wondering what residue a man like Brady could have. Maybe if they made it through this horror, she'd ask him.

Changing the subject, Brady said, "When we get there, it would be best if you let me do the talking." Seeing the dubious look on her face, he continued, "It has nothing to do with you being a woman, it's the fact that I've met these people already."

"What are you going to do?" she asked.

"You mean, if they don't leave?"

"Yeah, the thought had occurred to me," she said worriedly.

"Let's just see how it plays out, first, okay?" He turned the Jeep off the road into a narrow gravel drive. "Trust me," he said, holding her gaze a moment longer than she thought necessary.

Once around the sharp curve in the driveway, the cabin was in full view. Seeing it for the first time, Della gasped. For two days now, all she could think of was the cabin, almost as if seeing the cabin would be a panacea. Her chest tightened, she could feel her heart beating faster and for an instant it was too much.

That cabin, that beautiful wooden structure symbolized everything her life had become with Ash. That cabin meant beauty, serenity, calmness and most of all, security. Della felt movement on her lap. Looking down, she saw it was her own hands shaking. The overwhelming emotions threatened to overtake her. She couldn't let this happen. *Not now, not now,* she thought, as she reached a trembling hand towards the Jeep's door handle.

Brady hurriedly shut off the engine, jumped out of the driver's side and made his way around the Jeep until he was blocking her way.

"We decided that you would allow me to handle this, Della," he said, holding firmly, but not threatening, onto her forearm. "Remember?"

"You decided," she said, not breaking her gaze from the house. "I don't remember agreeing to anything."

"Damn it, Della." This time his grip tightened. "Listen to me on this, I know what I'm doing."

Della's eyes wavered for the first time from her cabin and rested upon Brady's hand on her arm. She let her gaze travel up from his calloused fingers, up his tan, muscled arm until she locked onto his dark eyes. For a few moments she studied him silently.

"Fine," she said, looking away. Then reaching out at the last moment, she touched his shoulder and said, "You just remember that is my cabin. Mine. You understand?"

It was his turn to study her face. "Alright."

Della stood at the Jeep, irritated at her inability to confront the strangers who stole her house. Not wanting to be completely left out of the loop, she followed Brady and stood at the bottom of the stairs while he climbed them up to the front porch and knocked on the door. Everywhere she looked, she saw Ash.

The railing she caressed beneath her fingertips instantly brought a memory crashing in on her. She could clearly see Ash standing there sanding the rough railing the day they had installed it. In his yellow swim trunks and no shirt, singing loudly and, as usual, off key, to an old country song that belted its way into the air from a radio plugged in nearby.

Della closed her eyes and for an instant felt Ash's presence with her. She could see his face staring at her, telling her to be strong and push through the pain. Instantly, she was overcome with images of her husband. His beautiful rugged face, his lopsided smile that always warmed her heart, the stubble across his strong jaw line that never seemed to go away, the soft reassuring feel of his hands on hers, the way he loved to hold her, the warmth of his kisses, the sexy way he growled when she'd teasingly rub against him at night when she'd climb into bed. Della shook her head to clear the memories away. She had to continue to be strong. Once she and the boys were safely in the cabin, then she could start to let her guard down a little, maybe.

At the top of the stairs, Della heard the sound of voices. She could see a short dark-haired woman and a taller brown-haired man. They looked familiar, although she couldn't quite place them.

"Evening Mr. and Mrs. Shields."

"Brady," the man said, and then looked around him down the stairs to where Della was standing. Seeing Della, the man looked quickly at his wife, then back at Della, and nodded as though nothing were wrong.

"I'm sorry to bother you folks, but we have a little situation that I'd like to see if we could clear up," Brady continued.

Della noticed his usual relaxed stance was gone and replaced by a confident air of authority, as if he'd done this before.

"What's the problem, Brady?" Mr. Shields asked.

"Mrs. Bishop." Brady motioned with his head towards Della, "has made a claim on this cabin. Says it's her family's." Brady took a moment and let his words sink in.

"Oh, is that Della Bishop?" Mrs. Shields said, leaning around Brady to wave and smiled a little too broadly.

"Yes, do you know Mrs. Bishop?" Brady asked.

"Well, yes, I mean no, but we knew her husband."

Straightening to his full height, Della noticed Brady was using his height to gain a position of power over Mr. Shields. "About the cabin," Brady redirected.

"Oh, yeah. Ash sold us the cabin two months ago," Mrs. Shields said, and then looking over at Della, added for Della's behalf, "I'm sorry honey, didn't Ash tell you?"

"What?" Della couldn't contain it any longer. She advanced up the stairway to her cabin and the intruders.

"I'm so sorry about your husband, sweetie," Mrs. Shields began as she lowered her eyelashes and softened her voice, "The world today is just ...," her voice trailed off as she wiped her face, at what Della believed to be the worst crying job she had seen in a long time.

"Ash is not dead," Della replied in an even tone, "and he never sold you our cabin."

"Whatever do you mean?" This time the man spoke up with feigned disbelief. "Of course he sold us the cabin. $70,000."

"Mr. Shields," Brady began, cutting off Della before she had a chance to tell them all how ridiculous this whole evening was becoming. "Do you happen to have any proof Mr. Bishop sold the house to you?"

The couple eyed each other for a moment before Mr. Shields spoke.

"Well, I'm sure we have the bill of sale somewhere."

"Great, if I could just have that, we'll get this all taken care of and get out of your hair for the evening," Brady said, walking towards the door.

Stepping in front of Brady and blocking the way, Mrs. Shields said, "We can't get it for you at the moment, we have a mess here. We just got here yesterday and we're still waist deep in boxes. Have no idea where to start looking."

Mr. Shields then added, "Will Ash be joining us soon? I'm sure he could clear all this up." The couple then looked at Della expectantly.

"We're not sure when Mr. Bishop will be joining us at Mt. Hope. He was away on business when this all occurred."

"Ooh," they said in unison, as if that suddenly explained everything.

"It's getting late and I can understand not wanting to go through all those boxes right now, but we do need to get this matter cleared up, so why don't we meet at my office at ten tomorrow morning," Brady said, placing a hand on the small of Della's back, gently guiding her to accept his proposal.

"That would be fine, Brady, we'll see you there."

"Again, Mrs. Bishop, I do hope Ash is okay and makes it here before…." Mrs. Shields again, wiped away nonexistent tears and hurried into the cabin with her husband right behind her.

Brady's hand continued to apply consistent pressure on her lower back until they were standing in front of the Jeep.

"What the hell's wrong with you?" Della asked incredulously. "Any blind man could see they were lying!"

"Yep," Brady answered, and opened the Jeep's passenger side door for her, motioning her to have a seat. She did so. He closed the door on her and walked around the front of the Jeep to the driver's side. Della watched open-mouthed, amazed that they were really leaving those people in her cabin.

"We're leaving?" she asked. "We're just leaving those people in my cabin? You're not going to do anything at all to them?" Della turned completely sideways in her seat, facing Brady.

"You believe them over me?" She was amazed. She couldn't believe that he had bought that whole trick pony act those two had just performed.

"I never said I believed them," Brady said, when she stopped long enough for him to speak.

"You're leaving them. Hello?"

"This is only for the night and we will get everything taken care of in the morning," he said calmingly.

"But why in the morning?" she asked. "Why didn't you just throw them out right there?"

"Della, you have to calm down," Brady said, after noticing how flushed her face had become and how agitated her movements were inside the Jeep.

"Calm down?" Her voice had raised an octave. "Calm down? You've got to be kidding me!"

Della reached around for the door handle and tried to open it, but the automatic door locks delayed her long enough for Brady to notice what she was trying to do and slam on the brakes.

"Della!" he shouted, as she forced open the door and flung herself out of the car, making contact with the gravel seconds after Brady stopped the Jeep. Instantly, she was up and wiping away the dirt from her jeans.

Della's arm hurt and she was certain she had twisted her ankle in her less than calm exit of the Jeep, but she refused to slow down for the pain. Those people were in her cabin, her's and Ash's. The cabin they had dreamed about, drawing out plans together. The cabin that they loved, that her boys loved.

She wasn't sure what she was going to do, but she knew she couldn't just walk away, leaving those people alone in her cabin.

"Della!" Brady had managed to exit the Jeep and was running after her. "Wait!"

The tears were flowing freely now and the pain from her arm and ankle made her wince with each step.

Couldn't he understand? she thought. *Didn't he know? That cabin. She had to be in that cabin. Ash. Ash.*

Her foot caught on something and she stumbled. Sitting on the gravel, Della tried wiping her face, but her hands were dusty and she felt the mixture of warm tears and dirt smear across her cheeks. Brady had caught up with her. Sitting down beside her, he handed her a piece of cloth from his back jean pocket. It was only a torn piece of cloth, but Della was grateful as she tried unsuccessfully to clean her face without a mirror. She couldn't stop the tears. She felt them moving, rolling in waves throughout her body, building with each new thought of Ash. She knew it wasn't about the cabin. But, somehow she had began to equate Ash with the cabin. Having it taken away from her was like having her husband taken away.

"Are you alright?" Brady asked, after a few minutes had passed.

Della couldn't speak. She drew her knees up to her chest and put her head down on them. It was useless to talk now, she knew she'd only sound like a babbling idiot. She expected to hear the dirt road crunching beneath his feet as he walked away, and looked up surprised when she realized he had not moved from her side.

Brady was a blur through her swollen and achy eyes, but she could still see the concern on his face.

"I'm sorry," she sobbed. "You probably think I'm a complete nut case."

She looked sideways at him, expecting him to say something, anything.

"Well, I don't blame you," she continued. "I think I'm a complete nut case."

"It's okay," he said, moving closer to her and taking the rag from her tightly clenched fist. Opening her fist, Della realized she had been squeezing it so tightly that she had drawn blood from her palm.

"We'll get through this," he said softly.

Brady folded the rag to find a clean spot and leaned close to her face. He brushed the wet, tear drenched wisps of hair from her face and used the rag to wipe her flushed cheeks.

"I'm sorry," she said again, feeling foolish and drained.

"Let's get you up and go check on those boys of yours," Brady told her.

He had apparently noticed her limping before and wrapped her arm around his neck, gently lifting her to her feet. Weak from the emotional outpour and the day's events, Della felt herself give way and she leaned into his body for support. Grateful he was there. Grateful to this stranger who had just witnessed her descent into a stereotypical female blubbering abyss. Grateful for the opportunity to rest on someone's strong shoulder. Grateful for his ability to understand her situation. Grateful.

As she was attempting to bring her gratitude into perspective, Brady stopped walking.

"What's...?" She had wanted to ask what was wrong, but Brady held up a hand to silence her.

Brady turned his head to listen. Della didn't need to. She heard it. A soft humming, reverberating through the trees. They turned around, looking for the noise. Nothing. The noise grew louder and suddenly the road grew darker as if the sun had ducked behind a cloud. Immediately, they both looked up. A dark black cloud was moving up the road towards them. From a distance, it looked to Della as if a rain cloud was headed their way. Only the single black cloud didn't move in unison with the other white clouds in the sky. It turned as if a flock of birds would turn; it behaved like a swarm of bees. But Della knew that cloud was hundreds of yards away and it would take millions of bees to make it look like that.

"What is that?" she asked Brady, feeling the fear starting to build within her.

"Come on," he said, and wrapped his arm back around her waist, dragging her, half running towards the Jeep. The noise was deafening as the cloud moved inexplicably fast in their direction. She could feel Brady's fear as he shoved her into the Jeep and ran around to the driver's side.

"Hurry!" she yelled, over the now roaring swarm.

"Make sure all the windows are closed!" he ordered, as he started the engine.

Gravel sprayed over the back window as Brady threw the Jeep into drive and stomped onto the gas pedal. Ahead a few feet was a thicket of trees with just enough space to pull the Jeep into. If they could make it there before the swarm, it just might hide them. Della watched in horror, as the black cloud grew larger and larger until she was certain day had been swallowed by night. Still, she sensed the swarm was further off than they thought. Brady pulled the Jeep under the protection of the thicket and turned off the engine. Sitting quietly, Della felt her heart pounding quicker as the humming grew louder and closer. Terrified, she squeezed her eyes shut and prayed. She prayed for the safety of herself and Brady and most of all, for the safety of her boys.

9

Only 126 miles until St. Louis, Ash thought to himself as he passed a mileage sign. He had already driven four days on I-55. The interstate drive was not a speedy one though. He and Emily had to switch cars every time they got to a point that was impassable. They now traveled in a Volkswagen Passat and the sun was setting. As always, they would have to locate somewhere to eat and some shelter until daybreak.

"Emily?" Ash softly asked.

"Yes," she responded. She still was, understandably, not over her mother's death.

"We're going to pull off at the next exit and try to find some food. It's starting to get dark." He quickly turned to her in the back seat and smiled.

"Okay," she whispered.

The miles they passed together were sluggish and occasionally terrifying, but as time went on, the number of infected had diminished. They had witnessed and smelled the appalling odor from the dead that littered the streets. It was a gruesome sight, but somehow they had learned to deal with it. More than a few times, they had run into normal people like themselves, just trying to get to their own destinations. But the talk was limited because their first concern was contracting the virus. For the past four days, Ash had heard nothing on the specifics of the virus. Ash's cell phone was somewhere back on I-55 near Chicago. It had never had service since the mayhem started and eventually the phone's battery went dead, so Ash tossed it.

"Here we go, keep an eye out, Emily," Ash said. He thought it was beneficial to keep her busy.

"Alright," Emily said, as she stuck her chin upward to see outside. She surveyed the area more like a professional would than a little girl. Ash steadily maneuvered around the vacant and wrecked cars. At last he saw a clearing, but a large dead woman blocked their way. He hated to run over dead bodies, but sometimes he had no choice. He couldn't get out and move her; it was too dangerous. The fear of contracting the virus was always present. They even traveled with all the car windows up and the air-conditioning on re-circulation. Not only because of the heat and the virus, but also the pungent odor from the dead was hard to take. There was no way around her. Ash slowly ran over her inch by inch, causing a loud popping sound followed by a gas release. The cracking of the bones as the car slid somewhat over the body made Ash's teeth clench. He turned to see Emily clutching her ears with both of her hands. The whole situation was grisly, as the back of the car bounced slightly and slid down her body as they cleared the dead woman's crushed carcass.

The Passat rounded the exit and merged onto the roadway leading to a gas station/convenient mart. The sign overhead read "Lucky's Pump and Go." The store looked ransacked and looted like all the others, but they always managed to scavenge up some groceries and toiletries.

Ash pulled in beside a gas pump and inspected the area before getting out.

"See anything?" he asked Emily.

"Nothing!" she replied promptly. She knew the drill, so she waited in the car while Ash stepped out and checked the pumps.

"Damn it," he said.

"Looks like we need another car for tomorrow. These pumps aren't working...no electricity," he said to Emily, as he opened her door and led her by the hand. They guardedly looked over their shoulders and around the vicinity for strangers.

"Stay right by my side," Ash said, as he slowly opened the door.

"Hello!" Ash then waited. "Is anyone here?"

"I guess it's safe Emily, but still keep an eye out?" he winked at her.

Emily let go of his hand as they gathered soft drinks, canned foods, and toilet paper. Ash found a road map. They quickly packed the Passat with what little they could scrounge up.

"Let's take one final look inside before we find a place to stay the night," Ash said.

Emily went straight for the candy and filled her pockets and even her socks. She then ventured to the rear of the store in search of toys.

Ash, on the other hand, rummaged around the clerk's counter in search of...

"Hell, yeah!" he howled. Ash finally found a firearm. *Hot damn,* he thought. A double barrel shotgun and two boxes of ammo. *I've hit the jackpot.* He was proud of himself, but that was short-lived as a squeal rang out from the back of the store.

"Help! Ash! Help!" Emily screamed.

"Emily?" Ash's heart leapt as he sprinted through the store's obstacle course of boxes, shelves, broken glass and other items.

When he reached the back of the store, he saw Emily crying as she looked up to him.

"It's in there!" She pointed to a closed door. She trembled as she sucked in each breath between crying.

"What is it?" He looked to Emily and then to the door.

"Just look!" she almost demanded under her sobs.

Ash checked his shotgun and found it loaded. The rest of the shells were in the front the store, so he hoped he could do with only two shots, if necessary.

Ash tasted his chalky lips as his tongue rolled over them. He heard a heinous cry from behind the door. A shiver traveled down his spine as he slowly and carefully turned the knob and opened the door.

What he saw was the most horrifying thing he had ever seen in his life. He was overwhelmed with fear, which then turned rapidly to sorrow. His eyes swelled with tears.

In the dimness of the closing day, in the back storage room lay a lifeless woman in her mid-twenties. Her gorged, motionless eyes were transfixed on Ash and the blue of her body told him she was no longer alive. She had veins that spider webbed up her neck and onto her cheek like a road map, but that was not the worst of it.

On the rigid cement floor was a newborn baby covered with bloody afterbirth and dirt. The umbilical cord was still attached to the baby boy. He seemed to shriek with anger as he looked at Ash.

Why? Ash thought.

The infant wiggled furiously and shrieked in a deep inhuman tone.

The baby tried inching on its back towards Ash, but was unable to move from the umbilical cord's strong clutch. Foaming crimson bubbles spewed from the boy as his eyes rolled to the back of head.

Ash kept his gun in check as he inched into the room and knelt down several steps from the baby. Ash was hypnotized by the baby, almost forgetting that it was infected.

"It's okay little one. I'm here to help you!" Ash said to the little wicked one.

Ash reached out, but quickly yanked his hand back. The baby made a gurgled hiss and reached out for Ash.

Ash backed up slowly.

"Emily?" He waited for her to look at him.

"Yes," She nodded.

"Look at me." Ash placed his finger under her chin and pulled her head up to look at him. He wiped her tears from her cheeks.

"What are you going to do?" she asked Ash.

"I don't want to lie to you, but the baby is infected and if I don't do something, the baby will suffer," Ash whispered.

"Are you going to kill the baby, like you did Mommy?" her quivering thin lips asked.

"Yes, and like your Mommy, it's the only thing I can do to help the baby," Ash paused. "Now, you stay right here. I'm going to close the door and you'll hear a big bang. Then I will come right out again."

She intently looked at him.

"Alright?" Ash said.

"Yes," she answered, and lowered her head again.

Ash shut the door behind him and noticed the baby staring directly at him making cooing sounds.

"Damn-it!" Ash raised his shotgun and eyed down the barrel at the baby boy. *What did he do to deserve this?* Ash asked himself. Tears ran down Ash's face as he aimed, closed his eyes and fired. A tremendous boom reverberated the entire stock room as the coos became silence. He turned and left the room, not looking at the destruction.

10

Della put her head on her lap, trying to become as small as possible, as if the swarm might see her through the thicket and the Jeep's roof. Although she was certain a normal bee or fly could not detect them, she could not shake the eerie feeling that this was not a normal insect. Squeezing her eyes tightly shut, she listened to the swarm's hum. It was rhythmic and repeated the same varying octaves. It reminded Della of Morse Code. Again, she shivered. This time it was more from the cooling of the temperature in the Jeep.

Turning to look at Brady, Della noticed the inside of the Jeep had a light covering of what looked to be frost. Confused, she opened her mouth to say something and was shocked to see her breath form into a white puffy cloud. Rubbing her arms to keep warm, her teeth began to chatter and she again felt certain that whatever was outside in that swarm wasn't something that would be easily explained. Brady reached a hand over and placed it upon Della's cool forearm. Once he had made eye contact, he pointed towards the sky and towards his ear. She had been so confused over the drop in temperature; Della had not noticed the humming had been growing distant. Then as suddenly as it had begun, it was gone and Della could see the light breaking its way through the heavy thicket.

"Is it g-g-gone?" she asked, her teeth still chattering.

"I think so, but let's wait a little bit to make sure," Brady whispered.

"What was that?" she asked.

"I heard on the radio before you came that this virus that's attacking everyone is evidently coming from those insects, like a horsefly or something close to it. I don't remember its name, something like spiderfly or spiderflies, or something weird like that. I wrote it all down at the office," Brady answered, rubbing his own arms, trying to rush his blood into the cooler areas.

The inside of the Jeep had warmed up considerably in the 90 degree heat of the New Mexico mountains. Whatever had caused the drastic cooling had apparently left with the swarm. Della turned her ear towards the outdoors and listened. She could no longer hear the swarms humming, nor could she see any traces of the insects outside her window.

"Brady, were those things headed towards the cabin?" Della's thoughts reverted to a few minutes earlier when they were standing outside on the cabin's front porch.

"Yeah, it looks that way."

"Oh my God, Brady!" Della screamed. She realized that it wasn't where the swarm was going that should have concerned her, but it was where the swarm had come from.

"That swarm came *up* the road!" She was trying to force the words out, but felt as if her mouth were full of peanut butter.

"The town, the boys, the swarm was coming *from* the town!" She finally managed to get out.

Recognition began to form in Brady's eyes. As quickly as he had done before when they were in danger of being discovered by the swarm, he yanked the gearshift into drive and punched the gas pedal. The Jeep fishtailed in the heavy gravel and dirt from the thicket, but finally surrendered to the horsepower of the Jeep and the determined driver.

"God, Brady, what if ..." Della gripped the dashboard and cursed her decision to leave them behind. She should have never let them out of her sight. *Ash wouldn't have made that mistake,* she thought. Not when things are so uncertain. He would have kept them within eyesight. Ash would have protected her boys. Della could feel the familiar hammering building behind her eyes.

"Stop," Brady said, looking at Della's worried expression. "Freaking yourself out right now won't help your boys," he said firmly.

"Hurry!" she pleaded, putting her hands to her face, trying to block out the images her mind was conjuring involuntarily.

"You've got to keep it together," Brady said again, this time firmer.

"Shut up and drive faster!" Della pleaded. She definitely didn't need him telling her to keep it together. But as her temper flared at him, she realized he had accomplished what he had intended. Her mind was clearer now and more focused. The anger had helped.

The town was not far from her cabin. She and Ash had decided that they liked the easy mile and half walk to the little town when they were choosing the perfect spot. The small gravel road wound its way around the lake and through a small valley before turning sharply to the left. Once around the curve, Della knew the town would be in plain view. Would she want to see that view? The memories of the mob scenes from Chicago that she had seen on television that first day came rushing back to her. Shaking her head, she tried to clear those awful images and sat closer to the dash, willing the Jeep to go faster.

The Jeep rounded the curve and stopped, suddenly causing Della to bump her head on the windshield.

"What the hell did you do that for?" she cried, rubbing her head.

Brady didn't answer, but got out of the Jeep and opened the back door.

"What are you doing?" she yelled, getting out of the Jeep and following him. "My children are possibly in serious danger with....God knows what those things are!"

"Just give me a sec, will ya?" he said, frustrated.

Della could see a large black steamer trunk in the back floorboard. With the lid open, she could see an array of guns and other weapons. Brady was busy checking the ammo inside of his shotgun.

"Here," he said, handing her the gun and stuffing shells into her jean pockets. "Do you know how to use one?" he asked hopefully.

"Yeah, but..." she began, thinking she could probably never use one of these weapons against another human being, no matter how frightening they became.

"Good, 'cause I don't have time to teach you," he said, grabbing two handguns and several clips out of the trunk before closing and locking the lid. Della found it odd that she hadn't noticed the trunk before. She had noticed that the back seats had been removed and the roll bar had more than a few dents on it, but nothing else had caught her attention. She supposed that was the reason the trunk and the floorboards were both painted black to help in its concealment.

"Remember the important thing is to brace yourself with the butt firmly against your shoulder and make sure your feet are firmly planted," he said, putting a clip into one of the handguns and placing it under his belt in the small of his back. "Its got a good kick to it, but it'll be easier for you to hit your target with than a handgun," he said, putting a shoulder holster on. He loaded the other handgun and placed it in the shoulder holster.

"Another thing you should remember is not to get splashed if you have to shoot these things. I heard the virus is transmitted through bodily fluids, so if you have to shoot, aim for center mass, plant your feet, and stay far enough away not to get splashed." Brady stopped and looked at Della, who was not sure she was remembering all his instructions. "You'll be okay, just stay with me," he said, putting a hand on her shoulder. "Trust me, okay?" He gave her shoulder a squeeze and Della nodded. Not certain she had any other options.

Before getting back into the Jeep, Brady zipped off the canvas top and placed it, Della assumed, purposely over the gun trunk. Then he gave Della a quick smile and opened her door for her. Given another circumstance, she thought she would see the humor in his gesture.

Brady put the Jeep in drive and slowly coasted down the gravel road. Della could see nothing. She scanned the porches for dead bodies, but saw none. The windows in the buildings seemed to be intact, no broken glass anywhere. Brady drove slowly to his office and turned the engine off. He stood up and looked around. Seeing no signs of his men who were supposed to be guarding the town, he reached for the gun under his arm and motioned for Della to follow him.

Della had no intention of staying alone in the Jeep. She didn't care where his men were, she wanted to cross the street and go into the lodge. She wasn't concerned for the welfare of anyone other than her two sons. Seeing no one near the lodge, she touched his shoulder and motioned towards the lodge.

"Wait," he said in hushed tones, and pointed towards an open door in the office and then put a finger to his lips to silence her. Holding his gun as if he had been born with it, Della watched the precision in his movements as he made his way towards the door. He motioned for Della to stay at the corner of the house while he checked inside. Holding onto her own gun, she raised her eyebrows questioningly, only to be told in firmer tones to follow his orders.

The small cabin had only one room, one door at the front, and two small side windows. It had been built originally as a fishing shack, but had been abandoned for years now. Brady had pushed through the multiple layers of cobwebs when he had arrived. The cabin was quiet and the town even quieter. That bothered Della. There should be some sort of noise now. She watched as Brady gently pushed open the door with his left hand while keeping his right hand on his gun. *He's done this before*, she thought. The movements came naturally to him. Watching him, she felt as if she were watching a ballet. Graceful. Something she was certain he didn't learn in the construction trade.

She held her breath as he entered the cabin. Expecting to hear movements from someone jumping him and hearing none, she relaxed. Maybe the house was clear. If it was, then they could go to the lodge and check on her sons.

"It's clear Della, you can come in now," he said in a hushed voice.

"Do you think it's possible the swarm passed this place by, that it maybe came from another direction or something?" she asked, once inside.

"It's possible, but we both saw where they were coming from." He shook his head and looked around again. "I'm not ruling anything out."

"Where do you think your men are if the swarm didn't come this way?" she asked the question she knew he was thinking.

"That's a good question," he said, holstering his gun under his arm and running both hands through his thick curly black hair. "A damn good question."

"Let's go check the lodge," she said, heading for the door.

Suddenly, a young man that Della was certain she had seen in town earlier stepped into the doorway, blocking the exit. His features were distorted and Della felt she was staring at a watercolor picture where the colors had begun to mix together. His neck was bent unnaturally to the left and a trickle of blood ran steadily from his left nostril.

"Della!" Brady grabbed her and slung her away from the man in the doorway, causing her to slam into the back wall. She turned to see Brady throw his desk over on its side and dive behind it.

"Get down!" he shouted at her.

The man, although Della was certain he was no longer human, gave a loud rasping scream and advanced, arms outstretched into the cabin. Brady grabbed both his guns and began firing them simultaneously. Each bullet causing the man to stumble a step or two backwards out the door. When Della realized that the bullets were not immobilizing the man, she handed Brady her shotgun. He pushed her down closer to the floor, out of splash distance and shot twice at the man. Della heard the sickening thud of the man as he hit the ground outside the cabin.

"Come on, let's go!" Brady said, shoving the shotgun back at Della and practically pulling her to her feet. "Reload!" he shouted.

Outside, they paused briefly to scan the road. Seeing nothing but the dead man's bullet-ridden body, Brady took off running towards the lodge, dragging Della behind him. Stopping on the porch, Della managed to reload the shotgun after dropping shells three times. Finally, Brady opened the lodge door and pulled her inside.

Della's heart was caught firmly in her throat as she looked around the large room. Couches were upturned, end tables on their sides, game pieces were strewn all across the floor and the cards Louie and his new friend were playing with were everywhere.

"Oh no," Della said, putting her hand to her mouth. "No, no, no...," she started to walk towards the kitchen in the back when she heard another loud guttural scream coming from the room next to the kitchen.

"Della, pull it together, I need your help." Brady had grabbed Della's face and forced her to face him. "Pick up your gun and follow me," he commanded.

Della did as she was told and realized she didn't remember dropping her shotgun. The screaming had turned into growling and Della could hear what sounded to be pieces of furniture thrown against the walls. Her stomach was sick. Sick with worry and sick from the sight of the bullet-ridden deformed young man they had just killed. She wanted to throw up, but Brady kept her moving close to him and close to the lodge walls.

The yuppies that had originally built the lodge had used only the finest oak and hardwoods in their construction, so the sound of a chair thrown through the wall told Della all she needed to know about the thrower's strength. Brady motioned for Della to crouch down and wait near the room's door. Della was grateful to stop, her knees had become weak and she was certain she could not face another grotesque walking dead person.

Curling into a ball, Della's head was just low enough to miss the shower of broken oak boards that came minutes after Brady entered the room. Della jumped up, brushing off the barrage of wood and saw Brady flying across the room into the far wall. Della watched as the gruff man who had driven them from the roadblock a few hours ago growled and rushed at the unconscious lump he had just thrown against the wall.

Horrified, Della reached quickly for her shotgun and tried to aim at the monster. Thinking only to save Brady from a horrible death, she pulled the trigger, forgetting the advice of planting her feet and bracing her shoulder. The force of the blast landed Della a few feet behind where she fired the shot, but she managed to remain on her feet. The shot had connected with her target, but only upon his shoulder. Angry, the man started towards Della, leaving Brady opportunity to get to his feet.

"Brady!" she screamed at him as he struggled to pull himself up.

"Brady, move, hurry!" she yelled. She wanted to fire her last round, but feared Brady would be too close to the point of impact. The man who no longer resembled a human closed in on her. Blood smeared across his face and dripped from his teeth and chin. She didn't want to think of where the blood had come from, although she was pretty certain she knew. The dead man raised his right hand and threw a lamp he had been clutching at Della. Ducking just in time, she saw Brady finally get to this feet and stumble backwards away from the predator.

Knowing she'd only have one chance, Della took a second to plant her feet like Brady told her, aimed her shotgun and fired. The blast separated the dead man's head from his shoulders and Della ducked as pieces of his head flew across the room. The man's body stood upright for what seemed like minutes before finally subsiding into a crumpled heap on the floor. Screaming, Della dropped the gun and frantically ran her fingers over her body trying to feel if she had inadvertently gotten some of the dead man's fluid on her.

"Brady! Brady!" she screamed, as she dropped to floor on her knees, sobbing.

"It's okay, Della." Brady had made his way around the mess the shotgun blast had made. Still in pain from his fight with the now dead man, he groaned as he lowered himself to the floor beside her.

"It's okay. You got him." Putting his arms around her and pulling her tightly into his chest, he gently rocked her and told her again she was safe.

"That was a couple of really good shots," he said, when her crying had quieted a little. "Kinda makes my instructions to you seem foolish," he grinned, trying to lighten the mood.

"We gotta find my boys, Brady," she said. "I'm not going to make it if I don't see them soon."

"Okay," he said, helping her to her feet.

Brushing the remains from the broken wall off his jeans he added, "I've got an idea where they might be if they're hiding."

Della pushed the tear-soaked strands from her face and wiped her eyes. Looking around at the mess, she bent over and picked up her gun, took two more shells from her front jean pocket and reloaded her shotgun.

"Let's go," she said.

11

Ash rose slowly from the front seat of his borrowed Chevy Blazer and stretched. His body was sore from the strange positions that he had slept in. Although sleeping wasn't exactly what he would call it. Napping was more like it. Thoughts of Della, Ricky and Louie bounced around in his mind, keeping him from any type of deep sleep. His thoughts alternated between joyous reunions at the cabin and horrifying images of their deaths.

He peered through the tinted windows to witness daybreak beginning to push through the dim obscurity of night. There was no one in sight, but as always, the abundance of dead bodies and devastation was all over. It was day nine and Ash assumed they would deal with the countless obstacles when passing through the heavily populated city of St. Louis. Ash's chest tightened in anticipation of facing the unknown.

He heard movement from the backseat and glanced back to see Emily repositioning herself in her sleep. Her long blond hair, now a mess, was probably well kept prior to all this chaos. As a ten-year-old, she needed to grow up fast. Ash encouraged her to talk more each day. He was amazed at how quickly he had come to care for her, as if she were his own.

Ash leaned over to the passenger seat, pulled out a can of Diet Cherry Coke from his backpack, and opened it slowly. He gulped down several times. Reaching over to the radio, which was always left on, he pressed the channel search button. The digital radio station numerals repeated rapidly through all channels available.

Maybe we'll get something this time, Ash thought, *especially being near a major city.* Ash pulled a Slim Jim beef stick from the dash, ripping the packaging down the middle. His weary eyes moved towards the radio and locked on the scrolling numbers as it passed repeatedly over vacant stations. The green digital numerical lights hypnotized Ash as he ate his breakfast.

Unexpectedly, the radio came to a standstill on 580AM. Ash stopped chewing and bent forward. Initially there was static, followed by brief silence. A female voice then came clearly from the speakers throughout the car. One thing was for certain as she began her story, this had to be the first time she had ever talked on the radio.

"Attention listeners." Her voice quivered across the airwaves. "Please standby for an update."

Ash swallowed the rest of the barely chewed Slim Jim and focused nervously on her every word. His mouth was dry as desert sand, but he didn't dare take a drink. He didn't want to miss a single word.

"A new virus started to turn up worldwide about nine days ago. Its origin is unknown. It seems that no one is immune from the deadly virus. The spiderfly, which the scientific community has dubbed it, is from all accounts a grotesque fly that resembles a brown recluse spider with wings. To an untrained eye, it looks similar to a common horsefly. Within hours of a bite, a person will become deathly ill and delirious, which results in an extreme rabid-like state. The infected person or even animal will then become violent and kill or destroy everything in its path. It's estimated that the infected can live approximately twenty-four to forty-eight hours. The infection is transferred by a bite from the insect or by bodily fluids from an infected person or animal. It's also estimated that over seventy-five percent of the world's population has died due to the virus. Please stay indoors and keep to yourself. Don't attempt to go outdoors or travel unless you have no other alternative. If you go outside, wear bug repellant and travel by car with all windows closed. At this time, it is only speculation that any bug repellents will be effective against these bugs. Please be patient during this tragic time and we will get information to you as we obtain it. Thank you." There was brief silence and then the recorded message started over again.

"Shit," Ash said under his breath. "All this time these bugs were all around us and I didn't even know." He leaned back and rested the back of his head against the window.

"So, that's what's making everyone go crazy and die?" Emily stuck her head up and placed her chin on the back of the front seat.

Ash jumped. He wasn't expecting Emily to awaken so soon.

"Yeah. It seems there are some creepy looking flies that are biting people and making them sick." Ash looked into her concerned hazel eyes as her heavy eyebrows pointed downward in the middle of her wrinkled forehead.

"What are we going to do now?" Emily asked.

"Emily, it's like I told you. I'm going to protect you and take care of you. You're part of my family now," Ash said.

"When will we get there?" she added.

"I'm not sure, but as soon as we possibly can." Ash hoped that satisfied her.

Emily brushed her hair from her face. "I'm hungry," she announced.

"How about a chocolate chip granola bar and some apple juice?" He smiled at her.

"Sure." She nodded.

Ash sat up to get her breakfast.

As he did so, on the outside of the window where his head had once rested, a small fly-like defile creature wildly bit at the window then flew madly away.

* * *

"Hop out!" Ash impatiently asked.

Emily met with Ash's outstretched hand.

They crisscrossed through the wrecked cars, decomposing bodies, and anything else that stood in their way. From the interstate, St. Louis looked like a ghost town. There were several fires in the distance, but the weirdest thing was the absence of noise.

"This is going to be a major feat this time," Ash said. Mountains of vehicles blocked the interstate rendering it barely impassable.

"Are we close to getting out of here?" Emily's tiny voice asked.

"Not yet? I'm still looking," Ash said breathlessly as he led her through two eighteen-wheelers that had jackknifed, hitting one another.

Ash thought that it was a little comical that he was grateful for the smell of diesel fuel or any fuel for that matter, because it helped mask the smell of rotting flesh. One of the eighteen-wheelers had an extreme noxious odor as they passed it. They saw the rotting carcasses of cows entangled throughout the wreckage.

At least there has been no sign of any infected people, Ash thought, *but who knows about the spiderflies.*

"We have to move faster and get inside a car soon." Ash took a quick breath. "I don't want to see either of us bit by one of those bugs."

They scrambled across the front seat of a Subaru Outback. It was the only passage to the other side of a giant pile-up that blocked the exit to I-44. According to Ash's map directions, which were safe in his backpack along with food, drink, medicines, and other items, I-44 is where they needed to go.

Emily stepped onto the pavement, followed by Ash. From under the car, something grabbed Ash's pant leg and yanked him fiercely to the ground.

"What the...," Ash yelled, as he searched for his shotgun that had fallen away from him. He kicked frantically into the shadow under the Subaru.

"Emily, get me my gun!" he shouted.

Emily was frozen, her eyes transfixed on the terror unfolding before her.

"Emily!" he yelled at the top of his lungs.

Her trance broke and she hastily ran over to the shotgun and gave it to Ash.

"Stand back Emily!" he hollered over the shadow's screams. Its grasp was inhumanly strong. What little he could see looked like a teenage girl. She had the similar washed out face and deep-set eyes as the others. Ash pulled his body away from the car, but fell right back on his ass. It was just enough time to get a head shot.

"Die!" Ash screamed, as he cocked the shotgun and pulled the trigger. The infected girl's head exploded. Her brain matter, skull fragments and blood splattered across the green metallic paint of the Outback's quarter panel. Her limp body collapsed to the hot asphalt. Ash sprung to his feet and checked to make sure he hadn't been bitten in all the commotion.

"Thank God," he said with a deep sigh.

He then turned his attention to Emily.

"Are you okay?" Ash asked.

Emily nodded her head.

Ash checked the area.

"Well I'll be..." he said as his mouth formed a crooked grin.

"What?" Emily nervously asked.

"Look over there." Ash pointed some sixty yards down the exit.

Hot damn, he thought cheerfully.

The two of them ran excitedly down the exit.

Ash opened the door and found the keys still in the ignition. The fuel gauge showed half a tank.

"Hell yes!" Ash couldn't keep his emotions from escaping. "What I always wanted... a Hummer."

12

Brady led Della through the tattered remains of the room and into the kitchen. The lodge had a restaurant style kitchen with long stainless steel tables and work area lining both walls. Incredibly, the room didn't have a single thing out of place. Evidently, the madness had not spread this far into the lodge.

Good, she thought, *maybe it hadn't reached my boys.*

Brady held up his hand to stop her and motioned for her to listen. At first she heard nothing, but then slowly Della began to hear tiny voices. They sounded muffled and far away, but just the same they sounded beautiful to her.

"Where?" she asked Brady.

"The walk-in freezer," he said, pointing towards the back of the kitchen.

"Be careful, there may be more infected people and we don't want to lead them to the children," he said, grabbing her arm, restraining her from rushing to the freezer.

Della nodded that she understood, but felt as if her heart were tearing in two. She wanted to run and jerk open that freezer door and see her sons' faces, to feel them in her arms, but she resisted. Brady was right, they had to be careful.

Standing silently in the middle of the kitchen, they listened again for any sign that there might be other 'things' inside the lodge. But heard nothing. Nothing but the tiny voices of young children that Della had to get to.

"Okay, let's go," Brady said, dropping his hand and motioning her forward, slowly.

The freezer was positioned between the back door and a room-sized pantry lined with empty shelves. With the electricity out, it made a perfect shelter. Brady knocked on the freezer and waited for a response. After a moment, a small knock replied. Grinning at Della, he stepped aside and allowed her to open the door. The heavy door complained about the movement but eventually opened.

"Mom!" In unison, Ricky's and Louie's ecstatic voices sounded wonderful to Della as the boys rushed instantly to her. Della dropped to her knees, pulling the boys into a tight hug, smothering both with kisses.

"Oh, baby, Mommy was so worried about you," Della said cupping her youngest face in her hands.

"And you, how's my big boy," she said, doing the same to Ricky, "Come here and give me another hug."

"Mom, what happened?"

"Where were you?"

"Did you see them?"

"Did you see the bugs?"

"Are they gone?"

"Can we come out of the freezer yet?"

The barrage of questions from Ricky and Louie were quickly echoed by the other children in the freezer. For the first time, Della looked at the others inside their makeshift shelter. Eight children, including her own, and two adults looked expectantly at Della and Brady.

"We're not sure about everything yet," Brady began, looking at the adults. "But I think it would be wise to stay near this freezer." Then, seeing the worried looks of the children, added, "Just in case."

"Mark, let Della and Stacey get these kids out in the kitchen and you and I finish searching the area."

"Della." Brady motioned for her to leave the group and come join them. "I'm not certain this place is safe. I know you don't want to leave your boys, but I think it would speed things up if you came with us. It looks like we're a little low on manpower."

Della looked over at her boys, who were watching her every move, certain they wouldn't like being left behind once again.

"I don't know, Brady," she began.

"Look, you know they're safe, and if we put some food and stuff in that freezer, they'll be safe while we're outside," he said.

"Okay. But give me a minute," she relented, and walked back to her sons.

Ricky and Louie sat close together on top of a long shiny steel table. They eyed her with suspicion and concern.

"Boys," she started, not really knowing how to explain, "I need to go with Brady and Mark to make sure there are no more...um, bugs outside."

"No, Mommy!" Louie cried, and wrapped his arms tightly around her waist.

"Stay here with us, Mom," Ricky pleaded.

Della hated to do this to them, after everything they had been through. She knew leaving them again would be terrifying for them.

"Guys, I know you're scared," Della began, "but Brady and Mark need my help and we need to make sure we're safe," she continued.

"Why don't you guys help me with this food and we'll set everything up in the freezer like a picnic, okay?" she said, trying to redirect and lighten the tone at the same time.

Looking over at Brady standing in the doorway, she said, "Do you think you guys could bring in some of the kid's games from the front room?"

"Sure, I'll get them," Brady said, and pointed at his watch, reminding her that they were running out of daylight.

Stacey had managed to quiet the kids a little and had them busy bringing food into the freezer. Louie still had his arms around Della's waist and showed no signs of letting go. Della kissed his head and ran her fingers through his hair, trying to untangle his tussled mess. She was getting ready to tell him she had to go when Ricky suddenly spoke up. "Come on, Louie," he said sliding off the table, "it looks like Stacey's going to need our help."

Della gave him a grateful smile and pulled him into another hug.

"I'll take care of him, Mom," he said. "Don't be gone too long, okay?" he continued, returning her hug.

Ricky carried Louie piggyback over to the freezer with the other children. Brady had returned with an armload of games and had remembered to grab a few couch pillows as well. It was a thoughtful act that Della noted with gratitude.

Glancing at Della, Brady motioned her over to the back door where he and Mark were standing. Walking away from her children once again made her weary.

"We'll need to go back to the Jeep for more ammo and guns," Brady was telling Mark when she joined them.

"Mark told me that the children never saw an infected person. They were inside when Stacey came running in screaming about the swarm and ushered the kids into the kitchen and, thank God, into the freezer." Brady filled Della in as the three crossed the road, heading for the Jeep.

"Ben must have come in and tore up the place when he couldn't find anyone," Della surmised.

"By my count, we're still missing three people," Mark said.

"Billy, Todd and Lisa," Brady nodded.

"If I could get a radio; mine broke when I was fighting with Ben," Brady said to Mark. "I'd try and get in touch with Billy at the road block."

"Here, try mine." Mark pulled his radio out from his front jean pocket.

"Great. I didn't know you had yours," Brady said, taking the radio from Mark. "Did you try to contact anyone?"

"No. When we first saw the swarm, I tried you, but all I got was static."

Della walked around the Jeep to where the dead man lay. Holding onto her gun tightly, she walked around the body studying it. Earlier she had thought the man's face had looked distorted, now, she could see why. Dozens of bite marks were covering his face. The size of the bites made Della shudder.

"Brady?" Della asked. "Did you see these?" she called him over and showed him what she had found.

"Yeah," Brady said after examining the body, "it looks like they got him good."

"That might explain why they changed so quickly," Mark said to Brady.

"What do you mean?" Della felt as if she had missed something important that the other two obviously knew.

"It was reported that the bites were taking an average of two to four hours to infect the victim," Mark started explaining. "But these men changed a lot quicker."

"So, what does that mean?" Della asked.

"What I'm thinking is...," Mark spoke up, and then hesitated and looked at Brady. "Feel free to correct me if I'm off base here."

Brady nodded and Mark continued, "If a person was bitten multiple times, like these men, it may have quickened the infection process." Mark stopped and looked up towards the sun.

"If we're going to do this we should hurry," he said.

* * *

The three split up to save time and Della was relatively glad she had chosen to search the road down to the roadblock. Being in the open made her feel somewhat safe.

The walk down to the roadblock had been uneventful and Della was grateful, but as she neared the man-made mountain in the road, she felt her body tensing. *What if Billy had been bitten?* she thought about the fresh faced young man she had been so angry with a few hours before and how odd it was that she was now worrying about his safety.

When she was within sight of the roadblock, she stopped. Putting her hand up to shade her eyes from the evening's setting sun, she scanned the site for Billy. Nothing. She stood silently for a moment and listened. Nothing. If he had been bitten and infected, she was certain she would hear him.

"Billy!" Della cupped her hands to her mouth and yelled.

Remaining still, she listened again. Still nothing.

"Billy!" she tried once more, louder.

This time she heard something. A rustling near the bottom of the pile. Grabbing two shells from her pocket, she loaded her gun, cursing under her breath for not having done so already. Della pulled the gun to her shoulder and waited. The rustling continued and now Della could see movement near a small pile of branches near the base.

"I've got a gun!" she yelled at the moving branches, feeling a little foolish.

"Don't shoot!" Billy emerged from the bottom of the pile covered in leaves and dirt.

"Billy!" Della put her gun down and started towards him.

"Thank God you're alright!" she continued. "Brady and Mark have been trying to radio you. Haven't you got it turned on?" she asked, stopping a few feet in front of him.

"I ...I...must of dropped it when I was running from those...." He looked apprehensively at the sky. "Did you see them?" he asked.

"Yeah," she said, nodding her head, "Brady and I were almost caught unprotected, but luckily we made it to the Jeep and hid from them."

Della helped the young man to his feet and brushed the roadblock debris from the back of his shirt.

"Did you hide in there?" Della asked him, pointing to the hole Billy had crawled out of a few minutes before.

"Uh-huh," he nodded, still searching the sky nervously.

"It's okay Billy," Della told him, placing a motherly hand on his shoulder.

Billy jerked from her touch and moved a few steps away from her.

"Billy, are you alright?" she asked, concern growing in the pit of her stomach. Something was not right here. She could feel it.

"I..I..I'm sorry," he managed to say.

Della noticed he was still shivering. Originally, she had thought he was just nervous when he emerged from beneath the pile. Now, however, she believed it was more than that. He behaved as if he were cold. Billy grabbed both of his arms in order to calm the shaking, but it was no use. His complexion had turned pasty white and sweat trickled down his face one droplet at a time.

"Billy," Della asked carefully. "Did any of those bugs bite you?"

"Yea…yeah," he said shaking. "A few…before I could get away."

Oh no. Della thought. *No, no, not this kid too!*

"Damn it!" She screamed at the sky. "What is this?" she yelled. "Is this a test? Is this a punishment?" She took her gun by the butt and threw it hard at the side of the roadblock. Watching it bounce off the tree limbs. "What am I supposed to do?" she yelled at the sky again.

"What the hell are we supposed to do with all this?" she asked again. "Wh…what's, wr...wrong with m...me?" Billy asked, sinking to his knees and grabbing his stomach.

"Oh, Billy," Della sighed.

Della tore off the bottom of her t-shirt and wiped the sweat from Billy's forehead. He was freezing. She laid him on the pavement and he curled into the fetal position. The shaking had slowed down, but his body temperature continued to drop. Realizing he did not have his radio, Della ran toward Billy's previous hiding place. *If I can just call for help,* she thought, *maybe he'd be all right.* Inside the hole, Della spotted the radio, or what was left of it. Three pieces of what used to be his radio lay smashed beneath the rubble.

"Damn!" she yelled.

Running back to Billy, she noticed that he had stopped moving.

"Billy, can you hear me?" she asked, as she rolled him onto his back so she could see his face.

Della got no response. His chest was still continuing to rise and fall, but only slightly. His brown, short hair was matted with a mixture of leaves and twigs. His face no longer held a painful expression; instead, he appeared to be sleeping. Della sat down next to him and wiped his face once again with her shirt. She could see no obvious signs of bites, but Billy was wearing a long sleeved t-shirt and long pants. The bite marks must be hidden beneath them, she thought.

Della knew he was changing. She was also aware of what he would become shortly. The thought caused her to shiver. A part of her wanted to run back up that road and sit inside that freezer with her sons until this entire horrible mess was over. But she knew she couldn't. She wouldn't. Forcing herself to remain seated beside him, she continued to wipe his face and hold his hand. *He was just a kid,* she thought. *Five or six years older than Ricky. He had a mother out there somewhere.* That mother would not want Della to let her son die alone. She tried putting herself in that mother's place, but it was too difficult. The hurt was overwhelming.

Billy's eyes suddenly opened, causing Della to jump in surprise. He opened his mouth to speak but produced nothing audible. She moved closer to hear.

"Thank you," he whispered.

"Shhh," she said, smiling at his young face. "Rest. Don't talk."

Billy squeezed her hand and caught her gaze. Spider-like black veins had started to fill his blue eyes. She knew it had started. *Still, he was human,* she thought as she saw the tears beginning to pool in the corners of his eyes.

He knows, she thought. *He knows what's happening to him.*

"I'm turning into one of those monsters..." his voice almost a whisper. "Aren't I?" he asked.

"God, Billy, I'm so sorry." Della wiped her eyes, willing herself not to cry.

Billy's eyes flickered towards the shotgun shells she had taken out of her pockets before sitting down, and then to her. Pleadingly.

"I can't do that Billy," she murmured. "Please, don't ask me to do that."

"Please," he gasped, as he grabbed her hand again, tighter this time.

Della looked at his face for a moment and wondered if she would be able to do what he was asking. She was a mother. How could she? Then she thought of Billy's mother. What would she want her to do?

Della wiped the tears away from Billy's face one last time and stood up. Looking down on the once vital and healthy teenager, Della sighed. It was a nightmare, and she was not entirely certain that she would be able to survive, even if she managed to elude the bugs.

Billy's eyes had closed and she knew he had accepted what she was preparing to do, but it made it no easier. Retrieving her gun from where she had angrily slung it minutes earlier, she walked heavily back to Billy.

She was worried that she wouldn't do it properly and cause the boy more pain. She went to the roadblock and found a couch cushion, put the barrel of the shotgun in the middle of the cushion and fired. She lifted the cushion and looked through a hole that was about three inches in diameter. Then she carried the cushion to where Billy was lying and laid it on him so the hole was centered over his heart. She put the shotgun barrel through the hole and paused. Again, Billy's eyes suddenly opened wide, now they were insane, primitive.

This time, Della was not shaken. "Good-bye Billy," she said, and pulled the trigger.

13

"Now, this is a whole lot better than sleeping in cars, isn't it?" Ash turned to Emily in the bed next to him.

There was no reply. She was fast asleep. *Emily deserved a good night's sleep in an actual bed,* he thought. Ash relaxed and gazed at the ceiling. The countless years of smoke and age that defined the neglected motel was insignificant right now. He was just glad to be lying flat on a reasonably comfortable bed.

Ash and Emily made good time after getting past St. Louis and having a Hummer helped them get over and through many of the obstacles. The last few days had taken their toll on the once-mighty midnight blue Hummer, but it still ran like a champ. Ash had siphoned gas from other vehicles to keep the gas-hog running, but it just made sense to keep traveling in it. During the past several days they rarely saw anyone except the infected people that chased the Hummer like mad dogs after a meat truck. Non-infected people were rare. Few would stop to speak for fear of contracting the virus, and even waving while you passed was too risky for fear of attracting unwanted attention.

They had been fortunate at one exit to find a Piggly-Wiggly supermarket and loaded up on food and other provisions without human contact. There was, however, plenty of death along the way, but that couldn't hurt you, apart from the stench. Ash tried every phone he saw, but could find no dial tone or service. He did manage to find some more shotgun shells and even a pistol that he pried from a dead police officer's hand. It was just like everything else. Not stealing, only surviving.

That brought them here, sleeping in double beds at the Grand Motel in Everton, Oklahoma. Ash had figured that they were about half-way to Mount Hope. He and Emily had barricaded the front door, closed the curtains, and remained as quiet as possible so they wouldn't draw any attention. Their room was at the back of the motel and the Hummer was parked sideways beside the door for a quick escape if necessary. They both ate a can of cold Dinty Moore Stew and washed it down with their favorite warm soft drinks. They washed themselves off with bottled water from the Piggly-Wiggly and motel soap.

Ash worried for his family. Thoughts of his past life experiences poured over his mind as he struggled to stay awake long enough to relive them. He remembered playing tickle monster with little Louie, assembling the pinewood derby car and racing it in the Cub Scouts' derby race with Ricky, and the last time he made love to Della. Tears ran down both sides of his face and settled in his ears, slightly tickling them. His thoughts became disjointed and scattered as sleep overtook him.

* * *

"What? What is it?" Ash responded in a rasping tone of voice. Half asleep and bewildered, it took him a few seconds to regain his wits. He heard whimpering from Emily's bed. He looked to the curtains in the blackened room and noticed that it was still dark outside.

"Emily, what's wrong?" He reached over to the nightstand between them, located a lighter and promptly lit a small candle. Ash's squinting eyes slowly focused on the crying girl who lay on the bed.

"Emily?" Ash sat beside her and stroked her hair. "What's wrong, honey?"

"I miss my Mommy," she said, muffled by her pillow.

"I know you do, sweetheart."

"I want her back!" she cried.

"Let me tell you something that I do know for certain. Your Mommy is up in Heaven looking down and thinking how proud she is of you. She is and will always be with you wherever you go. Your mother loves you very much and she doesn't want to see you sad." He paused momentarily. "Okay?"

"Okay." She climbed into Ash's arms and laid her head on his shoulders. Ash leaned back on the headboard and held her while she continued to lightly weep. He silently cried with her. He wouldn't let her see or hear him cry. Emily needed someone strong in her life right now. She was beginning to feel like the daughter he never had and he was becoming very close to her. He began to wonder if he would be able to keep her as his own child after the madness ended. He knew Della would accept her and love her, too. *Too?* For the first time, he admitted to himself that he loved Emily, perhaps as much as he loved Ricky and Louie.

14

After the blast, Della dropped the shotgun. The sound of the pellets entering Billy. The sound of them tearing him apart. The sound of the blast. It echoed over and over inside her head. She had forced herself to look at her destruction. Mainly to make sure she had accomplished her mission. *It was unimaginable what the force of a shotgun blast could to do to the human body,* she thought. How easily the human body can be shredded, as if it had the mettle of tissue paper trying to block the force of the rain.

Della stood quietly over Billy's body. She should take her clothes off, she thought. She was concerned about the fluids. Shedding herself of her worn-out, dirt-filled clothing, she let them drop to the pavement beside her gun. Deciding it might be better to retrieve clean clothing from her van, she made her way over the roadblock. She wished she could see the humor in the fact that she was now climbing over a mountainous furniture roadblock clad only in undergarments, but she couldn't.

The van was parked at the same place she had left it earlier that day. Although to Della, that moment was a lifetime ago.

Opening the driver's side door, she climbed into the seat and closed the door. Della stared out the windshield and clenched the steering wheel. She was aware of the pain in her hands, but ignored it and squeezed harder. She wanted to put the keys in the ignition, turn the van around and drive away from this mountain.

She wanted her boys.

Reaching over the back seat, Della dug through the bags until she found a pair of cargo shorts and an old *Eagles* concert t-shirt of Ash's. After dressing, she trekked back over the mountain, past Billy and the hole in his chest, past her pile of sweat and dirt-stained clothing, past her shotgun and scattered, spent shells and started the walk back to town.

Back to her boys.

15

"How much further till Texas?" Emily attempted to restrain a smile. Ash had informed her that Texas was the next State they would pass through before arriving in New Mexico.

"Well, it could be a couple more days. It just depends on the road conditions." Ash glanced to the passenger seat at the shy little girl.

"How many days till we get to your cabin?" she asked apprehensively, as though she already knew the answer.

"Emily, it's hard to say. Maybe in a couple of weeks." He winked at her. He had driven on through the night and finally made it to I-40. They still had weeks to go, but he had milestones in his head that kept him going, and reaching I-40 was one of them. Ash had some pretty good luck driving through Oklahoma. There were fewer obstructions on the roadways, which made for better time. The Hummer, thank God, made almost everything passable.

"Hold on!" Ash shouted, as his arm held Emily back in her seat.

The tires on the Hummer came to a screeching stop.

They both leaned forward and stared in bewilderment at the scene on the highway some forty yards away.

"Just sit still," Ash whispered.

"Is he alive?" Emily's quivering voice asked.

"I'm not sure."

"Let's go. He's going to come after us."

"Wait. I thought I saw him move."

"Please Ash, I'm scared."

"Don't worry, we're safe in here."

"What the...?" Ash watched as a boy slowly crawled across the interstate in front of them. He was facing the other way, making it impossible to tell if he had been infected. Ash had always driven on no matter what. *But what if the boy is okay? He's about the same age as Ricky. I can't just leave him here if he's not infected.* His mind swirled. What action should he take? He had to do something now!

Ash surveyed the scene outside, grabbed his shotgun and opened his door.

"Please don't go!" Emily almost ordered him to stay. The slight creases around her eyes conveyed her seriousness.

"It's alright. I have to check this one out. You'll be safe. Just wait here. Besides, I have a gun if he's one of them." He stepped outside and shut the door.

Ash made sure his shotgun was locked and loaded, and went to investigate. The sweat ran profusely over his tired body, especially his forehead when it found the midday sun that emitted a staggering 100 plus degree heat. He assessed the area around him as he locked in on his target. All those years of training had paid off as he tactically made his way to the young boy. Now he stood but a few yards from the boy.

"Hey! Are you alright son?" Ash yelled.

The boy stopped crawling and dropped to the hot asphalt. He moaned in agony.

Ash noticed the blood trail that the boy had left that stretched beyond his line of site.

Ash guardedly walked around the boy with gun ready in hand. He glanced around again and saw the Hummer, but could not see Emily because the reflection of the sun on the windshield made that impossible.

He now faced the young boy. The boy's eyes stared straight ahead and into Ash's black combat boots. He couldn't have been any older than thirteen years of age. His dark red hair was caked with his own blood, as his nose and mouth slowly expelled blood. He could see that he hadn't turned rabid. The blood's major point of origin was somewhere under the boy.

"I'm just going to turn you over," Ash said. He could see the boy's back rising and falling with each blood-curdling breath. He was trying to speak, but Ash could not make out his words because of the short heavy breathing.

Ash took his foot and pushed him slowly up till the force of his own weight flopped him onto his back. The boy yelped and winced in pain.

"Oh, dear God!" Ash could not help himself. The young man's entire underside had nearly been scraped to the bone. It looked like someone had dragged him on his stomach for miles. His clothes and skin had been torn away and all that remained of his little body was mutilated flesh, bones and gravel. It was a miserable sight. *Who could have done this to him*? It was torture at its worst.

"Son, you're gonna be alright," Ash lied.

The boy tried to speak to Ash through his bloody mouth. His voice was so low and gurgled that Ash bent down to hear him.

"What is it?" he asked. He wanted to kill whoever did this. He was saddened and sickened at the sight of this poor boy. And he had to hide all these emotions and look at his grotesque body as though everything was going to be okay.

"Helllp me! Itzz a trap!" he slowly spoke in broken English.

"What?" Ash asked, hearing a car in the distance revving its engine.

"Nooo!" Ash looked up to see his Hummer heading straight for them. He knew he had to act quickly though he didn't want to shoot and hurt Emily or cause it to wreck.

With no time to think, he acted on instinct. Ash stood his ground and pointed the barrel of the gun at the driver's side windshield. As it drew closer at top speed, Ash knew he could do nothing for the boy below. He stood ready and waited for his shot. He fired two rounds into the windshield and it shattered on impact. Ash jumped, barely clearing the massive vehicle that picked up the boy from the road. His frail body twisted brutally and then landed under the vehicle as he came to rest, misshapen and distorted. At last he felt no pain. His chewed up, deformed body was no longer alive to endure the suffering.

The Hummer, on the other hand, zigzagged about the road out of control. Then abruptly regained its control and sped down the interstate.

"No!" Ash screamed at the Hummer.

"Damn, you son of a bitch!" the words left his dry chapped lips. "Come back here! You have my little girl, you bastard!" He gazed over to the dead boy and then to where his Hummer had once sat. "Emily... Emily!"

Ash then watched painfully as the Hummer vanished from sight.

16

Della couldn't remember the walk back to town. She wasn't even sure what path she used to get there. She couldn't see anything but Billy's face, pleading with her to kill him. *How am I supposed to live with that?* she thought. The town was quiet and the setting sun had begun to cast long shadows across the ground.

"Della!" She heard Brady's voice, but it seemed to be coming from a long way off.

"Della!" This time, she felt Brady's hand grab her arm, stopping her and forcing her to turn and look at him.

"What happened?" he asked her. "Where's your gun?"

"Della..." Brady stopped, afraid to ask the question and even more afraid to hear the answer.

"Did you get bitten?"

Della knew she should say something. She knew he was worried about her. Still, she couldn't. She couldn't bring herself to look at another human being, knowing what she had done.

He won't understand, she thought. His voice echoed inside her head. He was asking more questions.

"Leave me alone," she finally forced the words out as she pulled her arm away and started for the lodge.

"Della, what's wrong with you?" he asked, catching up with her.

"Brady, please leave me alone," she was struggling to speak. "I can't do this right now."

"Can't do what?" he asked.

"Della, you have to tell me what happened." This time Brady grabbed both her arms and held them firmly as he forced her to look at him.

"Please." She could feel the tears starting and she bit into her lower lip hoping the pain would override her other emotions.

"No, damn it!" he said, shaking her slightly. "I need to know if you were bitten."

"No, I wasn't bitten," she said softly. "I wasn't the one bitten."

"Well, who then?"

"God, just leave it alone," she said, jerking her arms away from him again.

"Della!" This time he grabbed her firmly by the shoulders and shook.

"I have people here to worry about, and most of them are kids. I've got mutant bugs trying to pick us off one by one and most of my manpower has either turned into zombie cannibals or gone AWOL on me. I don't have time for theatrics right now." Brady's voice grew harder and for the first time, Della noticed his face change into a firmer more authoritative person.

"I'm sorry...," she started to explain, but was suddenly overcome with sadness and started to cry. "I'm....so....sorry," she said again in between sobs.

"Damn it, Della! This is not pulling it together!" Brady said, as he reluctantly helped her to the ground, knowing she'd be no use to him in this condition.

"I can't do this anymore," she sobbed. "I don't want to do this!"

"You think this is fun for me?" he asked angrily. "You think I like seeing my men killed off by some stupid fly I can't fight! You think I like this, Della? You think you're the only one here allowed to be scared or angry?" He ran his hands through his hair out of frustration.

"You don't get it, do you?" he asked her. "You don't have a choice now. You don't get to say 'stop'. You're right in the middle of this fight, baby, and like it or not, you've got to pull it together." He was trying to make her mad and she knew it. She knew she was acting like a child, but she also knew she was close to losing her mind.

"I killed Billy," she told him.

Brady met her eyes and stood quietly for a moment.

"He got bit and was dying," she forced the words out. "He asked me to."

"God, Della," Brady said, his face softening. "I'm sorry. That must have been horrible for you."

Grimacing, she said, "Oh yeah, horrible might be a good word for it."

"I know you want me to be this tough zombie killer, but I don't think I can." She paused trying to find the right words. "I'm a girly girl, Brady. I like painting my fingernails, watching sappy love stories on television, decorating my house, and baking cookies. For Christ sakes, Brady, I'm not Buffy the freakin' Vampire Slayer."

"I'm not asking you to become all commando on me, but I think you're selling yourself short," he said, with a hint of a smile on his lips. "Besides, I don't think Buffy would have handled herself any better than you did against that monster at the lodge. I saw the way you went up against him. I mean, you might have been scared, but you worked through it. You saved *my* life. Remember? It wasn't the other way around. I was the one about to become zombie food and you saved me."

Della looked at the ground and breathed deeply. She knew he was right, she just didn't know if she had the strength to do anything about it.

"It's getting late," he said, looking at the darkening sky. "Let's call it a day and see if we can get some rest."

"Sounds like the best idea I've heard in days," she relented, and let Brady pull her to her feet.

"And for the record, I think Buffy killed vampires not zombies," he said jokingly.

"Is that what these things are?" she asked. "Zombies?"

"Geez, I don't know," Brady said shaking his head. "I guess. I mean, I'm not an expert in the zombie field, but from everything I've seen on B movies, I'd have to say, yeah."

"Great, I'm stuck in a B movie," Della said, following Brady back to the lodge and back to her boys.

17

"Ash!" A small shrieking voice resounded into the air.

Ash whipped around in the direction of the voice. He stared anxiously over the immediate area.

"Yes?" he eagerly yelled back. *Could it be*? he thought.

"Ash?" the voice was nearer this time, but it was difficult to see around the vehicles that overwhelmed the interstate.

Ash sprinted in the direction of the voice. "Hello!" he shouted nervously.

"I'm over here!" she said, waving her hands to get his attention.

His eyes locked onto her under a wrecked Volkswagen Bug.

"Thank God!" he said jubilantly.

Ash ran to her. "Are you okay, sweetheart?" He pulled her out and into his arms.

"I am now. They threw me out and hurt my knee," she cried.

"It's alright now. I should have never left you alone. I swear it won't happen again," he tried to pacify her. He looked at her small, skinned-up knee and then proceeded to take off his dirty white t-shirt, leaving him bare-chested. He lightly patted the blood from her injury.

"Can you walk?" he asked. He had to get them to safety. They were exposed targets for the bugs.

"Yes, but it hurts." She cringed in pain as she attempted to stand, but fell back into Ash's lap. She placed her arms around his broad shoulders and held him tight.

"Please, don't leave me again." She wept, and hugged him even tighter.

"I won't. I promise." Ash also hugged her firmly.

"Oh no!" she cried out hysterically, looking over Ash's shoulder.

"What is it?"

Ash could see the terror in her eyes as her bottom lip quivered as she stared into the sky.

Ash knew it could mean only one thing. He twisted his head swiftly and saw the same horrifying sight that Emily had witnessed.

"Oh my God!" he barely got his words out.

On the horizon, a shadowy blanket, alive with evil, was covering the skies. The scene left Ash mesmerized. The deafening buzz was growing louder and was bearing in their direction. Then reality set in. Yes, it was a spectacular sight, but it was also a deadly sight. The darkness of millions of spiderflies out to inflict devastation and death.

"Let's go!" Emily squealed above the buzzing.

"Okay!" he said as he snapped out of his trance.

Ash immediately snatched up Emily and placed her in the Volkswagen Bug's back seat and then shut and locked all the doors, windows and vents. He recklessly looked for a key.

"There's no key," he said. Looking to Emily he whispered, "Stay down and don't make a sound. Maybe if they think no one is in here, they'll go away."

Emily nodded her head in agreement and curled up in the floor trying to make herself invisible, grimacing in pain while holding her knee.

Ash laid on his back across the uncomfortable small front seat and gazed out the windshield as the light from outside gradually disappeared. He waited and hoped they would fly past, but that was not to happen. A lone spiderfly gracefully landed on the windshield and leisurely scuttled down to Ash's line of sight. Watching Ash.

Damn, Ash thought. *These don't look like flies. They look like hideous spiders with wings.*

"Stay down and don't look," he whispered to Emily. There was no way he was going to let her see these frightening insects.

Ash pulled himself up to get a better look. Its long, slender, brown semi-transparent legs were covered with fine hairs. The leg span wasn't any bigger than the size of a quarter. A dark violin marking was perfectly distinct, as the neck of the violin pointed toward the dark brown swollen abdomen covered with an abundance of thin hairs that presented a velvety exterior. Its minuscule gruesome face had six bulging eyes that arranged in pairs in a semicircle. The extended fangs dangled from its wooly mouth, thirsting for blood. The translucent gray wings attached to the back resembled that of a horsefly.

The spiderflies landed one-by-one, quickly covering the car. For a brief second, Ash thought it a little comical that these "bugs" were attracted to the Volkswagen.

The resonating hum of thousands of wings and the miniature bites at the car's solid exterior permeated Ash's psyche. Next, came the harsh cold temperature within the car. The bitter cold was becoming unbearable, so Ash scrambled to the back seat and embraced the shivering Emily. There was no relieving their ears from the droning sounds of the creatures.

"Hang in there Emily. Hopefully, they'll go away soon," Ash said loudly as he noticed his breath had turned to vapor in the freezing car.

"I'm sleepy," Emily said.

"What's that honey?" he asked.

She didn't answer. Ash turned her around and lightly shook her.

"Stop," she grunted. "I'm sleepin'," she said, with a disgusted look on her pale face. Her teeth chattered behind her purplish blue lips.

Ash attempted unsuccessfully to awaken her. Struggling to stay awake himself, his body trembled uncontrollably from cold and fear.

Is this going to be how it ends, he thought. *Without even a fight.* He couldn't hang on. His eyes closed.

* * *

"Wake up! Wake up!" Emily yelled at Ash as she shook him.

Ash's mind reached for consciousness.

"Ash, get up!" she insisted.

"I'm up, give me a minute." Ash shook off a chill and sat up steadily.

"They're gone. Look out the window. They're gone Ash."

It took him a moment to figure out what had happened.

"How long has it been?"

"I don't know, but they're gone," she said.

It couldn't have been too long or we would have frozen to death, he thought.

Ash shook off another chill and looked intently around for signs of the bugs or other dangers. The sun had returned to them and the car was starting to get uncomfortably warm.

"We need to get out of here and find us a car." He managed a smile. "How's your knee?"

"It hurts a little. What if we run into those men that took our car?" she asked concerned.

"I hope we don't. They're probably long gone by now. But, if we do, then I'll deal with them." He paused and put his hand on her shoulder. "Don't worry, I'll protect you."

18

"Here's our cabin." Ash beamed with excitement.

"Is everyone inside?" Emily asked.

"They should be. Our van is here," Ash said, eager to get inside. In all honesty, he wanted to run up, throw open the door and embrace the family he missed so terribly. But he had to do this with caution. With things they way they were, you had to be prepared for anything.

"Did you put on your bug spray?" he inquired, yet again.

"Yes, I did." She paused. "Did you?"

"Yes darling," Ash spat back teasingly.

They both were in high spirits. After all, they had journeyed countless miles through the core of Hell itself to ultimately arrive at their destination. They were finally home.

They reached the porch and out of the mid-morning sun that was baking them like a sauna. They needed to hurry and get inside.

Ash placed his index finger over his lips and Emily nodded that she understood. They both stepped gently to the door with

Ash at the lead. He held his shotgun tightly at his side. The creaking of the floorboards made nearly as much sound as his heart rapidly hammering the warm blood throughout his body. He swallowed hard, gently turned the doorknob and pushed the door open. The door slightly creaked open about eight inches to reveal a shadowy interior. He felt Emily clutch firmly onto one of his back belt loops. They entered carefully and allowed their eyes to adjust to the darkness. Ash was taken aback to see that everything was similar to the way they had left it months ago. He flipped the light switch several times to no avail. *Yeah, so why would this place be any different,* he thought.

He wanted to yell out, but he knew it was a bad idea. As they checked all five rooms they found a cabin that was neat and tidy - as if no one had been there at all. But why was the van out front when his family was nowhere to be found? His heart pounded within his chest as the top of his head began to tingle.

Out back, he thought.

He gestured to Emily to follow him to the back door. She wasn't leaving his side; she had his belt loop to prove it. The back door was already open, except for the screen door. Ash could feel the warm, dry breeze gust in from outside. He stood weakened in the knees as he looked over his small patch of dry barren yard. It had never been a work of art, but he knew that eventually he would get some landscaping done on it. He just never had the time. The sparsely scattered trees shaded about twenty percent of the backyard, while dry dirt, weeds, and clumps of shrubbery covered the ground. The kids' small bikes, wagon and toys also added some disorder.

Ash then observed something on the far side of the yard, almost out of view because of the tall brush. Ash's instincts told him something was very wrong.

"Oh my God, no!" he said loudly, as he grabbed Emily by the hand and ran, leading her to the location. As he closed in on his target, he stopped abruptly and prayed his eyes were deceiving him. He ambled at a snail's pace, struggling to concentrate and remain calm.

"No!" Ash cried.

"Wh-what is it?" Emily stammered.

He wasn't listening. He let go of Emily and rushed to the spot and threw himself to the ground.

"Please no! God, please no!" Ash cried punching the ground in front of him. "Why? Why them?"

Emily could only watch in bewilderment.

"Nooooo! Damn you!" he roared into the air.

Ash's tear-filled eyes were transfixed on the terror. Two mounds of dirt lay before him. Each had two homemade wooden crosses with the names of his beloved sons, etched across them. Ash then let his head drop to the ground. Mentally and physically exhausted, he cried uncontrollably.

Emily trembled as she stood nearby and read the names. She understood his sadness. Tears welled up in her eyes. She hurt for Ash.

Suddenly, Ash jumped to his feet and looked around the yard intensely through the blur of tears.

"Della! Della!" he shrieked.

His mind clouded, however, realizing that Della was missing. His mind raced to find answers. Then it came to him, the only place that he hadn't checked. He sprinted to the back door with Emily quick on his heels. He flung open the screen door almost tearing it from its hinges, barely missing Emily. He went to the center of the hallway, bent over and lifted the handle to a hidden trap door to the cellar. It was the only place he hadn't checked and something told him she was there.

He started down the steep stairs and stopped before he was about to disappear into the room below.

"Emily, stay right there and wait for me," he spoke softly.

"Please, let me go with you. I'm scared." She trembled.

"I'm sorry honey, but you'll be safer up here. I'll only be a minute," he said firmly, and proceeded below.

Damn, I wish I had my flashlight, Ash thought. Then remembered the small light at the end of his key chain.

"Della?" he asked the darkness. He held the shotgun ready. "Della?"

Ash shined the small light around the room. His arsenal of guns was still held fast by the hooks on the pegboard wall. The numerous shelves were well stocked with food, water, ammunitions and other necessities for any emergency.

He heard something rustling in the opposite corner. Ash whipped his body around and pointed his flashlight at eye level. Nothing, but then he caught a glimpse of something moving below the outer rim of the light. He hastily moved his light downward.

"Della?" Ash called, as he struggled to read her features.

"Ash?" Della breathed heavily as her body rose and fell with each arduous breath.

"Della, are you ...." He started towards her.

"Please stay back," she moaned.

Ash had taken several steps and kept the light transfixed on her pale white face. He could see that her face was covered with bites. Her ashen face was entirely masked by the endless dark lines of arteries. She then lifted a pistol from her lap.

"No!" he begged her.

"I'm sorry," she said softly as tears ran from her pitch black eyes. She swiftly placed the gun's barrel in her mouth and pulled the trigger.

"Noooooo!" Ash screamed.

Ash sat up bumping his head on the car's steering wheel.

"Ow!" he cried as he winced in pain.

He assessed the dark surroundings, trying to regain his bearings. His sweat soaked clothes stuck to him like a second skin.

"Ash?" Emily's crackling voice asked from the back seat.

Ash jumped, again hitting his head. Emily scared him to death, but thankfully her voice brought him out of his nightmare.

"Yes," he said, turning to see her sitting up in the back seat, "I, uh...I just had a bad dream."

Emily yawned and took the palm of her hand to massage one of her sleepy eyes.

"You go back to sleep. I think I'm going to drive a bit."

He wiped the perspiration from his brow.

There is no way I can sleep after that, he thought. *I have to get to my family*. Ash started the truck and headed down the interstate more determined than ever to find his family. He and Emily had finally made it to Texas and approximately 440 miles separated them from Mount Hope, give or take a few. Best case scenario, they could make it there in a week. Maybe.

19

"Ash, what about that school bus?"

Ash turned to see what Emily was pointing at in her excitement.

"Hey, that's an idea." Ash smiled back. He hoped that there weren't any rotting corpses on board. That was the first prerequisite before borrowing any vehicle. The pungent smell would be overwhelming and the possibility of contamination was too great.

They stood in front of the bright yellow bus. Ash pounded on the closed door with the side of his fist. At once, the bus came alive with the buzzing of the spiderflies as they hurled themselves against the windows in order to escape the vehicle, and get to Ash and Emily. The web covered windows were quickly covered with thousands of the grotesque insects desperate to feast on human blood.

Emily squealed and clutched Ash's waist.

Ash immediately stepped back with Emily still attached to his side, his eyes frozen on the spectacle.

"Let's go!" she shouted at Ash.

Ash glanced down at Emily and didn't say a word. He took hold of her hand and rushed back into the Intrepid. Ash realized that he still had to obtain another car, but right now he had to get them to safety, just in case those bastards escaped the bus.

In the car, Ash could see that the incident had shaken Emily. He admired the way that the young girl was holding up under these circumstances. He thought about Barbara and wondered if she knew that she had done a great job of raising this child.

They sat silently for several minutes, and then Emily, still somewhat winded from their sprint from the school bus, asked, "Ash, when we get to New Mexico, how much farther till Mt. Hope?"

"A couple of days, maybe."

"A couple of days? How could there still be a couple of days?"

Ash could hear the frustration in Emily's voice.

"Hey now, I told you it was going to take a while."

Emily sniffed, "You said it would take a week. It's been three already."

"I know. I'm trying my best. But you know everything we've been through. I didn't expect the kind of problems we've had."

Emily turned her eyes to the floor mat below her feet. "I'm sorry."

"It's alright. We're both a little testy. We have almost 240 miles to go and it's not going fast enough," Ash said.

"I know. Let's not get off anymore exits and keep going till we get there," she offered.

"How about we find us a car first, get off one more exit and stock up on everything we can and then no more exits. We'll concentrate solely on getting to Mt. Hope, even if we have to drive during the night."

Ash touched her shoulder, "We can do it."

Emily nodded and even gave Ash a little smile.

"Let's just wait a bit and make sure those creepy insects have forgotten about us." Ash cleared his throat. "While were waiting, let's put on some more bug spray. Just in case."

* * *

Ash slowly drove the Intrepid away from the danger inside the bus in search of another vehicle.

Ash spotted it the same moment Emily did.

"Look, a big dump truck," sounding as if she had just hit the lottery.

"Good job. That should help us get there faster. If there are any cars are in the way, we'll just push em' aside."

"I hope it has keys," she said.

"You and me both," Ash agreed, and pulled up as close as he could get to the truck.

The dirty gray truck's side door read *Malangus Stone, Inc.*

"I'm going to have to make a run for it. Those cars have my path blocked."

"Can I go too?"

"You need to stay here, where it's safe. I have to check for keys."

"Please?"

Ash looked back into her pleading eyes. "I'm sorry Emily. It's too dangerous." Ash unbuckled his seatbelt and grabbed his shotgun.

"I'll only be a minute."

"Please hurry," she implored.

"I will," he assured her.

Ash surveyed the perimeter of the Intrepid before yanking the door handle and making a mad dash for the truck.

Ash ran with a burst of energy he hadn't felt in years. The gentle sprinkles of rain surprised him, but felt good against his warm face. He leaped to the first step of the big rig and knocked on the window. Nothing. He pulled the handle and was grateful to find it unlocked. Once inside he was pleased to see the cab was empty.

"I'll be dipped in buttermilk," Ash said contentedly. The ignition still held the keys. He tried several times to start her up and on the fourth attempt it turned over. Ash watched as the gas gauge continued to climb.

"Come on baby. Give me more gas," he ordered the gas gauge as it stopped short of full.

"Hot damn!" he said jubilantly.

He poked his head out to let Emily know everything was all right. He gave the thumbs up, but then noticed that Emily wasn't in the car.

"Damn." He looked in the general vicinity and saw no sign of her.

Ash clutched his shotgun, scaled down the steps and jumped to the hard pavement. His feet tingled slightly from the landing, but his only concern was locating Emily.

"Emily!" he hollered, at about that same time he heard a deep, guttural growl. Ash's head throbbed with the anticipation of encountering his next foe.

"Watch out! He's coming after you."

Ash could see Emily screaming from the cracked blood-smeared window of the Intrepid.

Out of the corner of his eye, Ash noticed something dark and huge. He swiftly spun around to see that it was a large black dog. Ash had a choice to make. Shoot the animal, run back to the truck, or run to the Intrepid. He chose the latter. He shouldered the shotgun and sprinted for the top of the car. As he reached the hood of the car, he could feel the shotgun slide off of his shoulder. He attempted to catch it, but was too late. It clanked hard on the pavement, but Ash couldn't stop to retrieve it because the large bear-like dog was at his heels and baring its teeth. He leaped on the hood and cried out in pain as he fell violently onto the car. The rabid dog held the heel of his boot and was determined to get the rest of him. The mad dog shook his leg viciously as Ash held tight and pulled himself up the windshield. Ash struck the dog's face with his other boot, but that didn't stop him. It snarled as though possessed by the devil himself. Ash maneuvered his foot inside the boot and forcefully pulled his foot from the boot and scurried to the roof. He clumsily turned to get a look at his attacker.

The hell-hound was definitely a product of the death bug and it wanted Ash and Emily. It was a large black mutt with a missing ear and freshly-exposed flesh from its head to the base of its neck. A glossy film covered its huge bulging eyes from which hate seemed to radiate. Its mouth was covered by bubbling saliva, which released a howl that was comparable to that of an ailing wolf that still had some fight left in him.

Ash nervously watched as over and over the crazed animal jumped into the air as its nails screeched down the side of the car and hit the pavement full force on its back, yelping in pain. The dog was determined to kill, but Ash had other plans.

"Stay in the car Emily!" he yelled over the barking.

"What?" she screamed.

"Stay in the car, okay?" he shouted.

"Okay," she yelled back.

Ash could see his shotgun only a few feet in front of the car.

The only way to get out of this, he thought, *is to kill that son of a bitch.*

Ash had to act fast. Balancing himself, he made his way to the rear of the car's roof. The growling dog watched his every move as it paced from side to side. Ash steadily took off his other boot and waved it just out of reach of the demented beast.

"Here boy! You want this? Well, go get it," Ash said, teasing the dog. He then tossed his boot over its head. The dog chased after the boot in a fury.

Without delay, Ash ran down the windshield onto the hood. He leaped to the hot asphalt and dove on the shotgun. If it had been any other circumstance, the pain would have forced him to take time to gather himself. Ash rapidly turned over onto his back and cocked the shotgun. He pointed the weapon at the rabid dog that was charging him with Ash's boot in his mouth. He squeezed the trigger and nothing happened. Ash turned the gun to its side and realized the safety was still on. Now the dog was within fifteen feet from Ash. He snapped off the safety and brought the shotgun up to his shoulder and fired. Most of the shot hit the dog in the chest and forced it into a backward somersault. As Ash lowered the shotgun, he could see the dog get up and continue its charge. The force of the shot blew the dog off of its feet, but didn't come near killing it. Ash quickly cocked the gun and fired again as the dog leaped into the air. The shot caught him dead on the face, eliminating anything resembling that of a dog. The faceless dog came to rest on Ash's chest. Ash yelled in disgust and quickly scooted out from under the limp, hefty animal and recocked. He shot it again. He had to make sure.

Ash glanced down at his blood-soaked clothes and then to Emily weeping in the car.

There was no time to waste. He ran to the car and tried opening the door.

"Unlock the door Emily," he tried to calm his voice.

"Okay," her little voice trembled as she leaned toward the passenger door and disengaged the lock.

"We have to go. Grab everything you can and let's get to the truck," Ash ordered.

20

"Do you think they're okay?" Della asked. "Maybe I should check on them again," she said as she started to stand up.

"Della, I don't think they've changed much since the last time you checked on them," Brady answered.

"I'm being overprotective," she sighed, "again."

"No," he said smiling, "not unless you think eight times in the last ten minutes is a little overkill."

Della settled back onto the couch and curled her legs underneath her. They had built a fire in the large fireplace in the lodge's second floor gathering room and it was hypnotic. The flames danced and popped inside the stone walls, casting amber shadows on the sleeping people gathered around it. They had decided that it would be best to stay together tonight, and as it was growing darker and the other cabins had yet to be searched, the lodge seemed the most logical place. Two larger rooms surrounding two smaller ones covered the second floor. They had placed the children off to the right of the fireplace where there were no doors or windows and where they would feel relatively safe. Close enough where the heat from the fireplace would keep them warm, but far enough away to keep them from the embers. To Della, having her sons out of arms reach added to her apprehension. Thankfully, most of the children had little difficulty falling asleep.

Brady had pulled a couch and oversized chair closer to the fire and insisted Della leave her children to dream their dreams and relax. Brady and Mark decided to trade off sleeping schedules to make sure the group was safe. Della was certain that Brady chose the first watch due to her mental status. She hated that. She hated being thought of as unstable. It reminded her of her childhood and that was one emotional state she never wished to be associated with. Unfortunately, she was not only revisiting that state of emotional collapse, she was completely immersed in it.

"Take this," Brady handed Della a pill and a can of warm soda, "it'll make you feel better."

"What is it?" she asked half-heartedly, not really caring, as long as it could dull her senses and allow her a few hours of uninterrupted sleep, free of evil bugs, zombies and the horror she had faced the past few days.

"It's just something to help you relax," he said, waiting to see her swallow the pill. Della had the urge to open her mouth and stick out her tongue. After her mother's death, her doctors had prescribed anti-depressants and after each dose she was required to show the nurses her empty mouth. *Strange, the moments in life when memories chose to reveal themselves,* she thought.

"The boys are sleeping and surrounded by other sleeping kids," Brady said, sitting down in the large chair next to the fire. "I'll keep an eye on things. You need to get some rest."

"I know," she said softly, "but I don't think I can. I don't think I'll ever be able to close my eyes again without seeing Billy."

Saying his name brought another wave of emotions rushing over her. She knew she would probably never forget the young man or keep herself from wondering what he might have done in his life if given the chance.

"That pill should start to work soon. It's pretty strong. I got it from Todd's supply. He owned a pharmacy and brought a lot of his supplies along. Just in case."

"Maybe I'll just lie down here and try to rest." Della slid down on the couch and pulled a blanket over her legs. She could feel a warm sensation beginning to spread slowly through her body. She opened her mouth to tell Brady that she was feeling better, but fell asleep before she could push the words out.

* * *

"Ash, where have you been?" Della mumbled through a sleepy haze. She rolled over and looked at the clock on her nightstand.

"It's one o'clock..." she groaned.

"We went to O'Charlies after the game to celebrate," Ash said, pulling off his softball jersey.

"Sorry I'm late," he said, and sat down on the bed.

"I take it the boys won?" she said rolling up on her elbow.

"Boys?" Ash feigned insult and said, "My dear lady, we are men. Men among men, champions among champions, warriors among warriors..."

"Drunk, horny, middle-aged men among drunk, horny, middle-aged men," she said lying back down.

"Ow. That hurt."

"Yeah, but it's true."

"Only partially," Ash said laughing, "I'm not middle-aged."

"So, the boys are at Mom's?" he asked, leaning close to her face.

"Umm-huh," she said, pushing him away.

"So, we have the house to ourselves?"

"Uh-huh."

"Free to make as much noise as we'd like?"

"Feel free to snore as loud as your heart desires."

"That's not exactly the noise I had in mind," he said, brushing his lips across hers.

"It's one o'clock, Ash."

"I can tell time."

"Evidently, you can't," she said, sitting up and pushing her hair from her face.

"Because if you could, you'd know that the sexy-hot-mama switch was turned off about three hours ago and the sleepy-grumpy-tired-irritable-been-up-since-five switch has been turned on. So, go away."

Ash grinned and moved closer to Della. "You mean there's a switch. A button?" he asked.

Della flopped back on her pillow and tried to pull the covers over her head. Ash stopped her by sliding beneath them and pulling her closer. Della lay flat on her back and stubbornly refused to move, forcing Ash to come to her. He propped himself up on his elbow, slid the other hand across her belly and placed his thigh upon hers.

"I never knew about this button," he said, leaning down to kiss her nose.

"Is this it?" he asked, and moved his mouth to her lips, touching them, brushing softly across them until coming down firmly to cover her mouth.

"Ash, you're a mess," she said, stopping him. "You'll mess up the sheets."

"That's what I had in mind."

"You know what I meant," she said, placing a hand on his bare chest. "Go take a shower."

"I will if you join me," he said, and playfully bit at her left earlobe.

"You're drunk," she said, smelling the beer on his breath, but knowing better. Ash never had more than two beers. It wasn't in his nature to lose control. She knew he was high on his game victory and the excitement that came with that.

"Drunk on love, baby," he said, doing his best Barry White imitation.

Della laughed in spite of herself.

"You changed the subject," he said, nibbling again on her ear. "Let's get back to that button of yours."

"Ash." Della felt her skin coming to life beneath his warm hand as he slowly stroked the skin under her gown.

"Is this it?" he asked softly, as he leaned over her and let his tongue and lips trace a path down her neck to her shoulder.

"No," she said, but her body was beginning to betray her. Her weight shifted automatically to allow him fuller access to her body.

"Well then, what about this?" he asked. "Is this the button?" Grabbing the thin purple strap of her nightgown with his teeth, he pulled it off her shoulder. Leaving it bare and exposed to his hungry mouth.

Shifting, he leaned over Della and let his mouth concentrate on the small sweet spot on her neck. It was her weakness and he knew it. A moan escaped her and despite her best intentions, she felt a smile tugging at the corners of her mouth.

"No? Well, we'll just have to try a few more buttons," Ash said, and kissed Della's mouth, playfully nipping her lower lip and quickly darting his tongue across her teeth. She could taste the beer on his breath, smell the scent of smoke from the bar and the mixture of dirt and sweat from the game. Della found the combination exhilarating. Ash was the most alive person she had ever met. Everything about him shouted his existence to the rest of the world. He tackled life with a zest and desire that made him irresistible.

"What about this one?" he asked, as he slipped the remaining strap of her gown off her shoulder and down her arm, revealing her breasts. Grinning, he lowered his mouth and kissed each nipple, taking only a second to lightly flick his tongue across its center, causing a whimper to escape from Della's lips as she arched her chest toward Ash, wanting more.

"What?" he said, in husky passionate tone. "That's not it either? Well, let's try again." This time lowering his mouth to her left breast, he pulled the nipple deep within his eager mouth while covering the right breast with his warm, insistent hand. Della felt the bed move as Ash repositioned himself to her side and felt his hand leave her breast and slide purposefully down her stomach coming to rest on her panties. He expertly hooked a finger under her waistband and in one smooth, fluid motion pulled them down past her knees, ankles and then tossed them across the room. His knee moved between her legs and urged them open. Moving his mouth to the other breast, he allowed his hand to roam over her mound, teasingly close to her lips, finally sliding deep within her.

Della opened her legs to allow him the freedom to explore and gave into her husband. Ash had made love to Della hundreds of times throughout their marriage and each time she was certain it would be impossible to top the last experience and each time she was surprisingly astonished. Knowing the spots that drove her over the edge, Ash took his time as a lover and enjoyed watching her writhing beneath him, begging for more. She loved how he had that control over her. How, with just a look or a throaty whisper, he could make her knees weak. She loved how his breath on her skin set her on fire. How his kisses lingered not only on her lips, but all over her body. Most of all, she loved how his control allowed her to give into and drown herself in pleasure.

"I think I might have found that button," he said, with his voice hot and raspy at the base of her throat.

She sighed heavily, struggling to think, struggling to maintain control.

Della brought her knees to her chest and held her breath, waiting for him to enter her. Her breath rapid and shallow, her heart beating faster than she was sure was safe, her body temperature feverish. She waited. She opened her eyes and locked onto Ash's as he hovered above her waiting to see her reaction. Wanting to see her love for him. Della moved her quivering hands from Ash's back and cupped his face. Savoring the fire in his eyes. The desire. Trying to burn the moment into her memory. Lowering his lips to her mouth, Ash entered only slightly and stopped. Unable to maintain control, Della wrapped her legs around his waist, dug her nails into his back and arched her back. She dropped her head back exposing her neck and begged for more.

Ash ran his tongue down her chin lightly and drove himself into her with a sudden force that caused her body to tremble involuntarily and her gasps of pleasure grew into louder more audible moans of ecstasy. Della hung onto Ash tighter and drew him into her deeper. She loved the feel of his muscled back and how it rippled with each thrust. She ran her fingers through his hair and down his spine and felt him quiver. Desperate, she clung to him and twisted him onto his back, mounting him in his favorite position. She knew he loved to watch her.

Della closed her eyes and moved in rhythm with his motion. The warmth of their bodies, the sensation of their lovemaking, the urgency of the moment overpowering her. Feeling the release beginning to build and move through her body, she relaxed and rode the familiar wave of ecstasy.

As the sensation began to fade, Della's head began to spin and pulsate. Her bedroom faded and she opened her eyes to find herself staring at the ceiling in the lodge. She was drenched in sweat, her blanket shoved down by her feet and her fingers aching from her grip on the couch cushions. Trembling, she tried to slow her breathing. Regrettably, she realized she had been dreaming of a former life and the reality she lived in now was still the same horror story she had been in a few hours earlier.

A slight stirring from her right left her paralyzed. In an instant, she realized where she was, and who was seated a few feet away from her. Awake and watching. Turning her head slightly, she saw Brady gazing motionless from his chair at her, the amber shadows illuminating his face.

21

"We need to talk about yesterday," Brady told Della. "When you finish up with Stacey, meet me downstairs."

Della watched as Brady walked across the room and out the door. *Great,* she thought miserably. She had been trying her best to avoid him. It hadn't been hard. There were so many things that needed her attention, including her sons. She had barely crossed paths with Brady all morning. She had busied herself by helping Stacey fix breakfast that Brady and Mark had managed to get from one of the cabins earlier that morning. The children were still shaken and docile from hiding in the freezer, but thankfully they had not been exposed to any of the infected people.

Lisa and Todd arrived before breakfast, looking exhausted. They had been scouting a nearby cabin when the swarm hit and were afraid to leave. They hid until dawn. Della realized the red-haired little boy, who had befriended Louie yesterday, was Todd and Lisa's son. With fiery red hair, dark brown eyes, and freckled skin, he very much resembled Todd, although it did look to Della that the boy's small build and glasses more resembled his mother than his father's heavy, solid frame. She was glad to see the family reunited, yet at the same time, she was surprised by her own jealousy, longing for her own joyous family reunion.

Knowing she could no longer postpone the embarrassing conversation Brady was certain to have with her, she kissed her boys and walked downstairs. Brady and Mark had been busy that morning bringing most of the maps and papers to the lodge from the cabin he had used yesterday as an office. They were reorganizing the papers when Della walked up.

"Looks like you've moved your office," Della said clearing her throat.

"It's always best to have a command center in a central location," Mark started to explain, but was cut off when Brady knocked a map off the table while standing up.

"Mark, why don't you go check on the rest of the group," Brady smiled at Della. "Mrs. Bishop and I need to work on some things."

"Sure thing, boss," Mark said, and quickly left the room.

Della could feel the air in the room around her. She suddenly felt claustrophobic and had to fight the urge to run outside.

"I hate it when he calls me boss," Brady grinned, "and I think he knows it."

Brady was trying to lighten the mood a bit, but Della wasn't going to bite, at least not yet.

"Have a seat." Brady motioned to a chair next to him.

"I think I'll stand," she said, wrapping her arms around herself as if she were cold.

"About yesterday...," Brady began.

"Look," Della interrupted, and began pacing and picking at the loose threading at the end of her shirt. "I know it must have been uncomfortable for you and I'm sorry, I should have never put you in that position." She stopped pacing and looked at him, waiting for an answer.

"No, actually it's part of my job. It was an inconvenience, but it's nothing we can't deal with. I assume it was uncomfortable for you, given the personal nature."

"What?" she asked confused. "What do you mean, part of your job?"

"Well, that's what I do. Handle situations like that when they arise. It's not always enjoyable, but like they say, someone has to do it." Brady hunched his shoulders and grinned at her.

"Oh my God! I can't believe you just said that." Horrified at what she just heard, Della suddenly wished the floor would open up and swallow her whole. "I...I...can't believe you. I thought maybe you'd be embarrassed by the situation, but never...what do you mean not always enjoyable? It was a dream! I can't help what I dream. Inconvenience?" Della turned her back on Brady and sat miserably down on the sofa across the room and covered her face with her hands.

"Oh." Della could hear Brady say and then heard him chuckle. "I understand now," he said.

Brady walked to the couch and pulled a chair upright that had been turned over in last night's fight. She felt him sit down close to her.

"There was a misunderstanding, Della." She could hear the smile in his voice.

"I was talking about the situation yesterday at your cabin with the Shields'. You – obviously – weren't."

Della pulled her hands from her face and looked skeptically at him. "The cabin? That's what you were talking about?"

"Yes, the cabin. I thought we should probably take another look at the site today, since we haven't heard from them. Not that I expected them to show up this morning."

"Oh. Okay." Della felt the crimson spreading across her cheeks, deepening with each grin that Brady directed at her.

"But," Brady began, "since you brought it up..." He let the sentence hang between them in the air.

"Oh please, don't you think I've had enough humiliation for the day, for the year?" she said, wishing the burning on her face would cease.

"The pill I gave you last night..." Again, Brady found it difficult to finish his sentence.

"What about the pill?"

"I was going to tell you last night, but you went to sleep so quickly, I assumed you wouldn't be affected by the side effect." Brady hung is head, but she could see he was still grinning.

"Brady, what the hell was in that pill?" Rising from the couch, she placed her hands on her hips and glared at him.

"It was a relaxant, called Prolax, and on the black market it has been known to..." his voiced trailed off and he stood to face her.

"To what?" she demanded.

"To lower your inhibitions, to increase the arousal component."

"God, Brady, you gave me ecstasy?"

"No, no, it wasn't that, but I've heard it does have some of the same advantages, or disadvantages. However you choose to look at it."

"How much did you ... No, never mind, don't answer that. Could we just forget it happened and go on? We do have other things going on here that need our attention."

"Of course, whatever dreams about your husband...it was about Ash right?"

"Yes! It was about Ash."

Brady grinned again at Della and turned and started back to his maps. Della looked questioningly at his back, opened her mouth to say something and then thought better of it. *Best to just leave the room,* she thought.

"Lucky man," said Brady, still facing the maps, "your husband."

22

The sign said that there was a McDonald's seven miles ahead in a city named Shamrock, Texas. Ash was feeling good about the way things had been going for the past day or two. They were thirty minutes inside of the Texas border and had not encountered the dead or dying for more than three hours. They had not even seen overturned or burning cars during that time. Of course, since they left Oklahoma City, they had been traveling through a very rural part of the Southwest, but it still helped to brighten Ash's attitude. It also helped Emily to get some much-needed sleep. Now, though, he needed to get another vehicle because they were running out of gas and he needed some relief. He had been cramping for at least an hour, but didn't want to make unnecessary stops. All of the eating cold canned food on-the-run was catching up to him. *Maybe Shamrock will bring us luck,* he thought. *We're way past due.* Ash knew, though, that stopping for any reason and for any amount of time was dangerous, especially in the evening, but sometimes there was no choice.

As the exit approached, Ash slowed the truck down to thirty. The carnage had exhausted him and he was becoming a bit gun-shy. As he pulled off the interstate, he considered whether or not to wake Emily. She was exhausted and needed sleep, but he needed her to be alert when they stopped. She didn't have the luxury of trying to bring her mind into focus when it was time to move. He gave her left shoulder a light shove. "Wake up, kiddo, we gotta stop."

Emily stirred, but didn't wake.

Ash pushed on her shoulder again. "C'mon, get up, you little snot. You need to be awake."

"Why?" Emily asked with a yawn, as she sat up.

"Because we have to stop. We have to get another car and I need to go potty."

"Go potty?" she said, as she rubbed her eyes. "I'm not two-years-old, ya' know."

Ash grinned and winked at Emily, "Yeah, I know. But, I've said 'go potty' since Ricky was a baby, so now I always say it. You should have heard the hard time I got at work for saying it."

Emily grinned and looked up at Ash. "I'll bet," she said, with another yawn.

Shamrock proved to be a rather quiet town, in the sense that people used to think of quiet towns. There were no wrecked cars in the middle of town, no broken store windows, and no alien marauders in the streets. The only thing that was different - and a little odd – was a concrete barricade that he had to maneuver around. Other than that, Shamrock looked like a small town that rolled up the sidewalks at 8:00 at night like most small towns once did. For a moment, Ash allowed himself to believe it was over. Things were back to normal. But then he realized that even a town as small as Shamrock would not be able to get things cleaned and repaired so quickly. *Is it possible that these people were completely spared? Are there other places like this? Is it because they are so isolated? Do they even know what's happened to the rest of the country, hell, the rest of the world?* The questions shot through Ash's mind like a Gatlin gun. *They even have...by God, they have electricity!*

There weren't a lot of lights on, just a few in the homes on the outskirts of town. The way that the light soaked the windows of the homes made Ash certain that they had to be overhead lights or several lamps. Candles and kerosene lamps don't create the manner of illumination that spreads evenly over a room. As he passed a small red brick house on his right, he saw a person standing in the window, staring at his truck. Then, the person threw a blanket or spread over the window, blackening the opening. Ash looked further up the road and noticed the neighbors following suit. Soon, every home in the area was black.

The town itself was completely dark.

"What happened, here?" Emily asked, almost in a whisper.

"I think the question is: What didn't happen here? It's like the horror going on in the world just passed these people by. There have been no changes; at least, it doesn't look like it."

"Can we stay here?"

Ash looked at Emily. He thought he saw a flicker of hope in her eyes. He thought he saw a plea for a normal life, an end to the insanity.

"We can stay here, tonight."

Emily hesitated, but Ash knew the question that was coming.

"But can we stay here, after?"

"No punkin'. I have to get to my family. I'm sorry."

Tears welled up in Emily's eyes. "I thought I was your family, now," she said, sobbing.

"You are part of my family, now. But I have two boys and a wife in New Mexico and they need me, and I need them, and I need you. Okay?"

"Okay," the young girl sniffed.

Ash drove slowly through town looking for a vehicle to take. Seeing electricity, he wondered if gas stations were working, but the only one he saw was burnt and destroyed. He wanted a truck, a big one, but it was slim pickens in this town. That was another oddity. There were cars here and there, but no more than you might have had in town before the madness started. Ash was ready to slam the accelerator or pop the truck into reverse as the situation warranted. With all of the hell they had been going through, the quiet of this town may have been the most eerie experience yet. *What is going on here?*

"Well, we're almost out of gas. I'm going to have to try one of these cars or at least take some fuel," he said, mostly to himself.

He pulled into a small parking lot that still had three cars and parked the Ram. He walked to the first of the three cars, a Volvo, and pulled the handle. Locked. *Locked?* Ash had actually forgotten what it was like to find a locked car door. He then went to the second car, a Toyota Camry, and again the car was locked. Ash shook his head in disbelief as he approached the last vehicle, this time an older Chevrolet Malibu. He found it unlocked, but no keys inside. *So the better cars are locked and the older one isn't. Just like the old days.* As Ash closed the Malibu's driver side door, something caught his attention on the console of the Malibu. It was a bill from West Texas Gas. The envelope did not have a postmark; the bill itself was dated less than two weeks prior. *The country was engulfed in this mess well before then. How could this guy get a bill? He has gas service? He has postal delivery?* As he looked closer at the bill, he noticed that it was actually a woman's – Lois Carrigan. He noticed with some amusement that Lois was one payment behind. *It's amazing what used to be important.*

From behind him, Ash heard crunching on the gravel lot. It was at that point that he realized that he had left his shotgun in the Ram. *Stupid! Stupid! Stupid!* He turned to face the noise and saw a man carefully approaching him. Because of the man's stealth, Ash knew that the stranger was not infected. The monsters didn't care who heard or saw them.

Ash put his hand out to motion the man to stop. "That's close enough, man."

"You need to come with me," the man whispered.

"I'm not going anywhere."

"Don't be stupid, you can't be on the streets. You need to turn your truck off. It'll be heard," the man said urgently.

Something about the man's tone and mannerisms told Ash that he had better do as he was told. "Where are we going?"

"My house. Now turn off that damn truck and let's get outta here!"

"I've got a little girl with me, too."

"What?" It was obvious the man was quickly becoming exasperated. "Why?"

"Why do you think?"

"Alright. Get her and let's go!"

23

Ash and Emily followed the man into his house through a side door. They had been cutting through the neighbor's yard by hiding in bushes and behind cars. It seemed like an odd precaution because none of that was going to stop the bugs from attacking, but Ash followed the man through his paces anyway. As they entered the home, Ash could see they had a few lamps on, although the windows were covered with thick blankets.

"Sorry about the cloak and dagger shit, but it's a dangerous time. My name is Alejandro, but I go by Alex. Come on in and have a seat," the man said with a slight Latino accent. Alex was about fifty-five with an ample spare tire around his mid-section. His once-black hair was now mostly gray and he carried a ready smile.

"I'd love to, but I really gotta pee."

"Oh, sure, yeah. Go down the hall there and it's the second door on the left."

Ash proceeded down the hall as instructed. When he arrived, he absent-mindedly reached for the light switch and clicked it. The light shown brightly from three decorative bulbs over the medicine cabinet. Ash stared at the lights for a moment, then turned them off and back on again. *Life used to be just this easy,* he thought.

When he finished his business, Ash returned to the living room and looked at the lamps. "You have electricity."

"Yes. We have power about fourteen to sixteen hours a day."

Ash felt a tug at his shirt. "I have to go, Ash," Emily said.

"Okay, I'll show you where," Ash said, as he led her down the hall.

"Will you stay with me?" Emily asked.

"Umm, I'll stay here in the hall."

Emily grinned, "That's what I meant."

When Ash and Emily returned to the living room, a woman about the same age as Ash was there.

"This is my daughter, Cara," Alex said.

Ash smiled at the woman, "Hi, Cara."

Cara returned the smile, "Hello." She then turned her attention to the little girl hiding behind Ash. "Who's this?"

"I'm sorry. I've been incredibly rude," Ash said. "My name is Ash Bishop, this is Emily."

Cara crossed the room, bent down and stuck her opened hand out to Emily. "Pleased to meet you."

Emily peeked around Ash's leg, but made no move to take Cara's hand.

"Don't be rude, cricket," Ash said.

Cara stood upright and put her hands on her hips. "That's alright. The world's gone crazy. She has a right to worry about strangers."

"How can you have electricity?"

"I will be happy to explain it to you, but I would think you'd be hungry."

"Yes, very," Ash said gratefully.

"Cara, do you mind making something for our visitors?"

"Not at all. It'd be my pleasure."

With Cara standing just a few feet away now, Ash could see that she was a strikingly beautiful woman. Not as dark as Alex, but with the type of features that make Latino women the subject of songs. Her eyes were a dark brown and her hair was just on the brown side of auburn. She had the kind of pouty lips that made Ash blush. He wouldn't have described her as voluptuous, but she was well proportioned and not short of any desirable traits.

She noticed Ash looking at her, smiled and said, "Let me find you two something to eat." She then turned and departed from the living room. Ash wanted to follow her and just look at her for awhile, but he thought that might be considered a little rude. With all the horror, he and Emily had faced lately, it was wonderful to be near beauty again.

When she left, Ash turned his attention back to Alex, who was smiling at him the way a father smiles with pride at his children. He motioned to a recliner with his left hand. "Please, Mr. Bishop, be seated."

Self-consciously, Ash sat in the recliner and Emily stood to his left. He looked at her and pointed to his lap. She gave him a broad smile and crawled into the chair with him.

"Where are you from, Mr. Bishop?"

"Ash, please. We're from Denver, but we were in Chicago when this hit." Ash knew that he was taking liberties by including Emily in his background, but he didn't feel like explaining at that moment.

"Chicago? Really? How long did it take you to get here?"

Ash could hear the banging of dishes and cookware in the kitchen and he longed to join Cara there. But he maintained his small talk with Alex. "About three weeks now. It was...hair-raising."

"I'm sure. Did you see any of the bugs?"

That's an odd question. "Of course. Hundreds...thousands of them."

"I've never seen any, but I hear they are gruesome," added Alex.

Ash was stunned. "You've never seen any? I thought they had covered the entire country, the entire world for that matter."

"That's what they say. But we've never seen them here."

Ash sat quiet and completely stunned. "I didn't know there were little pieces of paradise like this left."

Alex rubbed his temples and shook his head, "Paradise, right."

At the same moment that Ash caught the aroma of warm food wafting from the kitchen, Emily turned around and gave Ash a huge grin.

"Smells good, huh?"

"Yeah," Emily whispered.

"Ah, my Cara is a great cook. How long has it been since you've had warm food?"

"Not since I left Denver."

Alex furled his brow and looked at Ash, then Emily. Ash realized that he had left Emily out of that statement.

Ash looked at Emily, and back at Alex. "I'll explain it to you later."

"That's okay. Don't want to pry."

"Dinner's ready," came the call from the kitchen.

Alex got up from the couch and led the other two into the dining room. Ash saw that there were two places set. "Aren't you going to eat?" he asked both of them.

"We already ate," Cara said. "I hope you like it."

"It smells great."

The small dining room table sat four. Ash sat facing the kitchen and Emily sat next to him with her back to the living room. Alex went around the table and sat so he was directly facing Ash. Cara began bringing bowls into the dining room containing shredded roast beef, mashed potatoes, gravy, green beans and dinner rolls.

"I hope you don't mind leftovers," Cara said, as she sat in the seat next to Ash.

"I just can't tell you how much we appreciate this," Ash said, scooping potatoes into his plate. "It's been a long time since I've eaten anything close to this good."

Alex helped fill Emily's plate. She gave a quiet thank you and started digging in. Her eyes got wide with the first bite of roast beef.

"You like that, honey?" Cara smiled.

Emily never looked up from her food, she just nodded her head and kept eating.

The three adults chuckled and left her to her meal.

"This is good, Cara, thank you," said Ash.

"No problem at all."

"You have family?" Alex asked. "I mean, other than Emily."

"Yes. I have a wife and two sons." Ash wanted to look at Cara to get her reaction to that. *Don't be a fool,* he thought to himself. *You're married and you love your wife and sons. Don't let a pretty face disrupt what you need to do.* "They're in New Mexico, at least I hope so. We have a cabin there and Emily and I were heading that way, but we turned off the interstate looking for fuel."

"Is that what you were doing with those cars in the lot?" Alex asked.

"Yes."

"Then, you're lucky I came by. If you had been caught, you'd be toast. Both of you."

Ash thought about that while he chewed on a dinner roll. He swallowed his food and said, "That's just the way things are done now. At least outside of this part of Texas. You take what you can get when you can get it."

"That couldn't be further from the way things are done in Shamrock," Cara said. "You have to get permission here for every move you make."

Ash stopped chewing and looked at Alex and then Cara. "Permi..." Ash stopped talking long enough to swallow. "Sorry. Permission from whom?"

"The people who run this town," Alex said. "You mentioned in the living room that Shamrock was paradise on earth. You couldn't be more wrong. We have electricity several hours a day and we're not invaded by bugs. But all the horrors you've heard about Nazi Germany are happening right here in our little town. People disappear, some are arrested for the flimsiest of reasons. Personally, I would rather leave here and take my chances with the bugs."

"Well, I don't know about that," Ash said. "It's pretty intense. So, why don't you leave?"

"Did I mention Nazi Germany? You can't just leave."

"Why not? It was pretty easy coming in."

"I know," Alex said. "That's what's so strange. Near as I can tell, no one saw you arrive. No one knew you were here."

"How did you find out I was here?"

"I was taking the garbage out when I saw your truck slowly roll through. Your truck wasn't marked and you looked like you were looking for an address. You know someone new to town when you see him. Especially when there are no visitors."

"What do you mean, marked?"

"Cars in town have a large, glow in the dark sticker on the windshield that indicates that it's approved to be driven. There's only a handful or two of such cars."

"I didn't see any stickers on the cars in the lot."

"That's why they're in the lot. They can't be moved without the stickers."

"Why do people have cars, if they can't drive them?"

"I guess they saw no need to take the cars. There's a limited amount of fuel available and you could be shot for unauthorized driving. The authorities took the cars they needed from wherever they wanted and left everyone else's cars alone. But you can't drive them, so they sit in parking lots and driveways."

Ash took a couple of bites of green beans and tried to digest what he had been told. Then he looked up at Alex and said, "How do you know I'm not a plant?"

Alex smiled, "I thought about that, but I decided to take a chance. Obviously, the powers-that-be in Shamrock didn't know I would be taking out my trash when I did, and if they were looking for resistance members in Shamrock, which do exist, they'd be sorely disappointed because I'm definitely not one and I don't know any...at least, not that I know of."

"My question for you, Mr. Bishop, is, how did you get into town? Did anyone stop you, or try to stop you?"

"No. No one. We just rolled into town like we would any other. Except, of course, for the fact that there were no cars on their sides and burning, no broken store windows, and no infected people wandering the streets."

Alex shook his head, "Doesn't make any sense. Where were the barricades and guards?"

Ash looked up from his now-empty plate, "Now that you mention it, I did have to drive around some concrete barricades on the edge of town. But there was no one around them."

"Odd. Very strange," responded Alex. "These aren't guys who fall asleep on the job. They are almost literally Gestapo. They even wear red armbands with a symbol that's very similar to a swastika. I'm telling you, it's scary. But, there's no way they would have fallen asleep or left that post – unless they were ordered to, or somebody screwed up."

"You said that these guys are very Nazi-like," Ash said, choosing his words carefully, "but you're still here."

Alex's expression suddenly became very serious, "You mean, why didn't they kill a beaner like me?"

"Well, I wouldn't have put it that way."

"It's alright, I'm just messin' with you. The motivations of these guys don't seem to be racist. That's one way they're different from Nazis. They kill based on your ability to oppose them." Alex looked at Cara, reached over and squeezed her hand. "That's why they killed my wife, Michele. She was as white as you, but she was a professor of history at the community college. She was one of the first to go, almost three weeks ago."

"Man, Alex, I'm sorry."

"Cara and I were both brought in for questioning right after she died, but they let us go after a few hours. Not without a souvenir of our visit, though." Alex pulled his shirt up to expose a burn mark on his belly. Cara stood up, pulled her shirt up to reveal the same mark. "These were actually done with a branding iron, like my daughter and I are cattle."

Ash heard a whimper and looked over to see Emily staring wide-eyed at the burn marks.

Alex noticed her looking, too, and he and Cara pulled their shirts down. "Sorry, I wasn't thinking. But, do you understand, now, why I want to leave this place?"

"Sort of. But remember, you've only heard stories about what's happening out there. You haven't seen it first-hand.

And you've got one thing on your side here that the people everywhere else don't have – history. Nobody knows what to do about the damned bugs, but we've got history to show us what to do about oppressive governments."

"Well, we can't fight them," Alex said. "They took our guns, at least what they could find."

"Speaking of guns, I left my shotgun in the truck."

"You have a shotgun?"

Ash nodded his head.

"Rounds?"

Ash nodded again, "About thirty."

"Well, we're going to have to do something about your truck anyway. If they haven't already found it, they will. And then they'll tear this town apart. I should have thought of this before."

"When do you want to go?" asked Ash.

"Finished eating?" Alex asked back.

Ash picked up his plate to take it into the kitchen. He smiled at Cara and said, "I'm done. It was outstanding."

Cara intercepted his plate and said, "I'm glad you liked it."

"Let's get going," Alex said.

Ash walked around to where Emily was still sitting and squatted in front of her, "I'm going with Mr..."

"Contreras," Alex offered.

"I'm going with Mr. Contreras. Stay here with Cara. She's very nice and will take care of you."

"Are you coming back?" asked Emily.

"You bet. I promised to take you to New Mexico, remember?"

The young girl nodded, "I remember."

"Great. I'll see you in a little while," Ash said, standing. He looked at Cara and started to speak.

"She'll be fine," Cara said, before Ash could say anything.

Alex went into the living room and shut off the lamps. Then, he went to the front door and slowly opened it. He looked both ways and motioned Ash to follow. Stepping out into the cool Texas evening air, they moved to the left, careful to remain behind shrubbery that lined the front of the house.

"If you see a car, get as low as you can, as quick as you can," Alex whispered.

They came to the end of the house and shrubbery and faced the side street to Alex's corner lot.

"The lot is just on the other side of the house behind mine," Alex whispered. "Just stay low and move fa... Get down!"

Both men ducked behind Alex's shrubbery as headlights of a car turned down the side street. The car, a late model Grand Prix, Ash guessed, rolled slowly down the street and passed the spot where the men were hiding. About a block further, the car slowed, almost to a stop, and then continued.

"We might be in trouble," Alex whispered.

"Why?" Ash whispered back.

"That guy almost stopped right in front of the lot. That may mean nothing, but it might mean that he was looking to see if anyone returned to it. Just be careful."

The two men ran through Alex's side yard and to a magnolia tree in front of the neighbor's house. Across the street, Ash could see the gravel lot where his truck still sat in the dark.

"There it is," Ash whispered. "Let's hurry."

"Hang on," Alex replied, as he grabbed Ash's upper arm. "There might be people watching it. We have to be careful," he repeated.

Ash surveyed the area around the lot. To the left was a ditch right next to the road. Nobody would be hiding there because they would not have a clear view of the lot, which sat a couple of feet above the road. To the right and behind the lot were slight knolls that offered perfect vantage points if someone wanted to watch the lot.

Alex pointed to the lot and swept his arm to the right. "See the little crests behind the lot?" he asked Ash.

"Yeah, I was just looking at that," Ash answered.

"Behind those is another crest that sits up higher. We'd be able to see both of the smaller crests from there," Alex whispered.

"How do we get there?"

"To the right, we'll move to the end of the cul-de-sac, then cross behind those houses. We're going to have to hide in bushes and behind cars to get there, but if we don't, we could be in real danger."

"Lead the way," Ash said.

"Make sure you don't touch the cars, they may still be alarmed."

"Why?"

"Who knows, but we can't chance it," whispered Alex.

With Ash right behind him, Alex ran to the first car, a Lincoln Town Car, and crouched behind it. Ash was surprised and somewhat amused at how this slightly overweight, middle-aged man could move so quickly and gracefully. Alex looked through the windows of the car down the suburban street. Nothing. He then turned and ran for a Dodge Neon sitting in the next driveway.

When Ash crouched next to Alex behind the Neon, Alex turned to him, "I'm going to need a minute," he whispered through labored breathing.

"Okay. Take your time."

This time, Ash stretched up to look through the car's windows. Still nothing. He slouched back down and looked at Alex who was leaning against the Neon. "I thought you said not to touch the cars," he whispered.

"Don't be a smartass."

Ash chuckled at the older man, and leaned against the Neon as well.

After a few minutes, Alex got up on his knees and said, "I'm ready."

"You sure? Nobody's seen us, I'm sure of that. You can have a few more minutes."

"Nah. I'm okay. We need to get moving."

The next driveway did not have a car, so they moved toward a brick wall lining a small portion of the walk. About five feet from the wall, a car turned down the street. Both men immediately went down to the ground, making themselves as flat as possible. The occupants of the vehicle were shining a spotlight on the houses on the right side of the road, the side where Alex and Ash were lying. But as the car passed them, Ash could see that they were shining the lights too high, at the houses. Ash held his breath till the car passed, but he could hear slight moaning coming from his left, from Alex. Both men remained motionless until the driver made his round and departed the cul-de-sac. Ash hopped up and turned Alex over to his back.

"Are you alright, Alex?" Ash asked.

"The pain's back. It's pretty bad."

"We gotta go back."

"No. We can't. We may be in danger if we don't get to that truck."

"But you might be having a heart attack," Ash whispered urgently.

"No. I'll be all right. Just let me rest a minute."

Ash heard the unmistakable sound of someone unlatching their front door. He saw a flashlight flick on and a figure moving behind it toward him and Alex. *Shit!*

Although he knew it was too late, Ash got flat to the ground and waited.

"Don't even try it. I know you're there. I have a gun, so don't move."

The man approached and shone the light on Ash's face. "Who are you?"

Ash struggled for an explanation while he tried to shield himself against the light that was piercing his dilated eyes. The man moved his light to the other person lying in his yard. "Alejandro?"

"Yeah," Alex struggled to say.

"What are you doing out here, man. You could get yourself killed."

Alex was unable to catch his breath long enough to respond. The man swept his flashlight beam between Ash and Alex a few times, then clicked the light off.

He glared at Ash and said, "C'mon, help me get him inside."

Ash stood up and both men lifted Alex to his feet, then grabbed each arm and lifted them over their shoulders to help Alex into the man's house. The house was dark inside until the stranger shut the front door and turned on two living room lamps at a switch on the wall. They helped Alex to the couch and laid him down.

"You all right, Alejandro?" the man asked, after he saw Alex breathing heavily and sweating profusely.

Alex just nodded his head.

The man turned his attention to Ash. Ash could now see that the stranger was a black man, about six-foot-four, probably in his late forties. "So, what's the deal?"

"I rolled into town today. Alex saw the truck in the lot behind this cul-de-sac and got me back to his house where he fed me and told me about this town. He told me that we needed to go back and get the truck before it was spotted by anyone, so that's what we're doing."

"Well, he's right. You need to move it. But, you don't just roll into this town."

"So Alex told me, but that's exactly what happened."

The man turned and looked at Alex, who nodded his head. "Okay, I'm Terry. Alejandro and I have been friends for a long time. If he says you're okay, you must be okay," he said, as he stuck out his hand.

Ash grasped his hand. "I'm Ash. Can Alex stay here while I get my truck?"

"Sure."

"Great. Now, what am I going to do with the truck after I get it?"

Terry turned to Alex. "The Tucker place?"

Again, Alex just nodded.

"Turn left out of the parking lot. About fifty yards over, there's a gravel drive on the right, drive the truck up the drive, about forty or fifty feet, there will be an abandoned house with a garage that doesn't lock. Pull your truck in there. The house doesn't look abandoned, it's only been unoccupied for about two weeks. The owners were murdered and now it sits empty. Be careful in this neighborhood; some of these people will snitch on you. It's amazing how easy some people sell out. Believe me when I tell you, Ash, these guys don't mess around. If you are caught, you'll be killed or tortured."

Ash nodded, "I believe you. Take care of him. I'll be back as soon as I can."

"Oddly enough," Terry continued, "the best thing you can do if you're caught is resist. If you do, they'll probably just kill you on the spot, instead of after they've tortured you. They're evil, but not too smart."

Ash gave Terry a small grin and nodded.

Terry switched off the living room lamps, handed Ash the flashlight he was using and said, "You're probably going to need this, but go easy on it. Batteries are not that easily found nowadays. Now, go."

24

Thankfully, the drive to the cabin had gone quickly and quietly. She had resolved to ignore the subject and concentrate on the matter at hand. Although Brady had been respectful of her silence and professional in the conversation, she couldn't shake the feeling that he was enjoying the fact that she was uncomfortable around him.

As they drove, Della watched the passing scenery. This part of New Mexico was the most beautiful area of the world she had ever seen. Della had visited most of the United States and several foreign countries, but nothing compared to their New Mexico retreat, at least as far as she was concerned. This area sat on a plateau about six thousand feet above sea level and the Rocky Mountain basin hovered around the region like a guardian angel. It was breathtaking. When she and Ash first crested the plateau at Tewa Lake, they fell immediately in love with the area. It had always been a perfect spot.

As they pulled up to the cabin, Della noticed that the interlopers' blue Honda was missing from the driveway. "It looks like they're gone."

"Well, maybe they got out of here before the bugs came," Brady said unconvincingly.

"Do you think the cabin's safe?" she asked.

"Stay here and I'll go check it out," he said, opening the door.

Della sat in the car for a moment and watched Brady cross the yard and start up the staircase to the porch.

"You don't listen very well, do you?" he asked, when he noticed she had left the car and followed him.

"Never been one of my strong suits."

"Yeah, well stay behind me at least."

Instead of opening the front door, Brady walked around to the front window, cupped his hands around his eyes and peered inside. Della followed him and did the same. The inside of the cabin looked quiet. She could see mountains of half-opened boxes and crumpled newspaper packing scattered around the living room floor, but saw no sign of the dreaded bugs.

"Ready?" Brady asked.

Nodding, Della followed closely behind as Brady slowly opened the front door and stopped just inside of it. Standing quietly, they listened for signs of movement. Nothing but the slight ticking of the grandfather clock on the far wall was audible. Stepping further into the house, Brady closed the door behind them, fairly certain the cabin was bug-free. Della tensed as she gazed around the room. The living room was the cabin's largest room, designed to allow maximum sunlight into the house, and a large bay window served as the room's centerpiece. The far wall was covered in stone and surrounded a small but efficient fireplace. The rustic paneled walls were dark and complemented the stone. Della had decorated the cabin in coordinating dark greens and maroons, choosing rustic and woodsy furniture to complete the look. She recalled, happily, the frequent trips to the local flea markets looking for the right accessory to match the cabin's four rooms.

"It looks like they left right after we did," Della said.

"Probably scared we'd make them account for their lies," Brady answered.

"But why would they leave all their stuff?"

"Maybe they were thinking of coming back."

"Oh, no. You don't really think so, do you?" she asked worriedly.

"No, I don't think so," Brady said, and looked around at the dozens of boxes scattered throughout the house. "Maybe this stuff isn't theirs either," he surmised.

"You think they stole this stuff, too?" Della walked over to the nearest pile and started opening boxes. The first was filled with six porcelain dolls wrapped in paper. "These dolls haven't even been opened yet."

"Maybe they stole them from retailers," Brady said, frowning. "But why would they steal dolls when, if you're a thief, there are plenty of other stores open for the taking," he wondered.

"Let's see what's in the other boxes," Della said. In the second box, she found snack size bags of candy.

"Chocolate!" she squealed excitedly, and ripped open a bag of mini Hershey bars.

"Good?" Brady asked amusingly, as he watched her devour the first candy bar.

"Ummm," she replied, closing her eyes and enjoying the delicious smooth chocolate fill her mouth and engulf her senses.

"God, Della, you've got to quit that." A pained looked crossed Brady's face.

"What?"

"The moaning. The dream. The chocolate. It's killing me."

Della stopped chewing the bar and swallowed self-consciously. "Sorry."

"Let's just finish going through these boxes," Brady said, with his back to her.

The rest of the boxes contained a potpourri of odd items. They found several boxes of tissues, candy, and, oddest of all, new unwrapped toys. Della thought it would be a good idea if they hid the toys and saved them for special occasions such as birthdays. It would probably be impossible for them to leave the mountain any time in the near future. Thinking of birthdays made Della sad. Louie's birthday would be here in a few months and she wondered if she and the boys would have to spend it alone.

"Do you think it's safe to stay here tonight?" she asked, after surveying the rest of the cabin.

"I'm not sure," Brady said, studying the fireplace. "We'd have to make some adjustments to make sure it's closed up tight."

The kitchen was more of a mess than the living room. Cabinet doors stood open and boxes were strewn throughout the room. Most of the boxes contained clothing; many still had tags on them.

"We should take the clothing to town and see if anyone can use them," she called out to Brady.

Luckily, the intruders had left most of the cabin intact, including the hidden trap door to the basement, which had remained untouched. All of Della's kitchenware was still there. The small kitchen had one window and most of the appliances shared the same wall. A wooden picnic table stood against the other wall with a dark plaid tablecloth covering it. The bedrooms were relatively untouched. The boys' rooms had only a few boxes in it. The twin beds flanking opposing walls were made with animal print sheets and pillows. A large circular braided country rug warmed the room. She checked the closets and discovered the boys' extra clothing she had thought to leave at the cabin still remained. Several games and puzzles also littered the closet floor. *It would be good to have the boys here surrounded by their familiar things,* she thought.

25

Della pushed the barrage of toys and couch pillows out of her path with her foot and carried another load of laundry to the couch. The loads weren't that large, but she felt that by using the generator to power the washer and dryer on small loads was better than trying to overload them with large ones. Not that the boys were dirtying many clothes. Sitting down with the basket on her lap, Della watched her sons. Ricky sat on his knees, leaning over the back of the couch with his forehead against the window. The same position he sat in most of the day. Most of the week. Della wasn't sure if he was watching for signs of the bugs or for his father. *Probably a little of both,* she thought.

Louie sat on the rug in the middle of the living room surrounded by hot wheels and playing cards. *This is so hard on them,* she thought. Ash would know how to soothe their fears. He was always better at assuaging their anxieties. As Ricky had grown older, he had gravitated towards his dad, spending evening and weekends in the shop Ash had made in their basement. A boy's only haven, he had called it. Ricky had built more model cars, planes and boats than five boys his age. When Ash had arrived home early one afternoon with a ping-pong table strapped down in the bed of his truck, Della was certain her time with Ricky was drawing quickly to a close. Thankfully, Louie was still her baby. Where Ricky couldn't wait to wiggle out of her hugs, they never lasted long enough for Louie.

Now, watching her normally active sons lie around and do nothing, made her angry. They needed to be outside. They needed sunlight and fresh air, not locked away like prisoners. They needed their old life back. They needed their dad. She needed Ash. Thinking about their life and Ash had gotten harder as the days stretched into weeks. At first, she had taken comfort in her memories, drawing strength from their love, but day after day with no word or sight of Ash had begun to drain her. She also, had woke each morning with hope that this would be the day she would see Ash walk through her door. But as each night came and still no word, Della found it harder to hold on to hope.

It had been just over a month since Brady had given the all clear for them to move out of the lodge and into the cabin. Initially, the boys were excited to be near their personal belongings and into familiar territory. But that feeling didn't last long. Soon, the boys began to tire of endless days of stale cabin and filtered sunlight. Visits from the other children from town were infrequent. Della wished she had thought to bring more books, but at the time, reading material was not foremost on her mind. Thankfully, Mark and Brady had managed to bring her van up past the roadblock and to the cabin. Unpacking the van had been a chore, but at least it had given her something to do with her time. The boys had plenty of toys, but Della was most grateful for her and Ash's insight to stock the cabin with an overflowing supply of DVD's. The time the boys spent in front of the battery-powered television was a much-needed break for Della. Trying to keep Louie occupied and focused on something other than his desire to go outside was a daunting task. Ricky helped but quickly tired of Louie's choice of play.

Now, watching her sons' lethargic state, Della had an idea. Taking her radio to the far end of the cabin, Della tried contacting Lisa. Mark answered and Della explained to him her idea on how to help not only her cabin-fevered sons, but their community as a whole. Della was certain that the other children in their town were suffering from the same case of cabin fever as her sons. It had been almost three weeks since a bug was spotted in their area. Although Della was not ready to believe the evil things had left for good, she was willing to concede that it was now safer than it had been a few weeks earlier.

*   *   *

"I'm so glad you thought of this," Mark told Della.

The two stood inside the cabin watching the group of children scatter throughout the living room floor. Happy to be with one another, their voices growing louder with the excitement of being together, the children branched off into smaller groups, huddling around game boards and toys. Smiling, Della hoped the kids found a way to forget about their current situation and become normal children, at least for an afternoon.

"I'm going to head back," Mark began, "just call me when you want me to round the kids up for you."

Preparing to bolt from the house and sprint to his car, Mark grabbed his keys and put his hand on the door.

"Do you need me to send Brady up tonight for anything?" he asked.

"No," she said. Then added, "Well, the fireplace has been making some odd sounds; if he wants to come look at it, he can," she said, looking at the floor.

"I'll tell him. Take care, Della."

Della watched as he sprinted across the porch and down the stairs, taking them two and three at a time, until he was safely inside the car. Pausing before pulling out, he waved at her as he left.

"The fireplace is making odd noises?" she said aloud. "Get a grip, Della."

If Mark had known she was making flimsy excuses for Brady to come visit, he didn't let it show. Truth was, Brady had, for one reason or another, checked on her and the boys every night they had been in the cabin. Della found herself looking forward to his visits. Even the brief ones. It had been five weeks since she had last seen Ash. Almost as long since she'd heard his voice. The pictures she kept around the cabin were for the boys, but she seldom forced herself to look at them. Was he dead? She wasn't sure what the outside world had become since she had taken refuge on the mountain, but she was certain that if Ash were alive, he'd move Heaven and Hell to reach her. That knowledge increased her guilt about her feelings for Brady.

Brady was so incredibly different from Ash. Even their physical appearances were strikingly opposite. Where Ash stood just slightly taller than she, Brady was much taller. She was used to Ash's soft voice and mannerisms, whereas Brady's rugged, tough persona was sometimes hard to understand. She found it, and him, compelling. Although Della was still very much in love with her husband, her heart wondered what it would be like to open itself to another. To allow herself to love again. To be loved again.

26

Ash ran out the door and headed directly for a Pontiac Bonneville parked next to Terry's house – the first one at the end of the short street. Ash peaked down the street through the car's windows. This time, however, Ash paid close attention to the area's homes. With no activity within sight, Ash decided to go for it. He sprinted past the remaining houses at the end of the cul-de-sac and into the backyard of the house nearest his goal. While in full sprint, he was surprised, and grateful, that he didn't hear any dogs barking. He was certain a barking dog was going to give him away when he started this excursion. But there had been none.

About fifty feet past the last house, Ash found the small hill that Alex mentioned. He climbed the hill briskly, but he was no longer concerned about being spotted. Anybody in a car that entered the cul-de-sac, as well as the homeowners, would not be able to see him now. When he crested the hill, he crawled on his hands and knees to the brim of the hill and got down on his belly. He could see the lot below and the small knoll that overlooked it. However, he could not see if anyone was watching the car, so he put his head in his arms and waited to see if his night vision would improve. Resting, in the still of the warm night, Ash realized how tired he was. His head, heavy on his shoulders, ached and his back, taunt with stress, hurt with each movement. *It'll be good to get some well-earned sleep tonight,* he thought. He read somewhere that it takes about thirty minutes to get full night vision, and he left Terry's house maybe ten minutes before.

He heard the voices coming up from behind him. Ash lay as flat and still as he could, but the voices kept getting louder, heading right for him.

"There he is," said a voice, oddly familiar.

Ash could see light from a flashlight around his face. His heart was beating so fast and hard, it almost made him believe that an *Alien* might start bursting through his chest. Six men stood in front of him with rifles pointed at his chest. They stood him up and surrounded him, taunting him, trying to get him to run. Ash couldn't believe what he was seeing. They were wearing brown shirts with their trousers tucked in their boots. They wore red armbands, as Alex had said, but these symbols on the armbands didn't just look like swastikas, they were swastikas.

My God, it can't be, Ash thought. *Bugs are one thing, we can't do anything about that, but history should have taught us better than this.*

Between the six thugs, a man approached.

Must be the head shithead, Ash thought.

When the man came into view, Ash couldn't believe what he was seeing. Terry. The man who appeared to be such a guardian angel had turned him in. A black man had aided people who patterned their behavior after the most egregious racists the world has ever known.

"What happened to Alex?" Ash asked.

"Alejandro never did recover from his heart attack, poor soul," laughed Terry.

"I thought he was your friend," Ash yelled.

"You are one stupid white boy."

The men laughed heartily at Ash. Two of them shoved Ash to the ground and two others started kicking him in the chest, stomach, and head. Suddenly, they quit and helped him back to his feet, though they held his arms behind his back.

"We're not ready to kill you quite yet. You need to see something first."

"Let me go."

Ash could hear the small voice of a child. It took a few seconds for Ash to realize that it was Emily, being held by Cara.

No!

"Cara, what are you..."

Cara's laughter cut Ash's words short.

"Let her go, she can't be any threat to you!"

Again, the six men broke into raucous laughter. "Who cares," said one of them, "killing her will be fun."

"You Nazi faggots, let her go," Ash screamed, straining against the men holding him.

In a rapid, fluid motion, Cara exposed a large knife and sliced it across Emily's throat. Her blood ran down Cara's left arm, which was holding the young girl across the chest.

"No! No, no." Ash screamed and rolled over on his back. His eyes filling with tears, he put both hands over his mouth and tried to calm himself. He sat straight up and looked around. Quiet. No one around anywhere. He lay back down with his heart still pounding at his sternum. *A dream. Another damn dream. These dreams are going to kill me.*

He turned back over and surveyed the berm. His quick scan revealed no predators lurking in the shadows. The area was barren of trees or other obstacles.

He decided to go for it. He jumped up, wiped the tears from his eyes and slid-ran down the higher slope toward the lower. When he reached the bottom, he dashed for the next slope without a pause. When he reached the brim of the slope, he tripped over a rock and let out a small wail as he rolled down the hill. As he reached the lot, he rolled back to his feet, and sprinted to the truck as he dug his keys out of his jeans. He looked for the door key while he ran. He didn't want to use the electronic keyless entry because the blip it gave was unusually loud. Ash reached the truck, unlocked it, and slid behind the wheel. He sat in the truck, breathing harder than he ever had in his life. He looked through the windows and all of his mirrors expecting to find Nazis punks, laughing, with flashlights and swastika armbands, coming at him.

But there was nothing. Ash started the truck, slowly rolled out of the lot, and hesitated. Terry told him to turn right, but could he trust him? He struggled to clear his head. *It was just a dream. Alex didn't indicate that there was a problem. He couldn't talk, but he could gesture, grunt or something. You're being stupid. Besides, you have nowhere else to go,* he told himself. He turned right.

He said it was about fifty feet ahead, on the right. He drove slowly with the lights off, keeping his head on a swivel. He found a gravel driveway between two overgrown hedges about where Terry said it would be. He turned in and saw the house a few feet ahead. As he stopped the big truck and put it in park, he wondered whether or not he should keep the engine running. He decided to leave it on and he opened the truck door. He walked up to the garage, turned the knob, and pulled. The garage door gave way, but emitted a squeal that hung in the night air. *Damn it,* Ash thought. He decided to forego scanning the area again. *The best thing to do is get this truck hidden and get out of here.* He got back in the truck, pulled it into the garage, turned off the engine and hopped out. He ran to the garage door to close it and stopped. The truck was well-hidden and he was sure he wasn't seen. Ash grabbed the flashlight Terry had given him, his shotgun, and box of rounds and covertly searched the garage for weapons, tools, or anything else he could use.

After a few minutes of searching, Ash decided the cluttered garage did not provide anything useful for him, so he tried the door to the house. He was very surprised to find it unlocked. He was even more surprised to find that the house was mostly furnished. Although it had obviously been ransacked, it had not been cleared out. He thought about looking for guns, but knew that guns would have been one of the first things removed, so he headed for the kitchen. The first drawer he opened revealed about a dozen pieces of cutlery. *They might be as evil as Nazis, but they're not nearly as efficient,* Ash thought. He grabbed four of the largest knives in the drawer, but found he couldn't hold all four and the shotgun and hold the flashlight, so he put three of them back and headed for the door.

Ash closed the garage door, and stopped to get his bearings. *I came in from the left, so I go back left,* he thought. But he knew better than to follow the road. He remained about thirty feet from the road and hoped there would be no obstructions and he would be able to find the lot, or better yet, the knoll behind it.

About forty feet into his walk, he found himself in a thicket of trees, a rare sight in this part of Texas. When he came through the thicket, he found himself right behind a man sporting a rifle. Beyond the man, he saw four men milling about in the lot where he had earlier parked his truck.

Ash weighed his options. He could wait them out, but who knew how long that would be, and no doubt they were going to start scanning the area. He could try to travel around the lot and surrounding area. But he did not know what was beyond the upper knoll and with the dream he had moments ago still fresh, he didn't want to go that way. He knew it was irrational, but the thought of climbing that knoll again put a severe knot in his belly.

That left one option. Ash put everything but the knife on the ground and quietly ran out into the open at the man holding the rifle. The man turned and saw Ash just as he hit him. He put his left hand over the man's mouth at the same time he thrust the knife deep into his ribcage. The man groaned loudly, his eyes went wide first and then glassy. Ash helped him to the ground to avert noise, pulled the knife out of the dying man's body, and looked over the berm to see if the groan and slight scuffling alerted those below.

There was no sign from the men below that they knew what had happened, so Ash ran back to the edge of the thicket, grabbed his stuff and turned to run back to Terry's house. He was ten steps past the man he just killed when he stopped. *Idiot!* Ash turned again and ran back to the man. He rolled him over and grabbed the rifle that had fallen to the ground in the scuffle. He picked up the rifle and searched the man for rounds. He found three loaded magazines and stuffed them into his jean pockets. Again, Ash was in a dead sprint to Terry's house, at least as much of a sprint as he could muster with a rifle slung on his shoulder, a flashlight, shotgun, a box of shells and a bloody knife in his hand, and with three pockets stuffed with thirty-round rifle magazines. This time, Ash did not try to be covert. He just ran as hard as his legs and load would allow in a straight line to the house. About five feet from the door of the house, the door opened and Terry moved to the side so Ash could enter quickly. Once he was inside, Terry closed the door and flipped on the lights.

"What are you doing running out in...," Terry started to say. When he saw the bloody knife, his eyes grew wide and his jaw became rigid. "What the hell did you do?"

"I killed one of your Nazis," Ash said, bent over trying to catch his breath.

"You what? YOU WHAT? Are you out of your freakin' mind? You killed a gang member?"

"A gang member?" Ash asked, unloading his gear, still breathless.

"That's what they are, a damned gang from down South. Man, the shit's going to come down now. You killed one. Damn it, damn it, damn it," Terry said, as he paced the floor of his living room.

Ash turned his attention to Alex who was sitting up on the couch. "How you feeling?"

"I'm okay. Been better, but I'll survive."

"Well, we need...," Ash started to say.

"Did you steal this rifle and ammo, too?" asked Terry.

"In a manner of speaking, I took it off the dead guy," Ash answered.

"Just keeps gettin' better."

"What do you mean?" Ash asked.

"They're going to be looking for that rifle more than they're going to be looking for the man who killed their cohort."

"You don't know that," Alex spoke up.

"What do you mean?" Ash asked Alex.

Alex looked up at Ash and back down to the carpet, "Nobody has ever killed one of them. Hell, no one has even stood up to them, before tonight. We don't know how they'll react, but it can't be good."

"Shit no, it can't be good," Terry said, "but not because they give a damn about their people, it's because someone killed what's theirs. And a missing rifle, not to mention ammo? That's bad, real bad."

Ash began to help Terry pace. "My problem is how do I get out of here now?"

Terry gave Ash a sinister laugh. "You should never have gotten in here, there's no way you're getting out."

"How do you know how I got in here?"

"Alejandro told me," Terry said, now completely serious.

"Then you know I have to get back to my wife and kids. I still have several hundred miles to go through the heart of Hell. I don't have time for this shit!"

"Well, if that's the heart of hell, then this place is the asshole," Terry interjected. "Look, I feel for you, but leaving this place would endanger you and that little girl, as well as put a lot of people in Shamrock in serious danger."

"Hey, I feel for you, too. But I'm leaving, one way or another."

"The only way you're going to get out of here is in a hearse. You got in here by some unimaginable fluke. You won't find the same bizarre situation trying to leave. I really am sorry."

Ash stopped pacing and looked at Terry. There was no indication that the man was telling him anything but the truth. He sat on the couch and put his head in his hands. After a moment, he stood up and walked to a corner of the room so he could face both men. "If that's the case, we're going to have to change parameters. I don't think we have to let those fools dictate everything."

For the second time, Terry laughed at Ash, "What the hell are you going to do about it? You don't know anything about what's going on around here."

"I know what Alex told me."

"Sure. But you haven't lived it. There are people who are trying to organize and fight these fools, but it takes time – and a lot of resources. We don't have many resources."

"And I don't have much time. And neither do you. They were in the lot where my truck was parked. They know it's missing."

"And now they have a dead man, thanks to you."

"So, do you know who these people are?"

"What people?"

"The resistance."

Terry glared at Ash intensely. He then turned to Alex and back to Ash. "What if I do?"

"Look, I understand why you might not trust me, but I'm more than willing to help you take down those idiots for my own purposes. If there is a resistance movement, we need to speed up whatever timetable they're currently considering."

"Mister, look at things from my point of view. You roll into town without getting stopped, you go get your truck and hide it away, again without getting caught, and you come back with a rifle, ammo, and blood on a knife and your sleeve that you claim belonged to one of them. You're either one lucky son of a bitch, or a plant."

"Terry, I trust him and I'll tell you why," Alex said. "There's genuine affection between him and that little girl. I've seen it, it's real. He wouldn't put this girl in harm's way - make her a target of our ire, if he were detected – when he loves her like he does." Alex then turned his attention to Ash, "She's not your daughter, though, is she?"

"No. Her mother was bitten in Chicago. I didn't know her mother before the madness broke out, but we ended up on the run together. After she was bitten, she changed and I had to kill her. If I hadn't, she would have killed us. So, I sort of adopted her and promised to take her to New Mexico with me."

Terry continued his intense glare at Ash for a few moments. "It doesn't matter anyway. The resistance is not ready to go up against those guys."

"How do you know that?" Ash asked.

Terry sighed, "Because I'm part of it."

Alex stood up, "What?"

"Yeah, I'm in it, Alejandro."

"Why didn't I know this?"

"I wanted to involve you, old friend, but you were already a target and you had already been through Hell, you and Cara. I figured you'd be better off if you didn't know too much."

"Well, like it or not, I'm in it now, Terry," Alex said.

Terry shook his head, "Can't let you do that, Alejandro, it's too dangerous. Besides, you're not well."

"I'm well enough. You're not going to keep me out of it now."

"I'm in it, too," Ash said.

"The hell you are. I don't even know you. My friends would freak out if I brought someone in who just rolled into town yesterday. Alejandro trusts you, and that's good enough for me, but it won't be good enough for the others.

"How many others are there?"

"About forty."

"How many in leadership?"

"We don't really have a leader, in particular, but there are about a dozen who have stepped up."

"Does that include you?"

"Yeah."

"Can you get word to them to meet tomorrow?"

Terry's brow furled, "You know, you ask a lot of questions."

"I'm pressed for time, and so are you – now. We don't have the luxury of niceties."

"Yeah, I can get word to them, but it won't do any good, they ain't going to listen to you and they won't listen to me after they find out I invited you."

"I have some experience in this kind of thing. Give me a chance to talk to them, and if they tell me to get lost, I'll get lost."

Terry began pacing the floor again. Stopping to look at Ash every few minutes, considering Ash's words. "Okay," he finally said, "tomorrow at 6:30 a.m., here. I'll get the word out. Right now, you need to go back to Alejandro's house and get some sleep."

Ash wanted to ask Terry how he gets the word out, but feared that would trigger Terry's suspicious mind. "Okay," he said, "you ready, Alex?"

"Leave Alejandro here," Terry said. "He doesn't need to be running and hiding his way back in his condition.

"No, I'm alright," Alex said.

"No, Alejandro, if you're going to be with us, we need you healthy. Stay here and rest tonight."

Alex shifted his gaze between Ash and Terry. "Alright," he finally relented, "go ahead, Ash. Stay safe. Tell Cara what happened and I'll see her tomorrow."

The power in the house shut down as Ash walked to the front door. "I'm going to take the shotgun," he said, as Terry flipped on his flashlight. "I'll leave the rifle and rounds here. They'll just get in the way."

Terry turned off the flashlight, and Ash carefully looked both ways before sprinting toward the side road. He didn't hide behind cars and bushes this time. He simply sprinted toward the corner house, shotgun carried in his right hand and shells in the left, ready to hit the ground at any sound or movement. Stopping behind the Magnolia tree, he quickly scanned the side street, saw no traffic and bolted for the shrubbery that lined the front of Alejandro's house. About halfway between the shrubbery and the tree, Ash saw the headlights of a car approaching from behind. Throwing himself to the ground, he cringed as his left knee crashed on the butt of the shotgun. Painfully, he crawled forward to a shallow dip he discovered between the rows of houses.

A moment later, he heard a car roll toward his position. It stopped next to Ash, or so he thought. He was lying facing the houses instead of the road and cursed himself for his short-sightedness, but he didn't dare turn his head. Ash expected to hear car doors slamming closed and voices, but heard only the car engine revving again as the car lurched forward. As he heard it slowly pass his position, Ash now felt that he could safely move his head and look. The road adjacent to the alley was clear. He carefully crawled forward and saw the brake lights of the car at the end of Alex's street. The driver was shining a bright spotlight down the street. After what seemed hours, the car moved on. Ash jumped to his feet and limped toward the house, his knee aching from the fall.

As he approached the house, Ash considered running up to the door and bolting in. But, the door may be locked, which would create quite a clatter, and the lamps may be on, which would endanger everyone involved. He also considered looking for the side door where Alex brought them the first time, but he wasn't familiar enough with the house or the neighborhood to make that a good option. So Ash hid behind the shrubbery and crept to the door. When he arrived, he tried the door. Locked. *Actually, that's a good thing with Emily in there,* Ash thought. He lightly rapped on the door, hoping he wouldn't have to make too much noise. To his surprise, Cara answered the door quickly.

Ash stepped in the house and waited for Cara to close the door. She looked down the street and slowly closed the door.

"Where's dad?"

"Alex experienced some...pain while we were out there."

"What? Where is he? Did you leave him out there? What kind of pain?" Cara asked, becoming concerned and angry.

"He's okay. He's at the home of a black man named Terry."

"Yeah, I know him."

"He was having chest pains. Terry came out and found us and brought him inside. When I left, though, he was feeling much better. I think he's going to be fine. But Terry thought it would be better if we just left him there, for now."

Cara, now visibly more relaxed asked, "Did you get to your truck?"

"Yeah," Ash said, and held up the shotgun.

"Oh yeah, right. You had a shotgun in the truck."

"Yeah, but it may have been too late. After I hid the truck, there were four people in the lot milling around. They must have realized it was there and then gone." Ash paused. "I had to kill one," Ash said sheepishly.

It was at that point that Cara saw the blood on Ash's sleeve. A whispered "damn," was all she could muster.

"Where's Emily?" Ash asked.

"Asleep, in the spare room."

"Mind if I crash on the couch, after I check in on Em?" Ash asked.

"No, I'll get you some sheets and a pillow," said Cara, who refused to meet his eyes.

"Thanks. Oh, by the way, I'm meeting some people over at Terry's house in the morning. Can you watch Emily?"

"Sure. She's a great kid."

Ash went into the hall bathroom to wash himself. Allowing himself to feel the exhaustion that was gathering in his bones, he washed the blood off of his arms and his face. As he dried himself, he looked into the eyes of a man who had killed someone with his hands. This was no killer monster, it was a person. A diluted person, but still a person. *After this is all done, I'm going to have me a hard cry, maybe even a small breakdown, but not now. I don't have time now.*

27

"They're asleep," Della told Brady, as she gently closed their bedroom door.

"Did they wear themselves out?" he asked, trying to get a fire lit in the fireplace.

"Oh, yeah. You should have seen them," she grinned. "They were completely spent when the others finally went home."

"I'm glad they had a good day." he said.

"Me too. I just couldn't stand to watch them spend another day lying around miserable," she sighed.

Brady grabbed another log and placed it gently on the fire. It was really too warm for it, but Brady thought it best to keep it going through the night to make sure the bugs couldn't access the home through the chimney. Besides, it was basically the only light in the house at night. Della didn't want to use the oil in the lamps, so she rarely burned them. Now, with the fire flickering and casting dancing shadows across the floor, Della sat on the couch, curled her legs underneath her and watched Brady. His dark, wavy hair had grown below his collar and she was certain by the way he kept brushing it out of his face that he had rarely allowed it to grow that long.

He wore a blue denim shirt and jeans. She liked the way the shirt hung on his broad shoulders and the way the jeans lightly hugged his muscular legs. He made her anxious. She couldn't sit still when he was around. Nervous. She wasn't sure why. Yeah, right, she knew exactly why this man made her nervous. Why her legs trembled and her breath quickened. She wasn't a child and she knew exactly what parts of her body ached and called out his name. Only she wasn't ready to admit it to herself.

Brady turned and caught Della in mid-thought.

"I said, I didn't see anything wrong with the fireplace," he grinned.

"Oh, sorry. Caught me," she reddened.

"Deep thoughts?" he asked, moving over to the couch beside her.

"No. Yes. I don't know." She was grateful for the moving shadows hiding her frustration.

Brady sat quietly and looked at her. Della couldn't hold his gaze. Flustered, she started playing with her shirt buttons. Certain his gaze was allowing a glimpse into her traitorous soul, she fought the urge to look again at him.

"Della..." his voice deep and rich. Della could hear the passion. It moved her.

She continued to fiddle with her buttons, forcing herself to remain seated and not meet his glance. Willing herself the resolution to remain strong. Failing miserably.

"Look at me." Brady moved closer and took her hand.

"I can't," she whispered.

"Why?"

"I'm afraid if I do, I won't be able to look away."

"Then don't look away," his voice finding its way through Della's skin, like thousands of tiny matches, igniting her.

"Look at me." His hand covered her's and calmed her fidgeting. Then moved his hand to cup her face, forcing her to look at him.

Della raised her eyes to him and lost her breath. She knew she was losing her battle. Brady's eyes, dark and enticing, were now filled with longing.

"Della, do you know what you do to me?" he asked, his voice in hushed restrained tones.

"Brady... please...don't," Della's mind began to spin and feeling light-headed, she left the couch to stand in front of the fire. Wrapping her arms around herself, she shivered. Uncertain she was prepared to have this conversation. Doubtful she would ever be ready.

"I'm not sure what I'm supposed to say," she told him.

"You're not supposed to say anything," Brady said. Following her from the couch, Brady gently took her arms and turned her to face him.

"Brady...I'm married."

"Della, you and I both know the odds..."

"Don't," she said. "Don't finish that sentence."

"I know it hurts, but we're going to have to face the truth here."

"What truth, Brady?" she said, backing away from him.

"Della, don't get mad at me," he said, dropping his hands to his sides. "I'm just..."

"I know what you're doing Brady, and truthfully, I don't know what I'm feeling."

"Come here," he offered his hand to her.

"Sit down and talk about this," he said, sitting on the couch.

Hesitating slightly, she took his hand and sat beside him.

"I'm sorry, I didn't mean to upset you." Brady covered her hand with his.

"I know," she said, her hand warming between his, her body tingling with anticipation.

"I know you're hurting. I wish I could make it easier on you. Maybe I should have waited. It's only been..." his voiced faded.

"It hasn't been that long Brady. Only a month. I can't believe I'm already at the point where I'm having this conversation with another man when my husband's only been gone a month. What's wrong with me?"

"There's nothing wrong with you Della," Brady said. "In situations like ours, when there's extreme stress, people bond quicker with each other. Like soldiers in battle or police undercover. The stress quickens things. What we've been through in just a month is more than most people go through in a lifetime. It's only natural that you start to cling to someone."

"So what we're feeling isn't really real, it's just circumstances?" she asked, a little hurt.

"That's not what I meant," he said. "What's happening between us is real. At least it is on my part. But we're feeling it much sooner than we would if given a normal circumstance. Understand?"

"A part of me still feels awful about it."

Brady let go of her hand and hung his head. "I shouldn't have come."

Della wanted to say something to ease his discomfort, to let him know the turmoil that waged within her heart. But she couldn't, not yet.

"I'd better get back," he said, rising from the couch and walking to the door.

"Wait," Della said, following him to the door. "I don't want you to go."

Brady's eyes found hers and held her gaze unwaveringly.

"Della..." he said, pulling her to him.

"I don't want you to stay," she said softly.

"But you don't want me to leave either," he said, drawing her closer.

Della could feel his hot breath against her cheek. Feel the stubble of his strong jaw line, the softness of his lips as they lightly brushed her face.

"I'm sorry Brady," she forced herself to speak what she knew was in her heart. "I'm still in love with my husband. I'm not ready to give up on him or on our family," she told him, dropping her head, leaning into his chest.

Brady ran his hands up her arms, making her heart skip a beat and cupped her face, forcing her to look up at him once again. Running his thumbs over her lips and tracing a path seductively down her neck, he told her, "I'm not about to take you into my bed unless I know I can have you completely."

The path his thumbs and hands were making down her neck and arms were causing her to tremble. She could feel his hands on her, even after he removed them. She opened her mouth to tell him again she was sorry, but felt the words stop midway up her throat. He had left her speechless.

Looking to Brady for help, she saw a grin tugging at the corner of his mouth.

"I'm a patient man, Della," he said, kissing her forehead. "I'll wait," he said, kissing the tip of her nose.

"I'm positive the wait will be worthwhile," he whispered, so close to her ear that she could feel his breath, warm against her face. Brady turned and walked out of the cabin, leaving Della still speechless and trembling.

28

Ash woke up in a panic. He sat up on the couch and looked around the dark room. *Another damn dream.* This time, though, Ash was grateful that he couldn't remember it. He rubbed his face with his left hand and started to walk over to turn on the light. With the first step, a pain shot through his left knee. *Forgot about that,* he thought, limping to the switch. No light. The power was off. He stumbled around in the dark and found Alex's flashlight on an end table. He turned it on and headed for the bathroom for a shower. He looked at the watch and saw that it was 5:20.

In the bathroom, Ash sat the light on the counter on its bottom, so the beam would hit the ceiling and cause a dim overhead effect. He stripped off his clothes and turned on the water, hoping the water heater had enough hot water to at least keep his shower lukewarm. Thankfully, the water became warm to the touch and Ash got in and stuck his head under the stream. It had been too long, and it felt great. He found some soap and began to scrub. The aroma of the scented soap was almost as enticing as the hot meal he had eaten the night before.

After showering, Ash dried with a towel that was under the sink and reached for his clothes, which were no longer on the toilet seat where he left them. He looked around the room, unsure of what was going on, and saw clothes hanging from a hook on the bathroom door. Pulling the clothes off the hook, he inspected them. There was a shirt, trousers, underwear, and a belt, all nearly his size. *Well, I have to put something on,* he thought. Quickly donning the clothes, which were just slightly too large for him, he grabbed the flashlight and opened the door to find Cara in the hall.

"Enjoy your shower?"

"Yes, very much. I hope you don't mind."

"Of course not," she smiled. "I hope you don't mind that I stole your clothes. I'll wash them for you."

"Is that what happened? Were these clothes meant for me?"

"Yes. They were my husband's."

Ash furled his brow, "You're married?"

"I was. I'm a widow."

Ash was growing angry at the violence. "Was it the same guys who killed your mother?"

"No. He died about two years ago. Car accident."

"I'm sorry to hear about that." Ash's rage was assuaged, but he was surprised to find that he was actually disappointed. He wanted to have his anger fueled by the senseless killing of this beautiful woman's husband.

"Thank you. When are you supposed to be over at Terry's house?"

"Six-thirty."

"What time is it?"

Ash stared at his watch until the luminescent hands came into focus. "Five forty-five."

"Well, I can make you some coffee when the power comes back on at six," Cara offered.

"No. That's okay. I want to get there early. If you have a spare toothbrush, I'll just brush my teeth, put my shoes on, and get out of here."

Cara just nodded and moved past Ash into the bathroom. She opened a cabinet drawer and pulled out a toothbrush, still in its packaging. She handed it to Ash as he followed her into the bathroom and again moved past him back into the hall. Ash turned on the water to brush his teeth and realized that he had left the flashlight on, still shining its beam at the ceiling. As he brushed, he admonished himself for not thinking more strategically. Batteries were probably hard to come by, and he had left the flashlight on now for about thirty minutes.

As he finished and dried his mouth and hands on a face towel, Cara came in with a pair of white tube socks. "I hope these will work."

"They'll be fine, thanks," Ash said, as he grabbed the light and moved past Cara toward the living room.

He spotted his shoes at the end of the couch and sat down to put them on. Ash then realized that the couch had been stripped of the sheets and blankets that he had used. "You're busy in the mornings," he said to Cara.

"Just like things neat." She shrugged.

Shoes on, he bent over and grabbed the shotgun and shells from under the couch where he hid them the night before. "Take care of her. I'll see you as soon as I can."

"Wait," she warned. "People can move around freely at six o'clock. What time is it?"

"Five till."

"Well, give it five minutes. You won't be suspicious then."

"I'm going to have a shotgun. You don't think I'll be suspicious?"

Cara looked down at the firearm and sighed. "Do you have to take that now?"

Ash paused.

Cara continued, "You'll be able to get around just fine if you don't carry that thing around with you."

"Okay," Ash said, "you know best."

Ash looked at his watch. "It's six o'clock, catch you later."

"Hang on, Ash. It's not officially six o'clock till the pow…"

A small thump and the refrigerator hummed to life signaling the return of electricity into the home.

"Until the power comes on. There you go," she finished with a smile.

Ash unlocked the door and looked out carefully. People were beginning to leave their homes in the dawn's pristine light. Ash decided to follow Cara's advice and just be one of the crowd, hiding his face as much as possible without drawing attention. He strolled down Alex's front walk to the sidewalk and turned, warily walking up the road, trying to keep his eyes swiveling and his head fairly still.

Reaching the road where Terry lived, he made yet another right, putting him face-to-face with a man walking towards him. Ash excused himself and went around the man. The man watched as Ash walk around him. He didn't say anything, but Ash could feel the man's eyes on him as he walked away. Deciding to play it safe, Ash went two houses beyond Terry's house and turned up the drive, praying that no one would come out of the house. Near the front door of the house, Ash dared to look up the street. The man was still there, but had his back to Ash. Ash considered his options quickly. He could cut through the yards to Terry's house, use the sidewalk, or covertly use the shrubbery and other obstructions to stealthily return. He chose the second option and, as casually as possible, walked back to the sidewalk, over two houses and cut through Terry's yard to his front door, where once again, the door opened before Ash had a chance to knock. Ash entered the house to find Terry and Alex enjoying a cup of coffee.

"Some coffee?" Terry asked.

"Sounds great."

Terry turned toward the back of the house "Hey, babe. Fix me one more coffee, will ya?"

There was no response, but Ash could hear some clatter from the kitchen.

"Anybody see you?" Terry asked.

"Yeah. I ended up face-to-face with someone as I turned up your street. I tried to throw him off, but don't know if it worked or not," Ash said, as a short black woman handed him a mug of coffee.

"Sweety, this is Ash..."

"Bishop."

"Bishop. Ash, this is Georgia."

"A pleasure," said Ash.

"Mr. Bishop," Georgia said, as she turned and left the living room.

"She's a little wary around strangers. She's taken the last few weeks pretty hard."

"Understandable," Ash said. "You seem to be in a better mood than last night."

"Yeah, I started thinking about it. Your arrival here may have moved things forward quicker than I had hoped, but one way or another, it'll be over, and there's a lot of relief associated with that fact."

"So, you agree that there's not much time."

"There's not now," Alex said, "they've found your truck. They've probably found the dead guy by now. If they haven't, they're going to real soon, along with finding the missing rifle. Things have begun to move beyond our control, so we've got to be ready."

Terry added, "When I first found out about you, I was pissed. Now, I'm not so sure it was a bad thing."

A knock on the door. Terry opened the door and let in an older man, probably in his mid-60's and looked the type who has worked outdoors his whole life.

"Ray, this is Ash," Terry said.

"Ash," Ray said, sticking his hand out, "you're the one stirring the pot, eh?"

Ash shook his hand and said, "I guess so, but I didn't mean to be."

Another knock on the door. This time two men entered.

"Luis and Carlos. This is Ash. He's the reason I called this meeting."

Both men came over and shook Ash's hand, then noticed Alex sitting on a recliner and greeted him in Spanish.

Again, a knock at the door. Entering Terry's house were two women. Terry introduced them to Ash as Susan and Yvonne. Yvonne, a pleasant black woman, greeted him. Susan, a white woman who carried a dour expression, stayed back and eyed him suspiciously.

The fourth knock on Terry's front door brought three people, two black men and a Hispanic woman. The first black man introduced by Terry was Andre, a young man of about twenty-five with a quick smile and cutting wit. The second man, named Richard, was about Alex's age and had a take-charge, no-nonsense demeanor. The Hispanic woman's name was Isabella. She greeted Ash and told him that she went by Belle.

The twelve people milled around, pulling chairs in from the dining room, except Georgia, who stayed in the back rooms. Terry spoke up first. "We need to get started. It's 6:20 right now, and I thank all of you for showing up early. Bob, Jeff, and Keven won't be able to make this meeting, so we're ready." Everyone except Terry, Richard, and Ash sat down.

"This is Ash Bishop. He's from Chicago and he rolled into our fair town last night."

"Wait a minute," said Richard. "How the hell does someone just roll into town?"

"That seems to be the question," Ash said, before Terry could speak. "I don't know. There were barricades, but I went around them. There was nobody there to stop me."

There was a collective gasp from the attendees.

"Bullshit," said Susan. "I can't believe that nobody was at those barricades. This gang is sadistic first and efficient a close second."

"Apparently," Ash said, "they're not as efficient as they have led you to believe."

That statement prompted objections and guffaws from the others in the room.

"We don't say that lightly, mister," Richard said. "We've seen them in action. They're ruthlessly efficient. We have first-hand experience of them moving in and snatching people at the slightest infraction or on the flimsiest evidence and arresting them. Those people are never heard from again."

"Are those people guilty of what they are accused of?" Ash asked.

"We don't know. We're not privy to the truth. Usually, we hear rumors later about some trumped up charge," offered Carlos.

"So, why do you think that's efficient?"

Murmuring spread through the assembled group.

"You know, thinking about it," Andre began, "we think they're efficient because they told us they are."

"Bullshit." It was Susan again. "When all hell broke loose, we had no power, no gasoline, no food, no nothing. Nothing but chaos. For all of their shortcomings, they brought order to the town."

"You sound like you admire them," Ash said.

Susan stood, red-faced and said, "You don't come into this town and tell us what the hell to do! I don't admire them, but you weren't here. What they did efficiently is evident. You can kiss my ass!"

"C'mon, calm down Susan," Yvonne said.

"So they were efficient in that manner. That's not the same thing as being efficient in regard to security," Ash said.

"Well, we'll find out for sure, soon," Terry said.

"Why?" asked Carlos.

"Because they found his truck," Terry said.

"What?" asked Susan.

"Wait, it gets worse. He went out to get his truck and had to kill one of their guys."

"WHAT?"

"And took his rifle."

"WHAT?" This time it was almost the entire group.

"Who's responsible for bringing this puke into this group?" asked Susan.

"We don't have time for finger-pointing," Richard said. "We have to figure out what we're going to do."

"Where's their base?" Ash asked.

"City Hall," answered Alex.

"Then we need to draw up plans to attack them."

"Say what?" Andre asked. "You're outta your mind. That place is a fortress."

"Have you been there recently?"

"I ain't goin' near that place."

"Any of you been there recently?"

Members of the group looked at each other. Finally, Alex said, "That was where they took me and Cara."

"Did it seem like a fortress to you?" Ash asked.

"No. I wouldn't say that. There were several armed thugs around there, but it was short of a fortress."

"How many were there, armed people, that is."

"I don't know. I saw maybe fifteen or twenty."

"Are they all armed with an M-16, like the one I took?"

"Yes. They broke into the National Guard Armory. They mostly have M-16's."

"Automatic or only semi-automatic?" Ash asked.

"Modified to three-round bursts," Richard answered. "I've heard them fired. Those clowns fire those things all the time."

"Does that sound like an efficient army to you?"

Richard glared at Ash.

"I think we can make a plan to beat these guys, tonight," Ash said.

"Hey Ash, I know you're anxious to get out of here," Alex said, "but we don't have time to make plans for tonight."

"When will they start looking for me?" Ash asked Terry.

"Probably after sundown. It's their M.O.," Terry answered.

"Who do you think will be doing the searching?" Ash asked.

"What do you mean?" asked Alex.

"Will it be the ones in charge, or the peons?"

"Peons, for sure," Yvonne offered.

"Perfect. Yeah, they're going to be looking for me, but I'm going to be with you guys storming City Hall. With most of the thugs out, if we can get City Hall and disrupt their command structure, we can beat these clowns."

"But that will leave our homes and families exposed," Ray said.

"Yes, it will," Ash answered. "But only for a moment. As soon as we attack, word will go out to the lower level thugs to return and protect the mother ship. If things go well, we should have City Hall secured and will be able to fend off and defeat the others. If I'm guessing right, the lack of a command structure will cause panic among the other troops."

Silence hung over the room like a canopy.

"That's a lot of ifs," Richard finally said.

"Battlefields are always fluid," Ash said. "But the thing we can be sure of is that they are going to start looking for me. So, do we wait on them to come to us on their terms or take the battle to them on our terms?"

Again, the room was silent as the members of the group tried to digest what had been said.

Richard broke the silence again, "This was going to happen anyway. It makes sense, if we're committed to taking our town back, to do it now." He looked at his watch, "Those of us who work better get going. Get the word out while you're out. Luis, Andre, Belle – get the stash of weapons and smuggle them back here this afternoon. We go tonight at...eight?"

"Sounds about right. Should be starting to get dark about then, huh?" Ash asked.

"Yeah." Richard answered and climbed atop a chair to address the group. Ash noticed how the crowd easily deferred to Richard, allowing him to slip into the leadership role. "Operation begins at eight, we meet here at six. That might draw some attention, but we don't have much choice. Hopefully, the operation will be under way before anyone is the wiser. The rest of you make plans. This is going to be dangerous, people. They could kill us... and our families. If you're in, you're all the way in. If you're not, go on your way. No hard feelings. Anybody who wants out, leave now."

Members of the group looked to each other, but no one got up to leave.

"Okay. Let's move."

Terry walked to where Richard and Ash were standing. "I'm not going in to work today. I'll stay here and help plan."

"That won't make them suspicious?" Ash asked.

"No. People miss work frequently. Sometimes because they disappear and business owners and managers are afraid to ask questions."

"Okay with me," Ash said.

"Me, too," said Richard.

Ray, Richard, Alex, Terry, and Ash cleared off the dining room table, grabbed some paper, and began to plan their assault while the other members went off to work.

As discussion progressed, it became clear that a frontal assault with a near simultaneous strike on the back of the building would prove most likely to succeed. City Hall only had two doors and such a plan would force those in the building to defend both doors at once. A second group would be responsible for setting up defenses at the front of the building and possibly be ready to back up those attacking, should their defense be more secure than suspected. The members of the group estimated that maybe ten to twelve thugs would be in the building at the time of the assault. A resistance force of thirty-five to forty people could more than overcome that many defenders, especially in a surprise attack. They planned to have ten people attack the front of the building, while seven would take the back, mostly as a means of cutting off escape.

It was almost noon when they had worked out all of the details. They would be facing a force of about fifty all together. After meeting at Terry's at six, the flanking troops and the rear assault troops would leave little by little and wait, hidden, for dark. The main strike group would arrive at eight o'clock in two cars. Both cars were marked as legitimate and would not raise suspicion. Richard would command the main strike with Ash as his second. Terry would command the rear strike with Belle as his second. The remaining groups would take positions behind the barricades set up by the city's oppressive regime. Routinely, two guards up front manned City Hall, but they didn't use the barricades.

"You guys go back home," Terry told Alex and Ash. "See if you can get some rest. You'll need it." He then turned to Ray and Richard. "You guys can crash here; we have plenty of room."

"Okay, see you at six," Ash said, as he and Alex left.

They strolled down Terry's walk and turned left toward Alex's house. Ash looked hard at Alex as they walked.

"What?" Alex asked.

"You okay?"

"Yeah, I'm fine. I'll be alright."

"I noticed you volunteered for the assault team in there," Ash said.

"Just trying to do my part."

"The defensive flanks play a large part in this."

"Yeah." Alex walked for a bit without comment. "I just don't like to be treated like an old man," he finally said.

"We're just worried about your health."

"I know."

The two men walked the rest of the way in silence. Ash, wary of the spiderflies, still felt uneasy in the outdoors. Even in this relatively untouched town. The day was sunny and warm and felt good on Ash's face. It was the kind of pleasant summer day that always made him nostalgic. Thinking back to his childhood when he would spend summer days playing baseball with his friends or walking to his grandparents' house, three blocks away. The thoughts made Ash sad. His sons would likely never know those simple pleasures. It appeared that his sons, and everyone else's sons, might have to struggle their entire lives.

They turned on Alex's walk and headed for the door. Alex tried the doorknob and found it locked. He reached into his pocket for keys and came out empty. He was about to knock on the door when it opened. Cara stood aside and let both men in.

"How are you feeling, Dad?" Cara asked, as she shut the door.

"I'm much better. I was just trying to do too much at once," he answered.

"Well, rest on the couch for now."

"I don't need you babying me."

"Dad, just take it easy, please."

"Okay. But there's something I need to tell you, and you need to sit down."

"Oh God, what?"

"We're planning an assault tonight."

"What? Are you crazy? Who's we? You and Ash?"

"Along with about forty other people."

"That was what we were meeting with Terry about this morning," Ash offered.

"Terry?" Cara asked.

"Terry's one of the leaders of the resistance," Alex said.

"What? You knew about that?"

"No. Not till last night."

"So, what does this have to do with you?" Cara asked, almost in hysterics.

"When Ash was out last night, he killed a gang member and took his gun," Alex said.

"I know," she sighed. "He told me last night."

"Well, you know that'll bring house-to-house searches tonight. It's the best time to attack, when the goons are spread out through the neighborhoods."

"I still don't know what this has to do with you."

Emily, hearing Ash's voice from the bedroom, came into the living room and gave Ash a hug.

"This is our town. I can't sit idly by. I'm involved, like it or not," Alex said.

Cara turned to Ash. "Did you try to talk him out of it?"

"We all tried. He's very hard-headed. The best we could do was talking him out of being on the assault team," answered Ash.

"You volunteered for an assault team?" Cara was incredulous.

"Big mouth," Alex said to Ash.

"So what will you be doing?"

"Defensive flank. I'll be behind a barricade shooting."

Cara shook her head, crossed her arms and started pacing the floor. "Heart attack one day and try to save the world the next. I will never understand that macho crap."

"Cara, it's got nothing to do with being macho," Alex said. "As it stands now, there is nothing to prevent those guys from coming in and killing you on the spot. This may be the best chance we have of taking our town back. You're the only family I have left and if I can help prevent something from happening to you, then that's what I'm going to do."

Cara walked up to Alex and put her arms around him. "Please take care of yourself."

"I will."

"When are you going?"

"We meet at Terry's at six."

29

After eating a hefty lunch of lasagna and garlic bread, Ash and Alex took a nap. Ash didn't think he'd be able to sleep with the assault on City Hall on his mind, but he quickly fell asleep. Startled, he woke at five in the afternoon, but not because of bad dreams. He actually had a rather pleasant dream about him and Della, or was it Cara. He thought hard but couldn't remember. His unfamiliar surroundings caused him to be a little dazed at first.

"You wanted me to wake you," Cara said again.

Ash quickly found his bearings. "Yeah, thanks Cara."

Cara closed the bedroom door and Ash got dressed. Within the past sixteen hours, he'd gotten almost eight hours of sleep on warm, comfortable surfaces - a couch and a bed. He felt as refreshed as he had when he and Emily had stayed at that hotel room in Missouri. After dressing, he went down the hall and into the living room where he was surprised to find Terry and Richard talking to Alex.

"What's up?" Ash asked.

"Nothing," Terry began, "Well, if you call a commando type assault nothing. We're just keyed up, so we thought we'd see what you guys were doing. We didn't mean to wake you."

"You didn't. I asked Cara to wake me about now."

"There's been a slight change in plans. We've been going over this trying to make sure we have it down. We'll only have one chance. It has to work and it has to be tonight," Richard said. "I was talking to Belle today, and she said that there are plans to begin a house to house search for you and your truck tonight starting at 8:30."

"How does she know that?" Ash asked.

"Her sister works at City Hall. She's a secretary, but the goons apparently talk fairly open there. They've also moved curfew up to 8:00. That's been on the radio."

"Well, that doesn't change much," Ash said. We can begin our assault a half hour later."

"The word's already gone out," Terry said.

"It does make things a little more complicated though," Alex said. "Our people will be hidden for a longer time which makes it more likely that they'll be spotted, lose their nerve, or get antsy. These guys aren't professionals. Also, even driving approved vehicles, we could get stopped on the way to the building, especially since it will be after curfew."

Ash nodded. "Yeah, but there's no alternative. We'll have to do what we can to minimize the problems. From what I saw this morning, I think we're in pretty good shape."

Terry looked at his watch. "It's after five-thirty. We need to get to my place."

"I still have a shotgun and shells here under the couch," Ash told the others.

"We'll have to pick it up on the way to town tonight," Richard told him. "You can't just walk down the street with a shotgun."

"Cara," Alex called. "We're leaving, honey."

"Are you sure I can't talk you out of this?" she asked.

"No."

"Well, at least promise me that you'll take care of yourself Dad, if you have to do this. Please take care of yourself." Cara hugged him.

"I will, sweetheart."

"Thanks for the lasagna, Cara," Terry said. "It was great, as usual."

"Yeah, thanks," Ash and Richard agreed, almost in unison.

"You're welcome. Take care of my Dad."

"You bet," said Terry.

Ash got down on one knee and opened his arms toward Emily. She ran to him and hugged him around the neck.

"Where are you going?" she asked.

"I have to take care of some things. I'll see you a little later. Stay with Cara and be good for her, you hear?" he told her.

"Okay," she said with tears running down both cheeks.

She knows, Ash thought and hugged her again.

The men walked to Terry's house without speaking. They knew that they couldn't risk talking. They were too close to the operation to change plans now, but still in a situation where things could easily change.

After they entered the house, they began going over the plans one more time with Ray, who had been napping at Terry's house. Ash knew there was going to be some confusion among most of their people, so the leaders needed to have the plan down. During the run-through, there were quiet knocks at both the front and back doors.

Luis, Belle, and Andre knocked on the rear door at six-thirty. They entered the house with a cache of weapons along with various holsters, slings, pouches, and belts. The weapons were carted into the house in plastic garbage cans loaded onto four-wheel utility hand-trucks. They handed them out according to need. As Ash evaluated their inventory, he realized that they were razor thin. People would have to take fairly careful aim, or risk running out of ammunition.

"Where'd you guys get all of this," Ash asked Richard.

"Mostly stole them," he said. "When all hell broke loose, we broke into police station, guns shops or whatever when it became evident that we would have to defend for ourselves. When the gang took over, they confiscated all they could find, but we were able to hide these away."

After the weaponry was distributed, Richard stood on one of Terry's dining room chairs. "Let me have your attention. Your attention, please," he yelled above the commotion created by the large group of anxious people.

When the crowd quieted, Richard said, "Does everyone understand their assignment?"

The group members gave some manner of affirmative response.

"If you want out, leave now. We can still recover if you leave now," Richard said. "If you go with us, understand that you'll be in extreme danger. Some of you could be killed. But if you go, please don't break the line. If you go, see the operation through, okay? So, I say again, if you want out, now's the time."

Group members looked at each other, but no one was leaving or voicing objections.

"All right then. There are forty-one of us here, if I counted right. Twenty-nine men and twelve women. We represent all races, ages, former social and economic classes, and ethnic groups. We are America. The gangs' running this city aren't. We will take back our town and start anew. The costs may be high, but we will succeed because we have to, because we are right."

"Alright then," Richard said. "The cars are parked behind the house. We need to start sending people to town. You know where your hiding places are. Please stay there until your commander gives the signal to move. This is very important. Grab your weapons. I need the two rear commanders and their groups to load into the cars."

Quickly, ten people approached the back door and carefully headed for the cars. When the cars were full and pulled out, Richard, still on the chair, said, "We need to get the second group ready. When the cars return, head on out and get into your hiding positions. Pay close attention to your commanders. That's the best chance you have of coming out of this alive!"

Within minutes, the cars returned to pick up a second load. Terry ran out to talk to one of the drivers and then returned to the house.

"What was that about?" Ash asked.

"I wanted to see if he felt that anyone was paying undue attention to him," Terry answered.

"And?"

"He didn't think so."

Ash adjusted a web belt that he found in one of the plastic garbage bags and put it around his waist. He then stuffed a pouch with three clips and put one into his M-16. He pulled back on the charging handle and slammed the bolt closed before putting the safety on and looked at his watch. Seven forty-five. All he could do was hope that they could get everyone deployed fast enough.

"We need to get the rest of the groups and the rear assault team ready. The cars will be back any minute," Richard yelled, this time from the floor. "Alex, I need you to help the others find where they need to be."

Alex gave Richard a thumbs-up.

The remaining people silently got their gear packed and weapons ready. Richard broke the silence.

"You know, we have the hardest part of this. We have to secure the facility in order to allow the defensive units to set up. We have to be quick and precise. We'll probably have the most casualties. But, we set the tone and have an excellent chance for success. Remember, battle is fluid. If things don't go exactly according to plan, all is not lost. Just keep your eyes on me and Ash. I will lead Assault Team A and Ash will lead Assault Team B. Team A will take the bottom floor, heading first toward the police dispatch area. Team B goes upstairs to take the head honcho's office. If all goes well, we should have the place secured within five minutes. Kill them if you must. Any questions?"

No one said anything. They just looked at each other. Ash could see the fear in their eyes. They were mostly kids – early twenties, maybe younger. Two of them were women, girls really. He couldn't help but feel responsible for them. He's the one who rolled into town, albeit inadvertently. He was the one who hid the truck and killed the man. They wouldn't be going through this if it weren't for him. At least, not tonight.

The two cars pulled up to the house again and the drivers got out and loaded their gear. Ash looked at his watch. 8:15. Fifteen minutes. Ash went into the living room by himself and looked to the ceiling. *God, don't let these kids die because of me,* he prayed and returned to the dining room.

"Time to go," Richard said.

Richard got into one car and Ash the other. The cars pulled out and headed for town. Ash looked at the town as they rolled through. He realized that this power struggle was probably occurring in small towns all across America. Towns that were left untouched, somehow, by the bugs, were easy pickings for outlaw groups like the ones that had taken this town so easily. As the car rolled to a stop, the driver turned to Ash and said, "There it is."

The car stopped about twenty feet short of the building and one man got out of the back seat of Richard's car and one got out of Ash's car. They walked to the building with their Glocks resting in the back of their belts. As they approached, Ash looked at his watch. 8:28. Right *on time.*

The guards eyed them suspiciously as the men approached. Behind them, the cars squealed their tires. The sound distracted the guards long enough for the assault team members to grab their guns and shoot both of them in the temple. As the men threw the guards aside, both cars pulled up and the teams dispersed. They entered through the front doors and Richard led his team through the first floor corridors while Ash took his team up the stairs. Hitting the top, Ash heard gunfire from below. He wanted to turn and help, but he knew he had his own mission to accomplish.

At the top of the stairs were hallways going left and right. Two men came at him with pistols drawn, but the assault team members easily mowed them down. A few yards forward and on the right was the mayor's office. They moved to either side of the door while Ash set up in front of the door with his rifle. He saw two silhouettes in the smoked-glass window and opened fire with a three round burst, smashing the window. At the mayor's door, the woman, who was to the left of the door, reached over and turned the knob. The door opened, but only about two feet. A dead body was blocking the door. Ash put his shoulder low and held his rifle in front of him. He slammed into the door and pushed the body away from it. He then rolled into the room and fired a burst at a man who was on the other side of the door. He crumpled to the ground, dying with his eyes wide-open. They swept through the room looking in the bathroom and behind furniture, finding their man hiding behind a huge mahogany desk.

"Adolf?" Ash said.

The male team member ripped the cord off the back of the telephone and tied the man's wrists and ankles together, then ran out of the room to meet the other teams.

"Clear," Ash heard a team member yell.

Ash motioned for two men to clear the rest of the upper floor while the other three began to descend the steps, but the gunfire from below was too close, so Ash told his other team members to wait while he slowly went down to survey the situation. Richard's team was in the midst of a firefight. They had found positions behind a receptionist's desk, but it was being splintered by gunfire. Every movement of the team was bringing a hail of gunfire from the gang members. Ash, about a third of the way down the stairs, stood up and fired, killing five of the seven people. Ash watched the two scatter and waved for his team to descend with him.

Joining Richard, Ash saw that one of their guys had taken a round to the chest and was dead on the floor. Saddened, Ash sighed and stepped over him. At that moment, gunfire erupted in front of him, to the rear of the building. Both teams moved quickly through the building, but when they came upon a hallway running in two directions, they split again. Ash's team made short work of the hall. Afterwards they ran toward Richard's location to see if he needed help, thinking they heard firing from his position. As they approached the cross-hall, a person appeared from the rear of the building. One of Ash's team fired on the person and he went down. As they came upon him, they discovered that it was a member of the rear assault team, a young woman.

Damn! Ash thought.

Ash looked to his left and saw Terry approaching, shaking his head.

He looked up at Ash, "Rear's secure. I left three back there to defend it, but I doubt it's necessary." Terry looked back at the woman lying on the ground and shook his head.

"Well, let's see if Richard needs help," Ash said.

As both teams deployed, now eight people, one kid stood in front of the dead woman, unable to move.

He must have pulled the trigger, Ash thought.

He ran over the kid and pulled his arm. "Let's go. It's awful, but it happens a lot. It's not your fault. Let's move." Ash gave him a yank and he finally started to go. Soon, both men were in a dead sprint heading for Terry's team. By the time they got there, though, Richard had taken the area.

"I lost another one," Richard said, as he motioned to the other side of the dispatcher's office.

Ash nodded. "Let's see how they're doing up front."

All three teams, now eleven strong, ran for the front doors. At this point every assault team member had M-16's and were ready to end this. Ash and Richard were the first ones to the doors and peaked through. They had lost three people that they could see, but had inflicted heavy casualties. It appeared that the remaining gang members had taken position behind two cars.

All eleven members of the assault teams rushed through the doors, took positions behind the barricades and started a frontal assault on the gang's positions, firing their M-16s in three-round bursts at the cars. The additional firepower apparently made the gang members realize they couldn't win. Two of them stood at once with their hands up, but they were both shot several times.

"Hold your fire!" Richard yelled. "Stop firing!"

"C'mon out," he yelled. "Come out, and we don't kill you."

There was no movement on the other side of the cars.

Richard sighed. "Lock and load, guys."

"Wait!" was the call from behind the cars. "We're coming out. Don't shoot."

Three men emerged, hands in the air. "Don't shoot."

"Toss out your guns. Now!"

"Put your hands behind your head," Richard yelled to them. "Get face-down on the ground. Now!"

As the men complied, Richard leaned over to Ash and motioned for Terry and Carlos to lean in. "Take your team and flank to the left," he told Ash. "Go around the cars and make sure there's nobody else hiding behind them or inside them. Terry, you do the same with a right flank. Carlos, take a team of four into the building and make sure it's been completely cleared. There are three guys of the rear assault team still guarding the back door, bring them with you."

All three men nodded and headed off.

Both Ash and Terry's teams arrived at the cars at the same time and both gave an all-clear. Richard then took his team from behind the barricades and into the street with their firearms honed in. "Search them," he ordered his team.

He turned to Ash and Terry, "check their casualties, make sure their wounded aren't still armed." After the surrendered were searched, he used his rifle to point, "Cuff these two up." He put his foot into the back of the third one and gave him a light shove, "Stand up."

The man slowly got to his feet with his hands still clasped behind his head.

"Grab your radio and call the other idiots over here. Be careful what you say."

"There ain't nobody. They called everyone over here when you attacked. "

"Call them anyway," Richard insisted.

"I'm telling you, man, there ain't nobody."

Richard put the muzzle of the M-16 to the man's temple. "Humor me," he said.

"Okay, okay," he said as he reached into the car, grabbed his radio, and keyed it. "Patrol Charlie to any unit." He paused as static crossed his frequency. "Patrol Charlie to any unit, please respond." Again, only static. "Patrol Charlie to any unit, please respond," he said again. After another moment of static, the soldier turned to Richard. "See, there's nobody else."

"Great," said Richard. "Cuff him," he said to his troops.

Terry's team left City Hall pushing the former gang leader in front of him. The man fell to his knees and Terry kicked him in the back, hard enough to cause him to convulse. Terry's troops picked him up and walked him to Richard. Richard glared at him for several minutes.

Finally, he said, "I don't know you. In fact, I don't know any of you guys."

"So?" the man asked, defiantly.

"So, who the hell are you?"

"Your worst nightmare."

Richard thrust the butt of his M-16 into the man's nose, breaking it immediately and forcing blood from the nostrils in spurts. "Wrong answer, you were my worst nightmare. Now you're just another shithead in handcuffs. If I were you," Richard said, almost in a whisper, "I'd cooperate. You made a lot of these heavily armed people around you angry and they'd just as soon torture you for weeks and let you slowly die. I might be able to prevent that, but you better start talking."

Richard looked up to see his other two teams return and give the thumbs up.

The man tried unsuccessfully to spit the steady stream of blood flowing from his nose and out of his mouth as he glared at Richard.

Richard looked around to his people. "Anyone have a hanky?"

He was given several. Squatting down, Richard squeezed the bloody nose and wiped down toward the man's mouth. Screaming in pain, the man fell back on his side. One of Richard's team sat him back up.

"My nose is broken, you bastard!"

"Start talking. Where are you from?"

"Houston," the man said. "When the bugs came, we took off. Wound up here by accident. Man, your town was a mess. Total chaos. You guys let our gang walk in and take over. We even got some of you to help us," the man said, spitting again.

"What kind of gang?"

"What?"

"You said you guys were in a gang, what kind?" Richard repeated.

"A gang man, it's just a gang."

Richard stood quietly, waiting for more.

"Look, it wasn't a social club. We just ended up here. We had planned just to rob your banks, but you guys gave up your freedom so easily that we had total power in no time," the man said.

"Absolute power corrupts..."

"Whatever."

Richard stood. "Get this son of a bitch out of here. Lock him up with the others. Make sure you search him good. As a matter of fact, strip-search him. Maintain two armed guards on them at all times and don't give them anything till we figure out what we're going to do with them."

As the men were led out, Terry and Ash approached Richard. "We have seven dead," Terry said. "We also have three hurt, one real bad."

Richard sighed. "I'll talk to the families. We need to get the injured some medical care."

"One of the hurt, the bad one, is Alejandro," Terry said. "He had a heart attack."

"Oh no," Ash said. He ran past the troops, who were celebrating and found Alex behind one of barricades with his head resting on one of the women's laps. She was crying.

She looked up at Ash. "He's gone."

Ash turned and squatted with his back against the barricade. He held his M-16 in front of him and put his head down between his knees. *How am I going to explain to Cara that she's lost her father now?* Ash was surprised at how deeply Alex's death had touched him. He met him just 24 hours before, and now he was grief stricken. Part of that was knowing the pain that Cara had been through, with the loss of her husband and then her mother, and now her dad.

Terry came over to where Ash was crouched. "I'll tell Cara," he said.

Ash looked up to find his friend. "No, that's okay. I'll tell her. I have to go get Emily anyway."

"No. I've known her for a long time. I've helped see her through alot."

Ash nodded and got to his feet.

Terry reached his hand out to Ash. "We did it."

Ash managed a weak smile as he shook Terry's hand, "Yeah."

"You changed our lives. Thank you doesn't seem to quite say it."

"All I did was screw up bad enough to force your hand," Ash said.

Richard and Carlos approached as Terry and Ash were talking. "Can you stay?" Richard asked Ash.

"No. I wish I could, but I have to find my family."

"Of course."

"You have a real opportunity, here. You could make this town great."

"No," Richard said, "We could make it great, again."

Ash nodded and leaned his weapon against the barricade. He and Richard embraced, followed by Terry and Carlos. In turn, Ash hugged the rest of his team. He was surprised when Susan came towards him.

"I was wrong about you," she said.

"Well, the story I told was far-fetched, even if it was true."

"Are you sure you have to leave?"

"Yes. I really wish I didn't have to, but I need to see if my wife and kids are still alive."

"You'll come back and see us, won't you?" Luis asked.

"Count on it," Ash answered. "You guys are the finest people I've ever met."

"Maybe after you find your family, you can come back to stay," Carlos said.

Ash looked at Carlos and grinned. "Maybe. I don't know if there will be anything left of Denver after everything is said and done. Maybe. Right now," he said to the group surrounding him, "I need fuel for my truck."

"No problem," Richard said. "Let's go get your truck."

Ash removed his web belt, which still contained a full magazine. He waved goodbye to everyone as he got into the car with Richard.

"So where is it?" Richard asked.

"An empty house just beyond the lot behind Alex's house. I forgot what Alex called it."

"Tucker house."

"Yeah, that's it," Ash said.

At first, they rode in silence. After a few minutes, Richard asked, "Do you believe in God, Ash?"

Ash found the question odd and surprising. "Yeah, sure. Why?"

"I think maybe God sent you to us. I honestly don't know if we would have ever tried such a brazen attack if you hadn't shown up. We probably would have continued to resist through small attacks and disruptions, but I don't know if we would have ever had the courage to overthrow them."

"I think you underestimate yourselves," responded Ash.

They pulled into the driveway and up to the garage. Ash got out of the car, walked up to the garage door and pulled it open. He walked back to the car that Richard was driving. "Follow you?"

"Yeah. We'll head back to town."

Ash went back to the garage, started the truck and pulled out of the driveway behind Richard, turning toward Shamrock. When he got back to City Hall, he followed Richard to a fueling station.

"Used to be only authorized cars could refuel here. They closed all the gas stations," Richard said.

"Well, I appreciate this," Ash said as he refilled his truck. After he finished, he told Richard, "I'm going back to Alex's to get Emily."

Richard stuck his hand out again. "Take care of yourself, man. Don't get bitten."

"You got it, partner."

As Ash pulled up to Cara's house, he saw Terry's car up front. He got quickly out and ran to the house. Through the front door and saw Cara sitting on the living room couch with tears in her eyes and Terry sitting next to her.

"Get your truck?" Terry asked, almost in a whisper.

"Yeah. Fueled it up."

Emily came running in from the dining room and gave Ash a huge hug.

"You ready to get out of here, little girl?"

"Why don't you stay the night?" Cara sniffed.

Ash felt severe pain for the woman. "I appreciate it, but we should get going."

"No. You need a night's sleep. Stay. I insist," she said.

Ash looked down at Emily. "Okay."

"Well, I'm going to go ahead and head home. Georgia's gotta be panicked," Terry said.

"Take care of this town," Ash told him.

"Take care of yourself and that little girl," Terry said as he walked out the door.

"I'm going to bed," Cara said.

Ash grabbed her arm as she went by, "You okay?"

"No," she said as she turned toward Ash and cried on his chest.

Ash put his arms around her head and motioned for Emily to go on to bed. He held her for a while until the crying subsided. They stood silently for a moment till Ash said, "Do you have those pillows and blankets again?"

Cara gave Ash a nervous smile. "You don't have to sleep on the couch, if you don't want to."

"Cara, you've just had a traumatic loss. You need time."

Cara nodded, walked back to her bedroom, and closed the door.

Ash stood looking at the bedroom door for a minute. *If I went back there, no one would ever know. I love Della, but Cara is so beautiful – and right here. For all I know Della is dead. Strike that thought from your head, man, and go to bed.*

Ash went to the couch, found his sheets and pillow that Cara had left for him and made his bed. Lying down, he tried to relax, but after the day's activities, he felt wired and restless but eventually his body gave way to a peaceful sleep.

He rose at five-thirty and woke Emily. He considered waking Cara and telling her goodbye, but he decided against it. Grabbing his shotgun and shells from under the couch, he locked the doorknob before quietly closing the door. He and Emily got into the Ram pick-up and drove out of Shamrock. In many ways it made him sad. But it also made him nervous. Although he had been in Shamrock for only a day and a half, it had seemed like a lifetime and now he had to fight the bugs and marauders again. He wasn't sure if he remembered how.

30

The cabin floor popped and creaked under Della's feet as she tiptoed in to check on her sons. Ricky hadn't mentioned to Della that Louie had been leaving his bed in the middle of the night and crawling into Ricky's, but she knew. She assumed that Ricky needed the security of his brother as much as her youngest did. Now, seeing her sons curled together, Della wondered if their lives would ever return to normal. Della picked Louie up and, careful not to wake him, put him back in his bed. Although she was grateful to Ricky for comforting his brother, she was certain he wasn't getting a good night's rest. Louie had always been a rough sleeper. Many mornings, she had awakened with bruises when he was younger and still sleeping between her and Ash.

Closing their bedroom door behind her, she crossed the living room floor and turned on the oil lamp. The fire had slowed considerably and she added a few more logs to it. The blaze quickly caught the fresh logs and warmed the living room. Della lay down on the couch and pulled the quilt over her. Watching the hypnotic ballet of dancing flames, Della thought of Ash. Her guilt over what was occurring between Brady and herself left her ashamed. How many weeks had it been? A little over a month and already she was ready to jump into the arms of another man. Okay, not completely ready, but the thought had crossed her mind once or twice. If the situation were reversed, would Ash be so willing to give up on her? *No, probably not,* she thought miserably. *Or would he?* It was possible he was alive and simply stuck in another part of the country believing she was dead. *Was he going on with his life?* Ironically, that idea hurt her more than she was willing to admit. Closing her eyes, she tried to recall her last conversation with her husband, the memories sliding easily around her mind, while she drifted in and out of sleep.

* * *

Unable to sleep, Della sat with a cup of coffee in her hand still curled under her quilt. Her mind was restless. Her memories of Ash left her aching and in her sleep-deprived state, her mind began playing tricks by mingling Brady's face into her memories of Ash. Della let her mind wander to Brady. He was so different from anyone she had ever met. She had rarely been around anyone who spoke his mind so freely. She was fascinated by his honesty, captivated by his ability to speak directly to her soul.

Della heard the sound of a car pulling into the drive and held her breath. Brady limited his visits to evenings. *Ash?* Jumping from the couch, Della crossed the room quickly and jerked the door open.

"Hello, bitch." Della heard her voice before she saw the fist coming toward her face. Too late to duck, she felt the small woman's knuckles connect with her cheek.

"Remember me?" she said, as she pushed Della back into the cabin.

"Mrs. Shields?" Della said, holding her hand to her throbbing cheek.

"Oh, please call me Mary. I think we're past formalities, don't you?" The small, dark-haired woman swung again at Della, though missing this time when Della ducked and ran for safety behind the couch.

"What's wrong with you?" Della screamed.

"Me? You want to know what's wrong with me?" Mary stopped and scanned the room. Seeing the fireplace poker, she walked over and picked it up.

"Nothing's wrong with me that won't be fixed by killing you," she smiled, rubbing the poker along her palm.

"Mrs...," she began.

"MARY!" The intruder screamed and swung the poker against the lamp on the table, sending it crashing to the floor.

Della was certain the noise was going to bring her sons out of their rooms any second now and that terrified her.

"Mary, please, my sons are sleeping..." she nodded to the bedroom door.

"Do you honestly think I give a damn about your brats?" She laughed and swung the poker angrily at the matching lamp on the other end of the couch.

"Is this about the cabin?" Della tried to stall the woman while she quickly scanned the living room for a possible weapon to defend herself. Mary Shields was several inches shorter and probably thirty pounds lighter than Della. Her dark skin had an obvious Mediterranean distinctiveness. Even through the smeared make-up and her dishevelment, Della could still see her beauty. Under normal circumstances, Della was certain she could handle the petite woman, but not in her crazed state.

Laughing the same detached absurd laugh, Mary suddenly rushed the couch, climbed over the back, and swung her poker wildly. Della jumped back just in time to miss the poker's sharp bite and stumbled over Louie's cars, falling hard to the wooden floor. Screaming, Mary flew over the back of the couch and landed on top of Della. The poker dropped from her hand in the fall and slid across the floor, stopping near the door. If Mary knew she no longer possessed the weapon, she showed no signs of it. Della tried to bring her hands to her face to protect herself from the barrage of fists, but was overpowered by the frenzy of Mary's madness.

Suddenly, the woman was off Della and lying on her back. Mary stood immediately and began looking wildly around the room for the source of their interruption. Jumping to her feet, Della saw Ricky standing in front of the mad woman, clad only in his pajamas and bare feet, clutching his baseball bat tightly in both hands waiting for the small woman to move on him.

Screaming, the woman threw herself at Ricky, clawing at his face as Ricky swung the bat wildly, trying to connect with some part of the woman.

"No!" Della yelled, as she saw the woman attack her first born. Quickly, she grabbed the woman around the waist and threw her off her son, bouncing her hard against the cabin wall.

"Ricky, get out of here!" she screamed at her son, taking the bat and swinging it protectively in front of her.

"No! I'm not leaving you with her," he said, standing beside his mom.

"Go get Brady!" she yelled, and pushed him out the door.

"But…" he stammered, clearly torn, grabbing the keys to the van hanging next to the door.

"Hurry!" she screamed, her eyes fixed on her assailant.

Mary dove at Ricky and missed him as he ran across the porch and down the steps. Della gripped the bat with both hands and brought it down hard on the mad woman's back, causing her to scream out in pain. Della took advantage of the woman's brief immobility, grabbed the woman's legs, and dragged her back inside the doorway, slamming the door behind her. Again, the woman was on her feet. This time running for the poker that in the struggle had been kicked near the couch where she now stood. Della, seeing what Mary was going after, brought the bat down again on the crazed woman, this time missing her back and landing on her calf. Mary howled in pain, but reached the poker and rolled onto her back to swing it at Della. The hook of the poker caught Della's left thigh, tearing a gash in her skin through her pajamas. Startled, Della stumbled back and fell to the floor, struggling to hold onto the bat while pain roared up her thigh.

"I'm going to enjoy killing you," Mary said, now standing over Della.

"What's wrong with you?" Della asked, slowly backing away.

"What's wrong with you? What's wrong with you?" she said mockingly. "You sound like a damn parrot. There's nothing wrong with me. Nothing except that my life is ruined and it's... all...your...fault!" She paused between each word, hitting the couch.

"But, why?" Della asked, suddenly scared for Louie, alone in the bedroom.

"Why? You don't know why, huh? Bullshit, you don't know why. Tony is dead because of you, you bitch."

Della looked wide-eyed at her adversary and tightened her grip on the bat, "Your husband?"

"Your husband?" Mary mocked Della, "You know damn well who I'm talking about."

Della still wasn't certain that Mary was talking about her husband. "I only met your husband that one time, how could I have killed him?"

Mary laughed hysterically, "I didn't say you killed him, bitch, I said he's dead because of you."

Della held the bat in front of her and slowly rose to her knees, wincing in pain with each movement. Even with a bat in hand, she knew lying on the floor was a very vulnerable position. "We need to calm down, Mary, I don't know wh..."

Della saw the poker sweep down toward her in a horrifying arc. "Don't tell me to calm down!" Mary screamed, as the poker whipped past Della's face. "God, I hate shits like you! Everything comes so easy, doesn't it? Just go pout to some guy who's declared himself king of the mountain and he comes to evict us with a hard-on."

Della managed to get to her feet, despite the searing pain in her left thigh. Seeing Della rise, Mary swung the poker with a two-fisted backhand. This time, though, Della saw it coming and easily avoided it. As the poker came to a stop on Mary's right shoulder, Della swung the bat and caught her in the lower ribs. Mary fell to the floor and began to cry.

"It's just not fair, it's not fair. People like you get all the breaks. I don't even have my Tony now."

The woman's sobbing started to melt Della's heart. The woman lost her husband, if she needed someone to blame, that was fine with Della, as long as she didn't try to kill her. "Look, Mary, I'm sorry about your husband but..."

From the corner of her eye, Della saw Louie enter the room, rubbing his sleepy eyes. "Louie, stay out of here," Della yelled, but it was too late. Louie always woke up too groggy to follow directions well.

Louie crossed the room and Mary reached out, grabbed him and pulled him to the floor with her. "I don't want your sympathy, bitch. I want revenge!"

In one fluid motion, Mary rose to her knees, tossed the little boy two feet to her left and brought the poker up, intending to strike a fatal blow on the dazed boy's exposed head.

"No!" Della yelled, and swung the bat at Mary's head. The bat hit the poker and wrenched it from Mary's hand before she was able to swing it.

Apparently unfazed, she tried to grab Louie again, but the little boy had awoken enough to scamper out of the woman's reach and run to the kitchen.

Della's fury had now fully blossomed. She limped forward, swung the bat up again and caught Mary in the jaw, sending teeth and blood into the air. She then swung the bat back with both hands and hit Mary in the temple, crushing her skull and forcing bone fragments into her cranial cavity. Defeated by death, Mary collapsed.

Although Della's first instinct was to run to her frightened son and comfort him, she knew she couldn't let him see this woman's disfigured face. She seized a plastic tablecloth from the kitchen table and covered Mary's lifeless body. Then she went into the kitchen and found Louie hiding in the cabinets under the sink. Della pulled him out and wordlessly held him until he stopped shivering and crying. After he fell back asleep, she picked him up, struggled to carry him into the living room, laid him on the couch, and covered him up.

As she re-entered the kitchen, she heard the living room door open. She turned and walked back into the living room, half expecting to find another insane woman. But this time, it was Brady, with shotgun in hand, and Ricky. She ran and hugged her son, while Brady moved past her and into the cabin. When he saw Mary's body, he pulled the tablecloth back, looked at her for several seconds, and then replaced it.

He returned to the living room and leaned the shotgun against the entertainment center. "Isn't that Mrs. Shields?"

"Yes."

Brady slowly sat down on the couch next to Louie. "So. What happened?"

"I'm not sure. She broke in and starting yelling crazy stuff."

"That's what Ricky told me. What was she yelling?"

"She said I killed her husband. I only met the man once. I've never killed anyone." Della stopped and looked at the floor, remembering poor Billy and what it felt like to take a man's life. "Well..." she said sadly. "I didn't kill her husband though."

"I know you didn't."

"You do?" Della asked surprised.

"Yeah. Todd killed him."

"What?"

"He'd been bitten," Brady sighed heavily, "Todd had to."

"Why didn't you tell me?"

"Because it just happened tonight. Todd told me a few hours ago in the lodge. He said he didn't see Mary at the time. She must've found him later. I understand she was a bit of a loon, already."

Della raised her eyebrows at him, "Why do you say that?"

Brady grimaced, thought for a moment and said, "I didn't know her, but in talking to some of the folks around here, when they claimed your cabin, it seems she was a big dreamer. Never satisfied with her life. I guess her husband was a big disappointment to her, just being a small shopkeeper and all. They say she developed an elaborate fantasy life after awhile and she kept her husband busy trying to make her happy. I guess she just slowly lost it."

Della crossed her arms. "So, why didn't you tell me this before?"

"In retrospect, I obviously should have, but nothing anyone said indicated she was dangerous, just off-balance. I figured you had enough to worry about without worrying about some crazy lady."

Della looked away from Brady to the recliner and saw that Ricky had also fallen asleep again. Then she looked back to the dining room where the woman lay dead.

"What are we going to do about her?"

"Mrs. Shields? I guess I'll have to dispose of her body."

Della slowly stood up, in obvious pain and rubbed her face. "I'm exhausted. Do you need help moving the body?"

"No, it should only take a few minutes," he said, walking towards the body. "Will you be okay here?"

"Yeah," she said, rubbing the back of her neck. "I need to wash this mess off and I'm really tired."

"Are you hurt?" Brady asked, looking at her more carefully this time.

"Yeah, she got me with that poker once."

"Got you where?" Instantly, he was at her side. His arms were on her as he searched her for wounds.

"In the thigh," Della said, as she turned the back of her left leg toward Brady.

Brady immediately went to his knees and looked at the injury. Ignoring the splattering of Mary's blood that laced both legs of Della's pajamas, he said, "Della, that's bad. You need to have that looked at."

"I will tomorrow. Tonight I'm just going to clean it off and go to bed.

Brady nodded. "That might be a good idea. It's not like we have an emergency room around here anyway. I'll check on you again in the morning."

Della turned to her friend. "You know, you could stay. I don't want to be alone tonight."

"Okay," he said quietly.

"Go clean up and I should be back in a few minutes to help you move the boys."

"Get me a blanket and I'll sleep on the couch."

Della hesitated, not sure if she wanted him to sleep that far away from her or not. "Okay."

31

Della finished cleaning the blood from her leg and was unsuccessfully trying to bandage it when she heard Brady return from disposing of Mary Shields' body. After a few minutes, the bathroom door opened slowly and Brady stuck his hand around the door.

"Decent?" he asked.

"Sort of. Come on in," she told him. She had changed out of her bloody pajamas and into a comfortable oversized shirt, but she decided against pants for fear it would stick to her wound. She was too tired and hurt too much to care what Brady thought about her pink panties. Sitting on the side of the bathtub, Della had propped her leg up and was trying to apply gauze to her wound.

"Want some help?" he asked, seeing her struggle.

Nodding, she said, "Please, I can't seem to get the tape to stick."

Brady knelt beside her on the floor and pulled part of the bandage off, examining her injury. Gently, he used the washcloth to clean the area and replaced the bandage, carefully taping around the gash. Helping Della to her feet, Brady wrapped his arms around her waist and lifted her into his arms.

"Brady..."

"Shh... You shouldn't be walking on this now," he told her, as he carried her into the bedroom, softly placing her on the bed.

"Did you move the boys yet?" she asked, scooting back against the headboard.

"Yes, the cabin's locked up tight and the fire is fine. You should be set for the night."

"Aren't you staying?"

"Do you want me to stay?"

"Yes," she said quietly, "I don't want to be alone tonight."

Brady smiled and walked around the bed to the other side. Sitting beside Della, he took her hand in his and kissed it. "If you were mine, Della Bishop, I'd never let you out of my sight."

"Oh, really?" she smiled unconvincingly.

"Really," he brought her hand to his mouth again and began to kiss each finger, before turning her hand over and kissing the center of her palm.

"How are you doing?" he asked, noticing her shaking.

"I don't know," she said, pulling her hand away and rubbing them together as if she were cold.

"That was pretty brave. Going up against a crazy woman."

"I don't think I had a choice."

"No, I guess not, but it still doesn't make it any easier does it?"

"No." Having a hard time calming herself after the attack, Della could feel her insides quivering.

"I think I must be in shock," she said continuing to rub her hands. "I feel a little numb. Isn't that crazy? I should probably be a basket case right now, shouldn't I? Maybe the fact that I'm not is proof how crazy all this has made me."

"That's normal," Brady said, and took hold of her hands, quieting them. "I'll stay and keep an eye on things. Why don't you try and get some sleep."

"Do you think the boys will be okay?"

"When I moved them, they were sleeping hard. Kids are incredibly resilient."

"That's the truth. After everything they've seen and then tonight...I don't know how they're keeping it together. I can't believe they're sleeping."

"They'll be okay. They're pretty tough boys. Just like their mommy."

"Do you think they'll have nightmares?"

"I don't know, but I'll be here if they do," Brady positioned himself where Della could easily rest on his chest.

Closing her eyes, Della listened to the rhythmic beating of his heart through his shirt and relaxed.

"Della, I know you're tired, but there's something I need to tell you."

"Um?" she asked, with her eyes still closed.

"I think I'm falling in love with you."

"Brady..." Della sat up and looked into his eyes.

"Shh... I'm not asking you to say anything. I'm sure my feelings aren't news to you. But seeing you hurt and knowing how close I came to losing you, it made me crazy." Brady brought her hand back to his face and gently kissed it again. "You make me crazy."

"Brady...," she began.

"I have to tell you something and you can't interrupt or I'll never get it said."

"Okay," Della said apprehensively.

Della watched Brady mull over his words, carefully considering his next words to her. "Don't do that," she said, "just tell me."

After a moment, Brady said, "Mark and I have been talking, and I, we, think it's best if we try and get off the mountain."

"Why?" Della asked.

"Well, things have been stable for a while now and we have to see what's out there. What's left?"

Della sat quietly and waited for Brady to finish.

"Before I got into contracting, I was involved with the government."

"The government?"

"I was in security."

"What did you do?"

"A little of this and that. That's not really important now. What's important is what happens to our country right now." Brady paused to allow Della time to soak in what he had told her.

"Why didn't you tell me this before?" Della asked.

"Didn't really think it mattered."

"And now it does."

"Yes."

"I have to get back."

"What? Back to where?"

"To D.C.," Brady answered. "I have to return."

"Why? I know they haven't called you."

"No. I'm retired. But things have changed in the world, they'll need me."

For the second time, Della was open-mouthed, staring at Brady. "They told you to return to work if man-eating spider-insect thingies attacked the world?"

Della could tell that Brady was desperately trying to maintain his professionalism. "I'm going to have to return. The country will need people to step up and do their part."

Della chuckled in disbelief. "I can't believe what I'm hearing. Are you going to drive or fly? I don't believe there have been many flights out of Santa Fe International in recent days."

"Obviously, I'll have to drive," Brady said. "I don't expect it to be easy. In fact, I expect it to take several weeks, maybe months, but I have to go." Brady watched Della's astonished expression for a minute, and then added, "And I want you to go with me."

"You're insane."

"No. You and the kids would be sitting ducks here. I need to be able to watch over you."

"We are not leaving here. Ash. Ash might still be alive. I have to... we have to be here if he makes it."

"Della, you and I both know you don't believe Ash is still alive."

"No, I don't know that. Yeah, it's been a long time. Yeah, we're a long way from Chicago, but damnit, he could still be alive." Della ran her hands through her hair and said, "I can't completely give up on him. I can't. He's my husband."

"Besides, we have a shelter here that will protect us from whatever hits."

"For how long? You're going to run out of something you need eventually. What if the bugs or the creatures or whatever come back?"

"I'd sooner take my chances here than chasing around the country hoping not to run into anything bad," said Della. "Oh, Brady. Stay with us. You don't even know that there is a government. The President, Congress, the military, they may all have been killed, or worse."

"If you're certain that Ash is returning, why shouldn't I leave?" Brady asked.

Della winced at his candidness.

"I don't know. Because... Because, there are people here who care about you."

"Does that include you?" Brady asked hesitantly.

Della smiled broadly, "You know it does."

Della sat quietly and thought over the information Brady just gave her. "I don't know why you think you have to go back. I mean, I understand duty, honor and country, but you don't know if any of that exists, nowadays, including honor."

"That's one reason that I have to go. If there's a chance that we can reconstruct our government, our way of life, I have to help. It's who I am."

"Don't go, Brady. I don't think you'll make it."

"You stay here. You stay safe, Della. I'll come back for you and the boys when I can. I promise you that."

Della lay on Brady's chest and was quiet for a moment.

"I thought you said if I was yours, you'd never leave me," she said softly.

"Does that mean your mine?"

"I'll tell you when you get back," she said, closing her eyes once again, feeling the heaviness of the day closing in around her. Relaxing in the smell and feel of the man she had come to need and depend on so much in her life now. Thankful, he was there; she gave herself over to sleep.

* * *

"Wake up!" Brady shook Della awake.

"What's the matter?" she asked, trying to clear the cobwebs from her mind. She had been under deep. So deep, she was surprised to see the room full of sunlight. After last night's ordeal, they must have slept later than usual.

Brady had already left the bedroom and Della could hear him talking to someone in the living room.

Struggling to stand on her injured leg, Della hobbled towards the voices.

"I told you, man, they were just there!" It was Mark; he was pacing around the living room, obviously distressed.

Della hobbled down the hall toward the living room. "What's going on?" she asked the men.

Mark stopped pacing for a moment and looked at Brady.

"Go ahead, tell her," Brady said, nodding towards Della as she made her way into the room.

"A swarm got into the lodge."

"No!" Della sank to the couch and covered her hands in her face.

"How many?" Brady asked Mark.

"Everyone..." Mark started pacing again. "They were having breakfast; I was out on rounds. God, all those people...those kids...they're all gone." Mark's pacing had picked up again; his face was covered in tears and his shoulders shook violently.

"Nobody else made it to safety? Nobody made it to the freezer?" Della asked.

"No. Nobody."

"How do you know that for sure?"

"Because I saw it. God, don't you understand?"

"Calm down Mark, and tell us what happened. What did you see?" Brady had walked over to the distraught man and placed a comforting hand on his shoulder.

Mark took a deep breath and nodded. "I was approaching the lodge from the north when I saw the swarm leave," Mark said through tears. "I went into the lodge to see what happened...who survived. Everyone was bitten. They were already changing... I counted – everyone was there and infected. They were my friends, I couldn't bring myself to shoot them. We're all that's left."

"When?" Della asked.

"Not long ago, maybe half an hour," Mark answered.

Della stared at Brady. She had a dozen questions, but couldn't voice any of them. "What are we going to do?" was the only thing she could think to ask.

"I don't know. We need to see what our infected friends are gonna do first. If they decide to go in another direction, then they may die off before they find us."

"Wait and see? That's the best answer you have? My kids are in here! I can't sit here and hope nothing's going to happen. We need to be proactive."

"The one thing we know for sure about these...things, they're unpredictable. If we start going off half-cocked, we could be asking for trouble," Brady told her.

"Well, I can't sit and wait either," Mark said, in a voice barely above a whisper, as he looked out of the living room window. "I'm going after them."

"Brady, I agree with Mark. If we go out after them, then maybe we could pick them off one at a time." Della said.

Brady held his hands up, "Wait a minute. We at least have some measure of protection here. If you try to meet them on the street or at the lodge, you're meeting them on their turf. We can set up a defense here and try to hold them off."

Again, in a hushed voice, Mark said, "We better decide soon, they're coming this way."

"What? All of them?" Della asked, near hysteria as she approached the window with Brady.

"Looks like it," Mark answered.

"Damn, I left two rifles in the Jeep. I'm going to have to go out and get them." Brady reached into a holster on his belt and handed a .38 pistol to Della. "You've had a gun all this time?"

"Yeah."

Della thought about that for a moment, realized why he might be carrying a weapon, and then turned back toward the window.

"If they start getting near me, shoot them."

"Okay."

"In the head, preferably. In the heart, if you have to."

"Okay."

"You'd better move, if you're going to do this," Mark said, still scarcely more than whispering.

Without another word, Brady raced to the door and out to the Jeep. He pulled the handle and found he locked it. *Damn it!* He fumbled for the keys in his pocket and, for the first time since going outside, looked up the road toward the lodge. The mob was picking up the pace and coming right for him. He found the right key, inserted it into the lock and rotated the tumblers. He popped the door open and immediately found the rifles leaning against the console. He grabbed them both with one hand and snatched two boxes of rounds out of the back seat. Brady closed the Jeep's door and again looked toward the lodge. The mob was within fifty yards of the cabin and had picked up its pace again. Brady ran to the front of the cabin and Della opened the door as soon as he arrived. She locked the door behind him and they knelt down to load the rifles. As they loaded, Della heard the door unlock behind her. She turned and saw Mark opening the door with the pistol in his hand.

"What the hell are you doing? Close that door."

"I'm going after them," he replied.

"No! Come back in here and close that door!" she yelled, as he crossed the porch.

"Mark!" she yelled, but by the time she limped to the door, he was five yards from the house and going fast.

"Della, come in here and lock that door," Brady admonished.

She put her head against the doorframe, and sadly closed and locked the front door. "You could have saved him, you know."

"He's a grown man. He has a better chance of taking care of himself than you, in your condition, or your kids. I don't have time to wrestle him back in here and load these magazines."

Two shots rang out, then a few seconds of silence and two more shots. Then nothing.

Della ran to the window, but couldn't see Mark. He could have been behind some trees past the clearing or he could have...

Brady stood up with both rifles in hand and approached Della. "There were six rounds in that pistol. I think we have to assume the worst."

"Why would he do that?" she said, head in hands.

"He and Stacey were together. I guess seeing her change was too much."

"We need to concentrate on us right now. Okay, Della. I need you to focus on me."

"Okay."

"Ash built a basement in here, right? Where he kept his supplies?" he asked, shoving the couch up in front of the door.

"Yeah."

"Is there any way out of there besides that door?" He pointed towards the trap door in the hallway.

"No."

"Any windows?"

"No."

"We've got to make a decision fast. Do you want to hide or run?"

"I...God, Brady, I can't...I don't know what to do."

"Alright, here's what we're going to do. You take the boys and hide in the basement. Take the keys to the Jeep. I'll hide the door once you guys are safe, and I'll draw them away from the house. When you think enough time has passed, take the keys and get the boys out. It'll be safer if you can drive around long enough for them to die off."

"No Brady, I won't let you do that."

"Della, you don't have a choice. It's either me or your boys, which one?"

Della stared wordlessly at him.

"I didn't expect you to choose," he said.

"I don't know what to say."

"I know. Now listen to me, this is important," Brady stopped moving furniture to face Della.

"What?"

"You're gonna have to stay locked down there until you're absolutely certain the infected are far enough away from here. I can't protect you after this. I'll do my best to make them follow me."

"Brady…I…"

"Della, we're going to have to do this quickly. When this is over, I'll find you and you'll have a lifetime to finish that sentence."

Della looked again at the tall, dark-haired man who had captured her soul with his gentle and protective ways. Reaching up, she wrapped her fingers around his neck and brought his mouth down hard against hers.

"I'll be waiting for you Brady," she said, after catching her breath.

32

"Are you ready to go four wheelin'?" Ash said, grinning at his companion beside him.

"Yes sir," Emily replied.

"Well then, let's hit it." Ash shifted the gears to the deep red Dodge Ram truck and lurched forward onto the unnamed gravel road.

"This shortcut should get us to the cabin in a couple of hours," he told Emily and to reassure himself.

He was quite sure he remembered this route to the cabin because of all the times he had hiked it with Della. The only catch was when they reached Jamis Peak they would have to hoof it the rest of the way. That would leave them exposed to those damn fly creatures. It still would make for better time than driving the more traveled Route 53. Who knows what they might run into if they went that way?

"Ash?"

"Yes?"

"Why did we have to leave that city," she asked, pouting.

"I already told you, sweety. I have to find my family."

"I know, but they had warm food and water and beds."

"Did you like Cara?"

Emily smiled, "Yeah, and she liked you, too."

"Think so?" Ash asked, trying to conceal his grin.

"Mm hmm. She was sweet on you."

"I think you're teasing me, you little snot."

Emily gave Ash a big grin and turned toward the window.

Ash took a moment to look at the skyline as well. Straight ahead were ominous mountains in the distance with bulky white clouds that seemed to sit upon them.

"It's going to get a little bumpy, so buckle up. This road isn't going to stay graveled for very long," Ash said, looking upward to the midmorning sun-drenched sky for any signs of trouble. The kind of trouble that could darken the skies before they could effectively move. He shook off a chill and drove on into the desert en route to the family he missed.

* * *

"Well, here we are. Jamis Peak," Ash announced after the both of them had experienced the bumpiest ride of their lives.

"My insides are still moving," Emily said, as she held her stomach.

"Mine too, honey. Let's just be glad that it wasn't too long of a trip." Ash braked directly in front of Jamis Peak as the dust from the road caught up with them and momentarily consumed the truck.

Ash and Emily went straight to the task at hand. It was second nature to them now, to cover themselves with bug spray and collect all their belongings in backpacks for the mile and a half journey to their final destination.

"This is it, little one. We're going to have to move fast. We don't want to be caught by those spiderflies." Ash said with absolute seriousness. He wanted Emily to understand the gravity of this final obstacle.

Jamis Peak gradually sloped upwards to a height of twelve hundred and some feet before descending down the other side into another slope that was easily traversed. It wasn't anything that was dangerous, just time-consuming.

"At the top of the peak, we will be able to see the cabins of Mt. Hope and of our new home," he said.

She returned his smile.

"Are you ready?" Ash asked.

"Yes," Emily answered with great optimism.

"Let's go." Ash threw open the truck's squeaky door and they jumped down and jaunted up the sandy dirt path that led to the top of Jamis Peak. Their backpacks bounced vigorously with each step and grew heavier by the minute. Ash held his loaded shotgun over his shoulder as they journeyed further up the path.

"Can we stop and take a break?" Emily asked.

"Not yet, we're only halfway there." He looked at the beads of sweat that had rested on Emily's forehead and above her top lip.

"We'll rest when we get to the top. We gotta keep movin'. It isn't safe out here." Ash took her backpack to lighten her load and make the ascent easier, but he never slowed his fast pace. At times, he would help Emily by nudging her along in front of him.

"Oow! Damn it!" Ash shouted, grabbing the back of his neck as he fell to the ground. His hand smacked at his neck as he scrambled to hold onto rocks in order to keep his balance.

"What's wrong?" Emily cried. But her question went unanswered.

"Damn, Damn, Damn!" He knew what had happened.

He quickly brought his hand around to see what had bitten his neck. He immediately let out a piercing shriek. The grotesque spiderfly was still barely alive and was now biting at his hand. He held the misshapen bug in disbelief for a few seconds before he threw it to the ground and began stomping on it with his boot until it disappeared into unrecognizable pieces on the ground.

"This can't be happening," he cried out in irate disgust. Ash then looked into the terrified face of Emily before a frantic look skyward.

He saw only the rolling clouds against the light blue sky. He had to get Emily to Mt. Hope and soon was not soon enough.

"I'm going to be alright," he winced, trying to convince Emily. "We've got to hurry."

"But...," she paused, "What about you?"

"Don't worry about me. We don't have much time."

Ash could feel the venom coursing its way throughout his body. He felt weaker and the ill effects kicked in almost immediately. He began pushing himself and Emily relentlessly to reach the top of the peak. He had to make it there and point Emily in the right direction. Ash understood that he would not and could not go any further than the peak. Not only was his body telling him that, but his mind told him that Emily would be safer without him and what he was about to become. Ash was also aware of what he had to do before he turned.

They at last reached the top of Jamis Peak and Ash collapsed to the ground in sheer exhaustion. The venom was rapidly making its way through his body and he knew he had to get Emily to safety.

"Emily..." he paused, and then puked up his morning breakfast of cherry Pop Tarts mixed with pasty orange stomach acid. His breathing then became more erratic.

Emily stroked the top of his head to comfort him as he continued to violently vomit.

"Emily," he said, nearly out of breath. He pulled himself up from the ground to a sitting position. He surveyed the area before him with blurred vision, as he squinted he finally made out the cabins of Mt. Hope.

"There! See there," he pointed. His hand shook as he showed Emily the way.

Emily looked in that direction and became excited once she noticed the small toy-like houses that were plotted randomly along Mt. Hope's mountainside.

"Yes, I see them," she declared proudly.

"Good, you need to follow the path very carefully and never leave the path. You have to hurry, but be careful. Once you get to the bottom, I want you to run like crazy till you get there."

"But Ash. What about you?"

"I'm sorry Emily, but I can't go any further."

"But, I can't leave you here."

"You have to. I've been bitten and you know what happens next."

She bent down and hugged him tightly, burying her face in his shoulder. "I don't want to leave you," she cried, her voice muffled.

"I know, but we have no other choice." Ash was becoming delirious.

"Listen to me." He pulled her from him and stared into her heartbroken eyes. "You have to get going. Don't stop for anybody or anything till you get to the cabins. Ask for my wife,

Della, she will take care of you. Tell her that I love her, Louie and Ricky."

"Please, come with me," Emily interrupted, "I'm scared."

"Don't be. We have come a long way together and you've shown me that you're a brave young lady." Ash felt his world spinning, but stayed strong.

"You have to go now. You've been like a daughter to me and I love you. So, please do me one last favor and save yourself," he pleaded.

"Okay," she sobbed, "I love you too." Emily again hugged him tightly and promptly started down the summit. She didn't say another word. She couldn't.

Ash watched her for a few seconds before laying his head down in complete nauseous exhaustion.

33

Ash awoke from his sickened slumber, lying in his own vomit that encrusted his bloated face and matted hair. His lips were parched from the arid heat that emanated from the scorching soil. His tongue struggled to quench his dry lips, but could not because he was severely dehydrated. No longer could he think with reason or contemplate his next move. The sun's intense rays beat against his backside, blistering his drained body. His mind struggled to bring the vertigo to an end, but that was out of his control. He caught brilliant glimpses of his environment, but could not bring meaning to it. He was suffering enough to pray for his own death, but could not form sufficient coherent thoughts.

The winds on the slope began to violently blow and howl, like a pack of wolves. The sun began to brighten to the point of causing pain to Ash's eyes. Ash, in crazed bewilderment, somehow fought the virus' effects long enough to roll over onto his back. He squinted at the sun's magnificent glow, unable to lift his arm to shield its intensity.

Have I died? Am I going to Heaven or Hell? Ash stared intently at the glow that no longer hurt his eyes to view. He had no control of his physical being, but lay waiting for the inevitable. He knew he was going to die and he accepted that fate, as much as he could accept anything at that moment.

"Ash," a deep grandiose voice bellowed from the glow.

Ash was unable to speak, but squinted his eyes toward the light.

"I am Archangel Michael, highest to the heavenly host. Head of all magnificent angels in Heaven that crusade against evil. As so before, I am sent by our maker to fight against the ills of Satan and his army."

"Beelzebub, or Satan, has begun the apocalypse of free reign over all God's creations. Beelzebub has command over disease, as do flies congregate around the corpses of the dead, and spread disease from the dead to the living, thus he is known as - Lord of the Flies. As you are now witness to, Beelzebub has unleashed Hell's spawned flies from his loins to destroy the world. This is not within the will of God."

"As this night begins, there shall be no sunlight cast upon the Earth for three days. Relentless cold conditions will cause you to take shelter with others and keep warm over this time. This cold shall bring death to Beelzebub's flies."

"I will continue to lead the forces of Heaven and Earth to triumph over the powers of Hell. Ash, you were born with a supreme purpose for God. Together, good will overcome malevolent forces as we shall rid the world from this the evilest of evil. You, as well as others, were chosen by God to lead this new world and with this you are immune to the virus. You will survive because you must. It is the will of God."

The glow and the wild winds instantly disappeared, leaving Ash to gaze upward to where the voice once emanated. He felt a pleasing warmness overcome his body that rejuvenated his whole being. He lay his head down and closed his fatigued eyes. He felt at peace as he drifted into a deep sleep. As he slept, the blackened arteries from his bites gradually disappeared as so did the bite areas that had oozed puss from their inflamed swellings. Ash was healed by the grace of God.

34

Della wasn't sure how long they had been in the basement. She couldn't believe that in Ash's careful planning, he hadn't thought about putting in a clock or a watch or something so she could tell what time it was in their basement. She was certain it had only been a few hours, but to her it seemed like days. She didn't want to think of Brady and yet she couldn't force herself to think of anything else. She couldn't imagine anyone surviving the mob that had gathered outside. *All those poor people,* she thought. *All gone.* Lisa, Todd, Billy...the death was so much. *Too much.*

"Mom?" Della noticed Ricky had been speaking to her.

"I'm sorry, Ricky. What did you say?" she asked.

"Do you think it's safe to go upstairs?" he asked, looking apprehensively at the door at the top of the stairs.

"I don't know," Della admitted, "It's been a while since we've heard anything."

"Maybe they're gone," Ricky added.

"Maybe," she said quietly. "Let me go up and find out."

"I'll come with you Mom," Ricky said, quickly standing up.

"No, I'm not sure it's safe yet," she put her arm around her oldest. "I need you to stay here with Louie."

"Oh, Mom, you're always saying that. I don't want to stay here." Ricky moved towards the steps, put his hands on hips, and gave his mother his best look of consternation.

Della looked at her son. He was right. In the past month, he had experienced more than his share of horror. She knew that if she were to be attacked upstairs then her boys were most likely dead anyway. It didn't make sense not to take them with her.

"Okay," she relented, "but you've got to be responsible for Louie. Okay?"

"Okay, Mom," Ricky said, walking over to Louie and grabbing his hand.

"I don't need Ricky to hold my hand," Louie protested.

Della smiled at her two little brave boys, took a deep breath and started up the stairway. Pushing the door open, she stopped and listened for any sounds that would signify that there were still infected people in the area. Hearing nothing, she ushered her boys out of the doorway and into the living room. Surprisingly, the cabin had been left untouched. She walked to the window and cautiously looked out across the yard and down the road, uncertain what carnage she might see. Thankfully, the area was clear. But, that also meant no sign of Brady.

"What are we gonna do now, Mom?" Ricky asked.

Della stood quietly at the window watching the trees move slowly in the afternoon breeze. *That's a good question,* she thought. *What are we supposed to do now*?

Grabbing Brady's keys, she turned to the boys and said, "Let's go look for Brady, he may need our help."

Ricky and Louie nodded and followed her out of the cabin and down the steps to the Jeep.

"Louie, get in the back and lie down." Turning to Ricky, she loaded a rifle and handed it to him. "You remember how to use this, right?"

"Yeah, Mom," Ricky said, taking the gun from her. "Dad's been taking me to the range since I was little, ya' know. I know how to use a gun."

"Good, just remember to keep your finger off the trigger."

"I know, Mom," Ricky said.

"Keep a look out on that side," Della told him, and steered the Jeep down the road.

They had reached the edge of town when Ricky suddenly sat up straight, leaned out the window and pointed at the hillside.

"Look!"

Stopping the Jeep, Della looked where Ricky was pointing and saw a young blond-haired girl waving frantically, running down the hill towards them. Della could tell from her movements that the girl was scared.

"Do you think she's...," Ricky asked, trying to find the right word.

"I don't know. I don't think so. She's not acting strange like them. Who is she? Ricky, do you recognize her?" she asked her son.

"No. I've never seen her before."

Della opened the door and walked cautiously over to the girl. Getting closer, Della could see that the girl was crying and had been for some time, by the way her face was red and spotty. Tears ran freely from her bloodshot eyes.

"Hello."

The young girl dropped to the ground and tried to talk, but her sobbing prevented it. Della bent down and wrapped her arm around the girl's shoulder trying to quiet her shaking.

"Honey, where did you come from?" she asked.

The girl pointed up the hill and gasping said, "Up there..."

Confused, Della looked up in the direction the girl was pointing and said, "I didn't know there were cabins up there."

"Not...a...cabin...," the girl was still struggling to catch her air.

"Need... to find...Della," she said.

The mention of her name by this girl sent shockwaves through Della. "That's me, who are you? Why are you looking for me?" Della asked puzzled.

"Ash, I'm with Ash," the girl said.

"Oh my God!" Della dropped to her knees in front of the girl, grabbing the girl by both arms and shaking her. "Ash? My Ash? He's here? On the mountain?"

The girl's crying increased and she collapsed into Della.

"He's up there." She pointed up the hill.

"Oh, my God!" Della started up the hill.

"Wait!" the girl screamed after Della.

Pausing, Della turned and looked at the girl. "What?"

"He's...."

"He's what?" she demanded.

"Bitten," she said crying louder.

"No!" Della sank to the ground once again and covered her face.

"No, no, no! Don't let him be this close and not make it. This close...to me, he can't be...he can't be dead!" Della felt the familiar soft hands of her sons on her shoulders. Surprised that they had left the Jeep, she wasn't sure how much they had heard.

"Mom?" Ricky asked, concerned, "is it true?" She could see the tears starting to collect in his eyes.

"Oh, honey, I'm so sorry." She pulled both of her sons close and inhaled deeply, gathering strength in their little boy smell.

"What's your name?" Della asked the girl, when she managed to get up from her collapsed state.

"Emily," she answered softly.

"Emily, where's Ash?"

"We were up there and he got bit, and he sent me on to find you."

"Can you show me where?" Della asked.

Emily nodded and turned to go back up the hill. Della reached down and picked up Ricky's rifle and sighed.

"Why, Mom, if Dad's already been bit?" Ricky asked, his mom following behind her and Emily.

"Ricky, you and Louie can stay here if you want, but I have to see for myself. I have to see if there's anything I can do to help him."

"We're going with you, Mommy," Louie said.

Della couldn't focus on the ground in front of her and stumbled several times before Ricky took the rifle from her out of fear that she might accidentally shoot one of them or herself. She knew she should sit down and wait for the grief to engulf her, but she couldn't, she had to see. She had to see her husband. She was struggling with another emotion. She was shocked to find herself more angry than sad. Angry that she had lost her husband, angry that she was now walking up the side of mountain preparing to shoot her soul mate in order to keep him from turning into a monster and killing her kids or this little girl. Angry that she had been through so much in the last month.

* * *

After his encounter, Ash, though heeled, was a little wobbly. Ash figured that had more to do with the power of God than the power of the infection. He stood, bent over with his hands on his knees for about five minutes, waiting for his renewed energy to find its way back to all of his muscles and nerve endings. Finally, he stood and started walking toward his cabin, his Della, his family. His short journey started in a thicket of trees and undergrowth. As he cleared the trees, he saw a Jeep sitting on the road in front of him. He approached it and looked around for a moment. It had no keys, but had several guns in it, which, even in this day and age, was odd.

Well, stealing to survive is a way of life now, he thought. He turned his eyes toward the clouds and said aloud, "I hope this is okay." *These people are probably dead now anyway,* he thought. He grabbed a .22 Remington and some shells and set off. After about a half-mile walk, he found his cabin and was thrilled to find his conversion van parked out front. *She made it,* he thought, and he entered the front door. He found everything as he had remembered it. Della was an excellent housekeeper and finding the cabin so orderly made Ash feel at home for the first time in weeks.

* * *

Della was scrambling up the hill as fast as her boys and Emily would allow. She wanted to break out in a full run, but couldn't. The kids wouldn't be able to keep up, and she needed to be more cautious than that. Emily crested the hill with Della and with the boys closely behind. At the apex, Emily started looking around on the ground, like a bloodhound finding its scent. Della, sensing that Ash, or what used to be Ash, was nearby, grabbed the rifle back from Ricky. Emily went to a small clearing behind some trees and looked around in a circle.

"He was here. He's supposed to be here," the young girl said.

Della squatted near the spot where Emily was pointing. There was evidence that someone had been there. She found blood and that horrifying puss that was emitted by the infected. Ricky and Louie squatted with her. Ricky looked his mother in the eyes.

"What happened," he asked.

"I guess your Dad's gone," she said, sadly looking up at the sky as the tears started to flow. After weeks of not knowing, weeks of trying to convince herself not to give up hope and then when she had finally started to accepted the idea that Ash might really be gone from her and the children....this. She had allowed herself to believe that her husband was still alive and now the heartbreak was devastating. All of the pain of the past few weeks came at her at once. Della erupted into crying that went well beyond her control. Tears streamed as her belly spasmed with each breath. She bent over where her husband had died and fell to her side. A moment later, she felt the kids at her side. She sat up and fiercely hugged them. She was holding them so tight that Louie told her that he couldn't breathe. Della laughed at her child and the laughter cleared her head. A few feet away, Emily was crying hard as well. Della motioned for the girl to come to her. When she did, Della embraced her as well.

* * *

"Della? Della? Ricky? Louie?" he called out as he walked through the cabin. "Emily?" Again, there was no response. Could they be downstairs? He pulled open the door to the basement and shouted, "Hello. Anyone in here?" Nothing. "Well, where the...," the thought choked him.

Don't lose your cool, he thought to himself. *There's no evidence that anything bad has happened to her or the boys.*

He went back outside and searched the area around the building. Finding nothing, he headed back toward town. As he walked, he saw the owners of the Jeep climb back in. He started to trot forward and explain about lifting the rifle, but as he approached, he realized that the people loading themselves into the Jeep were his family.

* * *

Della and the three children finally got to their feet and meandered back down the hill. They arrived back at the Jeep and Della put the rifles in the back, loaded the kids into the Jeep and started the engine. Before she could put the vehicle into gear, she heard a familiar voice from behind her.

"Where've you been?"

She turned toward the sun and saw a silhouette. She put her left hand up to her brow to guard her eyes from the sun, but she still couldn't see the man.

"Where've you been, Della?"

This time she recognized the voice. "Ash? Oh, my God, Ash?"

"Yeah, who else?"

Her elation suddenly turned to fear and she grabbed a pistol next to her and pointed it at him.

"Della? What are you doing?"

"Emily told us you were bitten."

"Yeah, I was, but I'm okay.

Della motioned with the gun for Ash to move to his right so she could see him better. As he came into view, she could see that he looked relatively normal. "You look okay," she said hesitantly.

"I'm okay. I was healed."

"Healed," she repeated.

"Yeah, healed."

"How did that happen," she asked, gun still pointed at Ash's face.

Ash hesitated. "This will sound a little odd."

"Try me."

"God healed me," Ash said, after a minute.

"What?"

"God healed me, or rather a messenger of God."

"Did you see this messenger?"

"I told you this would sound a little odd. Yeah, I saw him. I think he was an angel."

"Did he have wings and a halo?"

"It doesn't work that way, Della."

"I didn't even know you believed in angels," Della said.

"I don't know if I did or not, but I do now. Look, Della, this might be an odd story, but am I crazy? Am I drooling, or barking at the moon or anything like that?"

"No. Maybe you guys have just changed your tactics."

"Della, first of all there are no 'you guys' and there are no tactics. This isn't a vast right-wing conspiracy. People made crazy through these insect bites don't have the capacity to have tactics. Put the gun down so we can talk."

Della slowly lowered the pistol. "Okay, but I'm going to hang on to it."

"Suit yourself. The fact is, I was bitten. Emily witnessed that. I did start to change. I vomited several times and could actually feel molecular changes occurring in my body. Then, I saw a bright light telling me that I would not die. At first, ironically enough, I thought that was one of the stages of becoming a...monster or whatever you want to call them, but it wasn't. He told me that I was cured because God was not ready for me to die."

"Why you?"

"It's just not me. Evidently, this angel appeared to a bunch of us. Don't know why yet. I'm just being used as a catalyst to fight Satan's evil plans. He also said that there will be three days of subfreezing temperatures to kill off the bugs, starting tonight."

"Ash, it's the middle of Summer. It's got to be ninety degrees out here."

"Then you'll find out real soon if what I say is true."

"Della, I've spent the last month in Hell, trying to get back to my family. To you. I'm sure this month hasn't been a picnic for you either, so do you think you could at least act like you're happy to see me?" he said tiredly.

Della didn't know if she believed Ash's story, but she no longer cared. She just wanted him to hold her. She walked up to him, put her arms around him, and put her head on his chest. "I have missed you so much."

"I've missed you too, baby."

When Della went to hug Ash, both boys jumped out of the truck and ran to hug their father. Ash bent down to accept their hugs and gave them a long squeeze. Emily stood next to the Jeep, unsure of how she fit in. After Ash released his sons, he motioned for her to come and hug him, too. She gave Ash a broad smile and ran to him for an embrace.

"Where were you headed?" Ash asked Della.

"I was looking for a friend who was out here," she answered.

"Well, let's go look."

"No. I have my family together again. I'm not going to chance losing you again."

Ash stopped and stared at Della. "Well, alright," he finally said. "Let's go back to the cabin." They loaded themselves back into the Jeep and turned it around.

"Who's the little girl," Della whispered.

"I'll tell you later," Ash whispered back.

On the hill's summit, Ash could see a person standing with a rifle in his hand. Ash looked back down to Della, who was driving. "Who's that?" Ash said as he pointed to the hilltop.

Della followed Ash's direction, "Who's what?"

Ash looked up the hill again, but found the man was gone.

"I thought I saw someone. I guess it was just a shadow."

Della glanced at the hill wondering if it was Brady that Ash had seen, but quickly dismissed it. *No one could have survived that mob, not even Brady.*

"So, how was your drive down?" Della said, trying to change the subject.

"Oh, pretty good. We made good time. But, there was a lot of road construction and we had a hard time finding a hotel room. We did spend a couple of fun-filled days in West Texas, so overall, not bad."

Della pulled up to the cabin. "Well, I'm glad things went well," she smiled, as they all left the vehicle. "We've been mostly lying around watching TV. We've had pizza delivered every night, watched some DVD's and played on the internet."

Ash stopped Della inside the door and kissed her deeply. "I missed you bad, sweety."

"I missed you, too." she said.

35

"Ash, are you sure about this?" Della's eyes expressed her uncertainty.

"Della," he said stoking the fire. "I'm serious about what I heard. I know it sounds crazy, but look at the state of the world right now. Anything seems possible. Only time will tell I guess. Until then, we have to be ready."

"Ricky," Ash yelled.

"Yeah Dad."

"You have towels firmly under all the doors?"

"Yeah."

"Good job. Make sure all the doors and windows are locked."

"Louie, is it still daylight outside?" Ash smiled, because Louie took his job seriously as the mission's lookout.

"Yes sir," the little boy said, saluting his Daddy.

Everyone was in high spirits since being reunited. All Ash wanted to do was embrace his family and smother them with affection, but the pressing matter of spiderflies made that out of the question.

"I'm happy you're back. I was becoming more and more concerned that I would never see you again." Della hugged her husband tightly.

"I missed you too. My love for you and our children kept me going." Their lips joined in a melting kiss that had them both yearning for more.

"Later," Della winked at Ash as she headed to the kitchen.

"How are you and Emily comin' along with dinner?" he asked.

"Great. She's a good little helper."

Walking back to the kitchen, Della noticed the two glasses she and Brady had used the previous night. It would be hard to forget and go on with her life. To go back to the way life had been before this nightmare. Before Brady. Nevertheless, hearing the laughter and familiar noise of her family drifting from the living room, Della silently thanked God for her miracle.

* * *

"Daddy, I hear something," Louie said as he hurried into the dining room.

"Shhh. Listen," Ash ordered.

A sound that they had drawn accustomed to, could be faintly heard outside.

They looked at one another, alternating their gaze to the ceiling.

"Damn. They're back," Ash glanced at everyone and stood up immediately from his unfinished meal.

He raced to the living room window, but froze instantly before he got any closer. The window was alive with insects. The glass was covered with a swarm of spiderflies, squirming and fighting to get in. Ash ran through the cabin, checking each window, but finding each was teeming with the repulsive insects.

"Ash, are they going to get in?" Emily's trembling voice asked.

"No," he said, still staring at the children's bedroom window. The window was full beyond capacity. The humming emanating from the creatures was deafening to their ears. The children clutched their ears and squeezed their eyes shut, hoping that it would make the bugs disappear.

"Daddy, make them go away!" Louie cried.

"Let's go to the basement." Ash shouted over the loudness. "We'll be safe down there. The bugs are definitively going to find a way in. They always do."

"Della, take them to the basement. I'll blow out all the candles and pull the screen across the fireplace," Ash yelled.

Della grabbed Louie and Emily's hands, while Ricky followed.

Ash rushed throughout the house, his heart beating a mile a minute as he hurriedly blew out candle after candle to keep the chance of burning down the cabin to a minimum. He covered the fireplace and fumbled around the darkened cabin with only the flames from the fireplace to light his way to the trap door. *What the...*Ash heard the cabin creaking through intense drone noise. Fear began to grow in the pit of Ash's stomach. *How many of those horrible insects would it take to make our cabin groan like that?* The thought caused him to shiver.

Ash's temples pounded. He heard the large front window begin to crack under the sheer weighted pressure of the death bugs. Immediately, he rushed through the shadowy cabin to the trap door. Jumping into the descended the staircase, he seized the trap door above, drawing it down above him just as he heard the crash of the glass windows hit the cabin floor. Ash slammed the trapped door shut and locked it moments before hearing the deafening whoosh signifying the insect's successful onslaught of the cabin's interior.

"It's going to be okay," he yelled down to the others waiting anxiously below for him. Ash closed and secured the second security door that vacuum-sealed the basement. The vendor that constructed the basement guaranteed that oxygen for a family of four would last thirty-plus days. Ash was gratified that he had prepared for an emergency. He had plenty of food, water, heaters, weapons, lanterns, a generator and other necessities to last more than the three days of darkness and wintriness that he was told would envelope the entire globe. *What will the world look like after this dark freeze,* he wondered.

* * *

Three days later, the trap door creaked partially open as the frosty air rushed in and cuffed Ash's rigid face. He peered over the cloud his breath produced due to the low temperatures. Three days had arrived at a snail's pace and he was thankful to witness the daylight that filled the cabin.

"There's daylight," he shouted down to his family.

"What about the bugs?" Della was the first to speak up.

"I'm going to take a look. Everyone stay put till I check it out," Ash said, as he pressed the trap door open. He felt particles and other debris fall around him as he cautiously left the safety of the basement. He pulled the door closed, but not before taking another glimpse at his family.

Ash struggled to focus on his surroundings. The blurriness from the sunlight gradually faded away leaving him to an appalling scene. The cabin was plagued with thousands of dead spiderflies. They were largely lying on their backs with their thin, almost translucent legs crossed inward to their abdomen.

"What the," Ash shrieked, as he frantically brushed the dead bugs from his shoulders and hair. Realizing that the dead things probably fell on him when he raised the trap door, he relaxed.

The crunching of frozen spiderflies under his boots brought an eerie, repulsive feeling over Ash as he proceeded through the multitude of cobwebs to the living room. There he was astonished at the sizeable mounds of dead spiderflies beside the fireplace that reached over five feet in some areas.

Ash maneuvered carefully through the countless deceased insects that were once the dominant factor and now a mere nuisance littering the floor. He unlocked the front door and brushed away cobwebs that now blanketed the doorway. He continued out the front door, rubbing his hands together to keep warm. Outside, the view was unbelievable. Dead spiderflies for as far as Ash could see and remnants of spider webs blanketed the area as if a massive snowstorm had hit. The sun's warmth was slowly thawing out the frozen terrain. Ash shivered uncontrollably. Knowing he had to get back downstairs and stay for at least another day before venturing back out, Ash turned back to the cabin. Hesitating, he looked up at the sky and said, "Thank you."

It would be good news that he would bring to his family, but there was much work left to do in this new world.

* * *

In a small home on the outskirts of Teays Valley, Virginia, a lonely man, who barely survived the extreme temperatures stares out his front bay window. A fire roars in his fireplace as he manages a smile. For he too, feels that a miracle has passed and the malevolent forces of the insects had finally met their match. Opening his door, he walks out onto the porch, covered with the deceased insects.

Inside, to the rear of the man's living room, sits a hand-made mahogany desk and on that desk rests a crystal lamp. Under the lamp shade, a small dark shadow leisurely scuttles to the top of the shade. It peers around the room with its many eyes and then takes flight for the opened door. The man turns to survey the surrounding madness. The tiny insect flies by the unsuspecting man and into the vast freedom of the outdoors. The man stops momentarily because he hears the familiar dreaded sound, but writes it off as paranoia, and unrightfully so.

Printed in the United States
28160LVS00002B/112-177